BROKEN ENGLISH

David Thompson

Henry Holt and Company
New York

Broken English

Copyright © 1987 by David Thompson

All rights reserved, including the right to reproduce this book or portions thereof in any form.

First published in the United States in 1988 by
Henry Holt and Company, Inc., 115 West 18th Street,
New York, New York 10011.

Library of Congress Catalog Card Number: 87-46185

ISBN 0-8050-0811-X

First American Edition

Designer: Ian Gillen

Printed in Canada

10 9 8 7 6 5 4 3 2 1

This is a work of fiction. Names, characters, places and incidents either are the product of the author's imagination or are used fictitiously. Any resemblance to actual events or locales or persons, living or dead, is entirely coincidental.

ISBN 0-8050-0811-X

AN PHOBLACHT, 1 September 1979

Execution of Soldier Mountbatten

In claiming responsibility for the execution of Lord Mountbatten (former Chief of the United Kingdom Defence Staff, cousin of the Queen of England and symbol of all that is imperial Britain) the Irish Republican Army stated that the bombing was a 'discriminate operation to bring to the attention of the English people the continuing occupation of our country. We will do exactly the same thing again — against prestige targets.'

THE TIMES, 13 May

Royal Tour Confirmed

WINDSOR CASTLE today confirmed that Prince Charles and his family would be touring Northern Ireland, arriving in Belfast on June 12th then travelling to Londonderry before embarking on a tour of the Republic. Prince Charles intends to visit Mullaghmore in County Sligo on the shores of Donegal Bay where Lord Mountbatten was assassinated in 1979. Special security precautions are in effect both in Ulster and in Eire. Unionist leaders regard this visit with promise, seeing it as a symbol of Britain's commitment to Northern Ireland called into question by them in light of the Anglo-Irish Accord. This dual mandate shared by Dublin and London 'so long as it is the wish of the majority' has been severely criticized by both Sinn Fein and the Unionist Party. Only the Social Democratic Labour Party has entreated the people of Ulster to 'give it a chance'.

DUBLIN

10 am, 1 Meitheamh

The hands were speaking.

Burke sat in the leather chair and watched the fidgeting hands of Feeney. It was not the college ring which betrayed his occupation — it was the hands: porcelain, hairless, manicured. He looked up at the man but there was nothing of importance in that man's face. There was a lot of sound and fury in his speech but it seemed to signify nothing. The skin sagged around his eyes then stretched itself tight over red checks on its way to his strawberry-textured nose. No, the importance, for Burke, was in the way the dentist kept pulling at the third finger of his right hand compulsively. Feeney was nervous.

He glanced over to Sullivan's hands across the table. They would approach another's mouth only to do damage. Sullivan was making more sense as he spoke, but his hands twisted quietly around the curve of the rubber-tipped cane which steadied his withered left leg. The movement made a sound like leather being rubbed on wood somewhere far away. Words drifted in and out of Burke's mind and he was answering various questions but still he was intent on the hands. Somewhere here there was a lie.

Sullivan slammed his fist on the table. "Goddamnit Burke, can't you give us an answer?"

Burke shuffled in the chair. "Why would you be needing me? It's a simple matter of this Lynch just coming across the border like any other day-tripper."

Feeney smiled at Burke mechanically. "It is important that Dr Lynch be safely escorted across the border. He is a respected member of the medical community in Belfast . . . "

"Until recently," Burke added.

"Until recently. There is an element of secrecy and of danger to his crossing and we would feel more secure if you were there."

Burke smiled back at Feeney. "Why don't you contact the IRA?"

Feeney's smile disappeared. "We can't deal with terrorists."

"You're dealing with me."

"Jesus, Burke!" Sullivan stood and ran his fingers through his hair, then removed his glasses. "This is no time to play little games. You've been in jail for three years and you have a lot more time coming. You've dropped your contact with the IRA and it seems clear you want to keep it that way. You want out of Ireland. You need money and a new identity. We can give you both — no trouble, just one job."

"Why not use the Garda?"

Sullivan walked over to the window then turned. "This is not an official action by the government here, and if the police were used it would open the door to extradition proceedings by the British. Besides, there's a limit to who we can trust."

Burke shrugged his shoulders and leaned back in the chair until it creaked. "I've got the same problem. And I can't even consider this job unless I know more."

Feeney squinted at Burke. "Both the Garda and British Intelligence would be very interested in your whereabouts. I don't see that you're in a position to bargain with us."

Burke chuckled and shook his head. "Don't fuck with me," he said softly, then turned to Feeney. "Don't *ever* fuck with me. If anyone comes after me you can believe that I'll get to you first. Now get out of here."

Sullivan nodded to Feeney and Feeney left, relieved to be out of Burke's sight. "All right Martin. You've had your show, now don't fuck with *me*. Lynch got into some trouble up in Belfast. The Prods would like to get their hands on him and the British aren't likely to offer him asylum. We went to considerable trouble to bust you out of the Maze. You give us what we want, we'll return the favour. You might say you owe us one already." Sullivan paused as Burke considered his words, then walked around the table to the chair beside Burke and dropped into it, resting his cane against the table. "Lynch is an old friend of Feeney's and he needs help. He also has information of great importance to this government and to the Accord."

"So he boards a tour bus or a train and crosses over. No one watches the border that closely."

"For him they will."

"And for me as well." Burke toyed with the idea. He had to get out and the money was good. "Just this one job and you'll have a passport and my ticket to Canada?"

"My word, Burke. Once we have Lynch's information you'll be on your way." They shook hands.

Burke strolled along Harry Street. It was already past noon and he was dry. He passed McDaid's and decided to stop for a Guinness. It was cool inside and surprisingly uncluttered with the regular dregs who posed at the tables in imitation of life. The few there appeared to Burke as decoys, set by the owners, to lure other regulars in for a landing.

He took his jar and sat in a dark corner alcove just off from the window so that he could keep an eye on who was entering. The Guinness went down well.

It seemed like a job without complications but something nagged at him. It wasn't that it was easy; an easy job never hurt anybody. He had recovered most of the strength stolen from him in Long Kesh and he felt up to it. He'd be working alone so he had no one who would slow him down, or let him down. Sullivan had given him the patrol schedule for the border, the chopper routine, even the placement of the urine detectors and motion sensors. He figured the M-16A2 was gratuitous but it gave him a comfortable feeling to have some firepower just in case.

But just in case of what? They didn't really need him. That was what bothered him. They could have had a more worthwhile favour. His skills were well known; for the same price it would have been just as easy for him to kill someone, though he was glad they hadn't asked. That would have been hard for him to do now. As for Lynch, he could have trotted across in any number of places. It wasn't as if he had the whole British army out for him, and if he had lived this long in Belfast he could get past the Prods. But there was no mention of the IRA helping him. He must have pissed off quite a few people to be in that kind of trouble.

And who were Feeney and Sullivan? Advisory group to the Government due to the Anglo-Irish Accord? Perhaps. Retired IRA members? Easily said. Officials, maybe. He hadn't run into many men their age when he was active. Being a member of the Provisional IRA was not synonymous with longevity. But there was an unsettling smell, a disquieting sound to the whole thing. Questions to be answered.

Maybe he was just looking for an excuse to procrastinate. In the last few days he had come up with a hundred reasons why it was right to get out of Ireland and just as many more as to why he should stay. He wondered if it was a fear of breaking finally with the past or a latent death wish. A British agent might corner him at any time. Or the Garda. Then it would be back to the Maze for life or worse, if there was anything worse. He would have to decide soon, before the decision was made for him. He toyed with various trails of logic, searching for the inescapable conclusion.

Dublin was properly named the 'black pool'. It was purgatory. He was out of the hell that was Belfast but was trapped here, indecisive, unable to move. He didn't need their help. He could have gone to Argentina but he was damned if he was about to learn Spanish and it would be his luck that they would take him for a Brit. Sullivan had suggested the United States but Canada was more to his liking. At least there they spoke his language. He was respected in the IRA but if he asked for official help there would be strings attached. And he was not in the mood to rejoin. The slogans on the walls had said 'You can kill the revolutionary, but you can never kill the revolution.' There was more truth to that than people let on. What the hell. By accepting the job he was forcing his own hand, finally. He'd do a baby-sitting job and they'd swing the papers for him. It was a good deal.

As Sullivan leaned against the railing, feeding the carp which swam under the bridge Michael Magee walked up to him. "Did he agree?"

Sullivan nodded.

"Good." They stood silently watching the water boil as the carp fought for the breadcrumbs.

"You and the lads did a good job springing him. When are you off to New York?"

Magee looked up at the grey sky. "Tonight. I'll finish things there and be back with the goods in a couple of days."

Sullivan acknowledged the information with a grunt. "And the lads are doing okay at the training camp?"

Magee reached into the bag for some crumbs as Sullivan waited for the answer. "They'll be ready."

Sullivan looked back to the surface of the river. "Then I'll see you in Belfast. I've got to keep an eye on things."

"Will there be any trouble getting him to go back up there?" Magee asked, leaning over the railing and catching a glimpse of his reflection in the troubled water.

Sullivan shook his head. "He'll be there. He'll be spotted when he does the job and so he'll have to do what we want so he can get out. We just have to make sure he's covered. I don't want him turning up arrested or dead before he's served his purpose." He dumped the last of the crumbs into the Liffey and clicked off into the gathering dusk. Magee watched him for a moment then zipped his leather jacket and sauntered down the street.

BELFAST

5:45 pm, 1 June

Dr Lynch leaned against a pillar at the Central Station in Belfast, tamping his pipe. He was dressed like a common country boy: work shoes and wool socks, brown pants and a green workshirt, tweed jacket and soft hat. He was indistinguishable from the many others who waited for the train South. Still he was nervous. Near the stairs to the platforms Lynch had spotted a man in a grey suit with a topcoat. He carried no bundles and was obviously English. Though he looked about 45 he seemed too athletic for a man that age and too much like a Military Intelligence operative to be anything but. And Lynch had seen him twice earlier in the day, in different parts of town. It was more than coincidence. But why would MI be looking for him? They couldn't have a line on his information; not yet. Unless the Prods had brought them in. He settled on that. The Prods certainly would not want anyone to know what he knew. Somehow, they had found out. But from whom? Not from McHenry. His life would be on the line too. And not from Feeney.

He could trust Feeney, not just because they were old friends but also because he knew where the bones were buried. He would be safe so long as he could get near the border, hole up until first light, then meet his mule. Knowledge was sometimes a dangerous thing. He lit a match and held it to his pipe. He had quit smoking cigarettes three years ago on his forty-seventh birthday but still required the occasional bowl. A black swarm of thick-legged ladies scuttled toward the track area, bags and boxes emptied after a day of selling at the market.

The announcer blared over the intercom, announcing the last train for parts south. The man in the grey top-coat stiffened as the train heading for the South was announced. So he was expecting Lynch to take that train. It was a slow train, a milk run in the truest sense of the phrase. There would be no one but farmers, their wives, and Dubliners heading back on the last train south. And himself. Normally it crossed the border without a passing glance from the authorities, but Lynch knew this day would be different. Still, it was his only way of getting there. And then there was that man.

Lynch wanted to get out of sight. Perhaps the man hadn't recognized him in these clothes. He made his way to the washroom and once inside, stood at the urinal as a janitor emptied the garbage barrel. Grunting, he heaved the heavy metal drum back into place, then left. The door opened and, out of the corner of his eye, Lynch saw that it was the MI-type. He listened as the man went to wash his hands. Lynch was just about ready to leave when the man spoke.

"Dr Lynch? I'd like a moment of your time."

Lynch zipped his pants. "You've got me mistaken for somebody else," he said and headed for the door. The MI-type pushed his way to the door and stood in front of it barring the exit. "No I don't. Some gentlemen have asked me to have you come and speak with them. They want to know about your trip to the South. They want to know what it means."

"It doesn't mean anything. I don't know what you're talking about and my name isn't Lynch. Now if you don't mind, I've got a train to catch." Lynch moved toward him intending to push his way past and out the door.

The man pulled out a knife and flicked it open. "But I do mind. My employers made it clear that you were not to leave. So you can drop the shit and come with me. If there's any trouble, I'll open your guts. Now which will it be."

Lynch backed away and the man approached him. "Hold on a minute. I'll come, but you've made a mistake." Then he seized the opportunity and made a play for the door. The man was quick and grabbed him by the arm, bashing him into the wall face first, then swung him around and put the knife to his throat. "No, you've made the mistake."

"Okay, okay." Lynch ceased his struggle in a gesture of surrender. It was amazing how much minute detail could often be grasped in such a short time. This man was not MI so he must be a member of a Prod butcher squad. If he didn't find some way out he'd soon be dead. Whether he talked or not.

The man's watch ticked loudly. His breath moved the hair on Lynch's forehead. He relaxed the pressure on the knife and drew it away slightly. Lynch's arm swept up and slashed at the man's hands, knocking the knife through the air in a graceful arc. They scuffled across the floor and crashed into a cubicle. Lynch had managed to twist as they fell, and landed heavily, knocking the Prod's head against the toilet bowl. He lay inert on the floor half-in and half-out of the stall. Lynch dragged him to the garbage barrel and dumped him inside. He picked up the knife with a paper towel, walked back over and felt along his adversary's neck for the jugular. Then, with a quick slice, he sent him on a long journey. He took a bundle of paper towels and crumpled them over the body, camouflaging it.

Lynch washed his hands and checked his watch. 5:55. He would make that train.

BELFAST

6 pm, 1 June

Johnson stroked the damp stock of his FN. The set-up at this check-point bothered him. He had to watch the east roof for snipers but he had no wall at his back, just the steel post of a chain-link fence. Even though Andrews covered him from the other side of the street he was still vulnerable. Nobody ever saw the first shot, they just responded to it. By that time he'd be on the ground with his brains scattered around him, courtesy of the Irish fucking Republican Army. That must be why they used paratroopers as check-point lookouts — much easier to pull down their red berets over what was left of a face and avoid the embarrassing publicity on the telly. After all, brains on the grass just looked like so much cauliflower squashed by a boot.

How much longer would they have to stay here? It was always the same thing. Set up a road block, check the Paddies for weapons, get spit on at best, then move on. They never found anything. It was 'presence' the OC had explained. 'Presence'! Fuck 'presence'! And fuck Ireland! He stared at Andrews. Andrews lit a cigarette.

Sean crawled along the roof above Andrews and Johnson. In his small hands he held two toy grenades and some firecrackers. A waste of good toys, but he had told his brother he would help him. He wondered if Tim was ready. He snuggled down behind the facade by the corner of the building as he had been told and took out some matches. This would be great. And afterwards he could feed Tim's pigeons. That was a rare pleasure. Tim was so possessive when it came to those pigeons. And he was always afraid that Sean would leave the coop open and a rat would get in or that the birds would get out. But Sean knew how to care for them. And he enjoyed just sitting in the coop, having them roost on him, dig the corn out of his pockets, coo in his ear. Now that they were planning on moving down the street Tim would have to build a new coop. Sean hoped the janitor at the new building would let him. But then no one could say no to Tim: he had the face of an angel and more blarney than any one human had a right to possess.

The bells of St Patrick's began to sound the Angelus. Dezy would be helping the Father with that. He wished that he could tell Dezy about this later, when they were playing, but his brother had sworn him to secrecy. Older brothers had a way of spoiling things. He lit the long fuse on the firecrackers, dropped the toy grenades over the facade and ran like hell for the stairs.

It happened too fast. Andrews saw the two grenades hit. He hesitated for an instant, wondering which way to move, wondering if this was really happening. Then his military training hit home. He dove to the ground to avoid being caught in the concussion arc then rolled to the other side of the street in a fluid motion, ending on the other side, on his feet, beside Johnson. They sprang behind a car for cover. Nothing happened. Then the firecrackers went off. With their FN's at their shoulders they checked the roof line, squatting behind the car, not realizing that their backs weren't covered.

Tim and a friend stood up in the ditch they had crawled along, pumped three rounds from their revolvers into the heads and backs of the two soldiers, then disappeared.

Sean hit the street half a block from the car. The two soldiers lay crumpled on the street as other soldiers ran toward them while still others covered the area. He'd missed it. It had happened too fast. And why was there cauliflower on the roof of that car?

AT McDAID'S

6 pm, 1 Meitheamh

Burke stirred in his chair and took another drink of Guinness, still thinking more than he really wanted to. Thinking about the past. He had wanted to lose himself in the last few years and had had trouble doing so. Now he wanted to remember and it was hard.

In his mind's eye was his father, sitting at the kitchen table, in the dark of night, in the midst of one of the many lengthy conversations they shared in the years after his mother's death, paraphrasing his favourite philosopher — Popeye. "You is what you is an' that's all what you is."

Burke's father, a lawyer, was one of a handful of Catholic professionals in Derry, having received his training in the South where being a Catholic was not a handicap. Not that they had been religious, but in Ireland it was impossible to sit on the fence. His mother — he remembered her soft voice, her beautiful dark hair and the stories she would tell him in the quiet dark of summer night. She had died when he was six. His father had not remarried and had developed a camaraderie with his only son. They often sat long into the night, talking of history and politics. It was during these long, treasured evenings that Martin learned of his grandfather. Stories such as those, and the blood in his veins, shaped much of his life.

His people had been Ultonians originally but had been driven from that most rebellious of provinces 'to Hell or Connaught' by the forces of Cromwell. Some of his ancestors had fought in the Battle of the Boyne in 1690 when the English, under King William of Orange, had defeated the Irish. Others had been involved in numerous revolts against the English Overlords and the Protestant Presbyterians who, though they faithfully served the English, were held in contempt only one step above the Irish Catholics by their English masters.

His grandfar, Seamus Burke, had come to Dublin at an early age, looking for work as a common labourer. As a Catholic in the South when it was under English domination any higher education was denied him, but he was free to embrace higher ideals. He was a quiet, strong-willed young man and, in the Spring of 1916, at the age of 17, he was there at the steps of the General Post Office. From the Easter Rising on he was active in the IRA. It was then that he met his wife Fiona. She was two years older than he and, though she, by blood, belonged to the English Ascendancy, her family was strongly Republican; her ancestors had been instrumental in the establishment of the United Irishmen. She was a fiery supporter of The Cause. To them there was no need for religion and it did not form a part of their marriage and their life together, nor was it passed to their son Liam.

Martin thought of the picture of his grandfather which had been with him always, at least until he had been taken into custody. Seamus stood, well-dressed and proud, his bedroll slung over his shoulder and his rifle by his side. When some Republicans lost faith and compromised with the English it was natural that there would be civil war. And he was part of it, in the Flying Columns and at the trouble in Cork in '22. Liam, Martin's father, had been born then. Martin remembered tales his father had told of his grandmother reloading rifles, pausing to give birth, then returning to the barricades. Acknowledging the embellishments, it was an intense time, and those caught in the movement were intense people.

He also remembered tales of the English burning whole villages in the night and the morning finding villagers huddling half-naked and wet in the hills and valleys around their lost homes. They were tales of the Irish starving, spiritually and physically, under the English yoke.

Liam was ten when his parents were killed in a street battle in Cork with enemies they had made during the Civil War. He was taken in by well-off relatives in Dublin and lived there until he received his Law degree from Trinity. In 1947, on a trip to Londonderry he met Nuala, Martin's mother. They were married and settled in Derry but a car accident in 1958 put an end to their plans. Martin sometimes felt he missed his mother as much as his father did, but he knew that that was impossible. His father had compensated for the loss by throwing himself into work, defending the Catholics of Derry, fighting for a peaceful, legal means to end the strife.

While Liam was a peaceful man, Martin had inherited a touch of the spirit of his grandfather. His father had sent him to Trinity to study the law, but the ghosts of Wolfe Tone and others walked those halls: men of books and bullets, and that was their legacy to boys like Martin. He flirted with the IRA and, following the internments of 1971, committed himself to training at a farm near Drogheda. His instructor was a Vietnam vet whose nickname was The Doctor. Burke's skill with weaponry drew the Doctor's attention and they became close friends. They spent days sweating on the training fields and nights drinking and talking.

The Doctor was a short, powerfully-built man who had, in his youth, been captivated by tales of the Irish struggle against the English which his grandfather had brought from Eire to America. After his discharge it was natural that his love of adventure had brought him to Ireland to make use of his special skills. But Ireland could not hold him. As he put it, he needed to get back to 'busting caps for real'. In the fall of 1972 he signed on with a mercenary group heading for Africa and Burke went with him.

Burke had hesitated to leave Eire to fight in a foreign land, but he reasoned he was simply following the long tradition of the Wild Geese. For centuries Irishmen had left their home shores to fight as mercenaries in the armies of Europe, of Russia, of America, and of England. They had served with Napoleon and with Wellington at Waterloo, with Lee and with Grant in the American Civil War, with the British in India. Someday, as the legend had it, the Wild Geese would return and Eire would be freed. But that day would be long in coming, and for now Burke decided he would go: adventure beckoned and there was much money to be made.

The Doctor made the arms preparations and the banking arrangements. Martin told his father only that he was going to South Africa on the prospect of some work. But as they stood at the airport in Dublin, Martin could see that his father knew the truth. They parted without a word.

As soon as they hit Salisbury the Doctor sought out a tattoo artist and had a black snake needled into him, its tail on his right breast, its body snaking around and across his back, with its head, fangs bared, tongue striking, on his left breast. Martin got drunk. They were ready to fight.

After acclimatization training and some bouts of serious drinking, they moved into Mozambique with a hunting party. The Portuguese authorities had the operations down to a fine art. They would pinpoint an area of rebel Frelimo activity and drop the boys in by helicopter in squads of four to search and destroy. Burke became an animal of sorts, depending on his senses to preserve him long enough for his reasoning powers to work out an effective kill strategy. He and the Doctor were inseparable and invincible. Many times they were the only ones from their squad to break out to the pick-up zones.

In an operation in the summer of '73 a slight miscalculation was made. Usually they would start a skirmish with Frelimo rearguard, push to a base camp, mortar the place to the ground, then back out. On this night three four-man squads were dropped into the middle of a camp occupied by more than three hundred Frelimo Guerillas. The squads raced through alleyways, rolling grenades to their flanks and setting down random fire fore and aft until they linked up. The camp was a hornets' nest and, when the ammo dump went up, the rebels thought they were under massive attack and threw everything they had at the squads. Fires blazed everywhere and everyone was busting caps furiously. It was more than a nightmare.

The Doctor called in the choppers for some rocket support and, as that hit, they began their bustout. It took ten minutes and it seemed like hours. None of the squad members were unscathed. The Doctor took two slugs in his left leg and Burke had a knife plunged into his right shoulder. Of the twelve, four got out of the camp alive, but Derek, a kid from England, died on the chopper before they made it back to their base.

For two days in Manica, a town in the white-zone near the Rhodesian border, Burke and the Doctor burned their brains with enough whiskey to kill men who were not already dead. On the third day they strolled in the early light. A black girl, large young breasts hanging out of her light cotton dress, propositioned the Doctor and he took her in tow. They ducked into her shanty and Burke continued along to the nearest alley. He stood, taking a piss, watching the sun through the clouds. Suddenly there was a scream from the shack. Grabbing his Thompson, Burke tore down the street, busted through the shanty door-curtain, and rolled across the floor of the hut. He saw no one in the darkness but could hear a moaning from the bed. His eyes grew accustomed to the gloom and he stood. There, on the bed before him, lay the Doctor, naked except for his boots, his dog tags, and his field hat. His stomach had been torn open by repeated knife thrusts and his intestines were glistening on the cot. Blood seeped from his mouth. He looked at Burke for a moment, then his eyes took on that glazed stare of the dead. Burke squatted on the floor, staring across at his friend. Then he moved quietly to the darkest corner of the room and waited. Two sets of bare feet padded cautiously to the door and the curtain parted. The girl and a man entered from the bright sunlight. Burke cut them in half with his machine gun.

After the Doctor died the adventure dulled for Burke. For awhile the others in his group had thought he might lose his edge, but his efficiency actually increased. He had stopped feeling. One raid was indistinguishable from the next: he was a well-oiled killing machine. He played out his contract year, collected his bonus and the Doctor's death benefit, then headed for Ireland.

He rolled into Derry and entered the war zone he had grown up in and had sought to leave behind. Barricades were everywhere. British troops roamed the streets, and child's play was dangerous fun. And when he reached his father's house he walked in on a wake. Liam had been speaking at a rally the day before when it turned into a riot. Special Air Services troops had been called in to contain the situation. It was a bullet from an SAS rifle that had put an end to Liam's efforts. Martin looked down on this peaceful man and his blood raged. He had been busy fighting other wars when there was a war to be fought on his own doorstep. Late into the night he sat talking with an old friend of his father's named Finnerty who had spent his life in the IRA and now lived in Belfast.

Finn was a jolly sort of man though years of heavy drinking had left their mark on his face and general physical appearance. He looked pregnant except for the lack of any healthy glow, and his hair was an unkempt yellowed-white, but his eyes were younger than a child's. He stood with Burke at the graveside the next day as a British chopper hovered overhead taking pictures.

Finnerty took him to Belfast where he was re-introduced to the IRA. His experience made him useful to the movement both in the field and in training camps. But somehow it was not enough for him. In 1975 a sizeable group of actives split into the marxist-oriented Irish National Liberation Army and both INLA and the Provos restructured into the cell structure of terrorist organizations around the world. Burke remained with the IRA but on the fringe. He set up his own three man cell with Finnerty and a young volunteer named Hennessey, a gangly youth with a head for figures who had already raised money smuggling British subsidized butter to the Republic. Together they worked on a series of very useful arms deals. As well, Burke focussed the anger which had been building inside. It was a personal campaign against the British.

His targets were chosen to intensify fear among the British soldiery. He would frag a single soldier's bed in a British barracks or follow, for weeks, a soldier known to have killed a Provisional or a supporter then, in the proper moment, strike. At first it meant a great deal to him, a means of avenging his father's murder. Gradually, however, he came to despise his role. The struggle showed signs of becoming a long-term, modern guerilla action and he had seen the devastating effects of such a way of life on a people. Day after day he saw all of the Irish people reduced to victims. Night by night he saw his own culpability increase. He was no longer part of the solution, he was part of the problem. He was a folk hero, a great warrior for the cause. He was a demon, a murdering Fenian bastard. It depended on which Irishman you listened to. He supported the revolution but the cost pained him. He reached the point where he could no longer play the executioner and in 1982 he stopped. But even his continued involvement in the supply of arms proved a burden. He could not abandon his task but he knew soon it would be impossible for him to continue. Then, at an arms deal in '84 he had been arrested. The prison was his sanctuary, the beatings his penance. In a way, he was relieved to be freed from the responsibility of action. In the Maze his only task had been to stay alive and sane. Now his only task was to do what had to be done to get to hell out of Ireland. He paid his bill and left.

ON THE RAILS

6:45 pm, 1 June

Lynch tried to make himself comfortable but he found it next to impossible. He had forgotten how hard the seats were. The two priests and the old lady in the car were regaling him with their snoring. He was at least spared the forced conversation which was too often the price of rail travel.

He was glad that Feeney had arranged for someone experienced to get him across. It had been impossible to rest in the last few days and he was tired of hiding. They would have found him sooner or later. He needed the protection that Feeney could offer. He had thought the train might be the safest way to get near the border. Too often cars were stopped on lonely country roads and people were shot when the British or the Prods 'returned fire'. However the agent at the station had proved him wrong. Even if they didn't find his body right away the British would be crawling all over the border. But the risk was necessary. People knew that he knew what was up and his life was worth nothing. Feeney could help him and would be glad to in exchange for what he had found out. He had thought of trying to contact some Provisionals in the North but he was not sure where they might stand and he certainly couldn't go to the British authorities. He had contacted Feeney out of a sense of urgency mixed with panic. This way he would avoid knee-capping or imprisonment. This way he would live.

He checked his watch. It wouldn't be long now.

After the train had passed Newry he had been stricken with the fear that agents could be onboard and might lift him before he could get off. When the tea lady had entered the car his heart had palpitated. He would have to jump, and before the train reached Killeen. He would find a barn or some other refuge on a nearby farm where he could spend the night. He wished he had brought some food with him but he would have to forgo sustenance until he was safely across. Armagh was a relatively safe place but he did not want to risk contact with the Brits or with anyone else. This game was too dangerous to trust anyone but Feeney. He would hole up, get some much needed sleep and in the morning it would be a short walk to the border.

The others in the car had been asleep for the last few stops and the conductor hadn't been in either. If anyone was shown his picture and questioned it would be assumed that he had gotten off somewhere up the line.

He rose quietly and made his way to the end of the car then stepped out out onto the catwalk and moved down to the bottom step. Checking the rapidly passing countryside for a likely spot to bail out he noticed that the train was approaching a grassy curve near a crossing and had begun to slow. He would not find a better spot. With a quick prayer to St Christopher and St Patrick and to anyone else who might be about at that ungodly hour he flung himself with all his might, as the train rounded the corner. If only St Patrick had driven out the stones instead of the snakes.

He tried to execute a controlled roll as he hit the ground but impetus propelled him into an ungovernable somersault. He came to a stop finally and lay there, waiting to make sure no one had seen him. He looked up at the peaceful sky and was seized with a sudden desire to just remain there on his back forever. Then a dull pain arose in many parts of his body. He gathered himself together, checking slowly to see that no bones had been broken, got to his feet, dusted himself and crossed the fence to the road. He checked the sky for helicopters and the road for vehicles. The British had a habit of running 'eagle patrols' in this area: helicopter assisted road patrols. He had to get off the road and settled for the night, maybe have a bowl of tobacco before sleeping. Down the road and off back in the trees he spied a rundown shack which might have been a dwelling-house at one time. If he found no signs of recent habitation, that would suffice. As he picked up the pace he rubbed his gluteus maximus. It was nice country for raising stones.

BELFAST

9:15 pm, 1 June

Meagan O'Farrell stood outside of McKeirnan's Furniture and checked her watch. Bob Gentleman was late again. She realised that it was a long way from the Ministry of Intelligence Headquarters on the outskirts of Belfast to their meeting place but she had said 9 o'clock. As long as the rain which had been threatening all day didn't arrive it would be fine. She just hated waiting. And she wouldn't wait much longer. Gentleman had been useful. It was always a good idea to keep an eye on what Brit Intelligence was up to and what better way than to screw a courier. It killed two birds with one stone. But lately he had been busy and she had been unable to get together with him long enough to get any information. And she desperately needed that information.

She looked up to see Gentleman coming down the street. He was handsome, even out of uniform, though overpoweringly British: blond hair and moustache, upright, six foot frame, blue eyes, strong arms. The only thing un-British about him was his passion. She pulled her jacket closed and stepped into the street.

"Bob," she shouted and waved. They embraced in mid-street. "I thought maybe you'd forgotten."

"Sorry I'm late but Hedley had his ass in an uproar again. It's the Tour. No one's getting leave."

"It's ok." She pulled his arm around her shoulder and they headed off down the darkening street. "What do you say to a drink before we go to my place?"

"We'll have to postpone that too. There's another meeting at eleven. I just came 'cause I didn't want to stand you up but I have to get back. I can probably get back after that but it'll be late."

Meagan pulled his arm off her shoulder. "Jesus Bob, what's the point? You've got no time but you want to crawl into my bed in the middle of the night. I can keep myself warm you know."

Bob looked down at her as they walked. "It's really out of my hands. Hedley has Wilkes and Barton from SAS and some other bigwigs coming in. They've been twitchy ever since Burke busted out." Meagan didn't respond. "I might get a day next week and after the tour I'll have a weekend coming. Maybe we could go to Dublin?"

Meagan looked up at him. "That would be nice," she said sarcastically.

Bob put his arm back around her shoulder. "Come on Meg. You know it's not my fault. Let's get a drink then I'll walk you to your place."

They ducked into the nearest pub. It was smokey and crowded at the bar so Gentleman ordered a lager and lime for Meagan and a whiskey for himself. As they sat down at a free table Meagan noticed two rough characters eyeing them. They had obviously heard Gentleman's accent and it was clear they weren't impressed, with him or with her. She turned to Bob as he sipped his whiskey. "So why all the SAS? Isn't Burke out of the country by now?"

"Probably. But they've got the SAS in to run down some doctor. He's supposed to have some important information about something but we don't know what. So Hedley wants to try and bring him in. His ass is in a sling if there's any major trouble during the Tour. But seriously, what do you think about Dublin? I want to get out of this town." He stroked her neck, then leaned over and kissed her.

Behind her Peadar looked up drunkenly and nudged his friend. "Padraig, take a gander at that little slut there. Being oh so friendly with that fuckin' Brit."

Padraig focussed in. "Needs her fuckin' head caved, the slimy little cunt."

Meg moved nervously. It was obvious that the drool from the next table was having an impact on Bob. Neither of them would admit that they had heard it, but she could see that his anger and ego might force a confrontation, and that was something she needed to avoid. "So will they get him?"

"Get who?" Bob asked, his mind on what he had been overhearing from the other table. "Oh, Lynch. Well, he's supposed to be crossing to the South tomorrow. That's all we have. But you know the SAS. They'll probably get him."

Meagan saw him glance at the two men again. "It's getting late," she suggested, "hadn't we better go?"

Gentleman stood agreeably. He was under strict orders, as were all members of MI staff, to avoid any confrontation with the more unstable elements of the populace. He'd been foolish to go into this pub in the first place. But, no harm done. They walked outside into the mist of a Belfast night and headed for her apartment. Neither of them noticed Peadar and Padraig had followed them.

Peadar wiped the froth of a downed jar of Guinness from his upper lip with his coat-sleeve. "You take out the Brit. I want her." He handed Padraig a snub-nose .38 as they followed the two at a distance. "It's ok, I've got another for myself."

They turned into Meagan's street dark from the lack of street lights and stopped in front of the rundown tenement-house. Gentleman held her in his arms and kissed her, whispering, "I really have to run but I'll see you later. I'm going to call from the station on the next block and get a jeep to pick me up." He kissed her again, then walked off down the street. Meagan turned and entered the foyer.

Peadar and Padraig popped up from behind a veranda on the next building like two weasels in a Disney horror story. With silent signals Padraig was off down the street trailing Gentleman while Peadar leaped up the stairs and into Meagan's foyer. He surprised her as she was fumbling in her purse for her keys. She backed against the wall, recognizing him from the pub. He drew his revolver from his coat and approached her, menacingly.

"Well, well. I've always wanted to see what kind of woman it is that prefers English cock." He jammed the gun between her legs, making her wince in pain. "Maybe he could use a hole with a smaller bore."

Meagan tasted the edge of fear in her mouth. This situation was unlike any she'd had to deal with before. The man was obviously drunk and even when sober was probably dangerous. Now he was without whatever control he might normally have had. He was a 'Brady', one of those thugs who have no ties with the real IRA but masquerade under its banner. She had to plan, and plan quickly.

He stepped back a couple of feet and motioned with the revolver for her to take off her skirt. "Why don't you just drop the skirt before I blow it off."

Meagan looked to the doorway.

"And don't be looking for your knight to come chargin' in to the rescue. Padraig will be takin' care of him."

Meagan undid her skirt. It fell to the floor and she stepped out of it. She wore no slip and now stood in her panties with her turtleneck sweater and short coat still on.

"The sweater and coat, too, love. Nice and slow."

She removed the coat. Slowly she pulled one arm out of the sweater, revealing a firm breast, unencumbered by a bra. She hesitated at removing the entire sweater as that would reveal her shoulder-holster. Her mind searched for some way out, but a maniac with a gun had to be treated with deference.

Peadar moved forward and her moment came almost too quickly for her to take advantage of it. The barrel of his pistol angled away from her as he fondled her. She grabbed the revolver with her left hand and forced his left hand against her breast with her right, her knee flew up into his groin and the gun dropped from his hand. He doubled over and, in doing so, set his jaw in line for a devastating kick which sent him reeling, unconscious, into the doorway.

She pulled her clothes on quickly, took her gloves from her purse, and retrieved his revolver. Cautiously she checked the street outside, then, all being clear, she grabbed the crumpled form in the foyer in a fire-man's hold and quickly carried him across the street, laying him just inside the mouth of an alley. She placed his gun in his hand then drew her Beretta, fitted it with a silencer from her purse and stepped back about four feet. The weapon spat into the crumpled pile of clothing and flesh and a red patch appeared on either side of Peadar's head. It would be just one more body found in the morning, one more statistic that nobody really noticed.

Suddenly she thought of Bob. She raced down the street and across an alley toward the call station where he would be waiting. She stopped dead in her tracks. He was standing ahead of her under a street lamp on the next street, patiently waiting in his regular military stance, hands clasped behind his back.

But further behind his back, between him and Meagan, crouched Padraig, taking aim with his newly acquired .38. Meagan, assumed the position, legs apart, crouched, steadying her silenced Beretta on her left arm at her elbow, her back arched. She took direct aim on Padraig's head. To hit him anywhere else would have been easier, but he would have cried out, or shot, or both. If she missed she might hit Bob and she would surely alert both of them.

There was no time for such thoughts now. There was only time for action. She squeezed the trigger and Padraig collapsed without a sound.

She dropped her pistol down a sewer grate, stuffed her gloves in her purse and ran through the dark alley, past the dead man, toward Bob. He heard her approach and turned nervously as she arrived in his circle of light.

"Meagan. What are you doing here? It's not very safe."

"I know, but after you left I started thinking. Why don't I wait for you at your apartment? I really do want to see you tonight. And I don't want to be alone."

The jeep Gentleman had called for pulled up. He led her into it. "That sounds fine. I don't like you being alone around here either. I wish you'd move. It's a dangerous neighbourhood."

Meagan snuggled beside Bob as the driver glanced back in the rear-view mirror. She smiled up at Gentleman. "Maybe I will."

MIHQ, BELFAST

11:45 pm, 1 June

Hedley paced back and forth in front of the blackboard staring at what was written on it. Colonel Barton sat off to the side, in combat fatigues, a cigarette dangling from his mouth, ready and waiting. Wilkes watched them both with some interest. He didn't really like the Supremo. If he had been an ex-SAS man it might have made a difference but this MI bureaucrat had been out of the field for so long that he was probably mouldering inside that three-piece suit of his. Barton was more his kind of man. He loved action, and Wilkes knew that he did not share the Supremo's affection for the Accord. The British Army and Britain had been made fools of for too long by weak-kneed politicians and bastard Fenians. And too many good men had been wasted by hobbling them with civilian authorities. What was needed was action, strong action, before it was too late. And action would be taken. He had been in contact with a man who had a plan which would free his men to act. And all it would cost was a figurehead.

He glanced at his watch. It was getting late. If Barton was going to intercept this paddy he'd have to get into his chopper and get to Armagh. The troops were already deployed and the best CRW squads were waiting but they needed Barton's direction at the proper time. Wilkes desperately wanted to get home to bed. Morning came soon enough and he had important business transactions to discuss. He had also decided that he would speak with Barton after the operation. A man like that could be useful.

Hedley paused. There was so little information. Their Catholic informants seemed to know nothing and their Protestants only that Lynch had run afoul of some Protestant faction somehow and was on a hit list. Someone had heard that he was headed for the South and intended to cross somewhere to the east of Crossmaglen. Why, he had no idea. He also had no idea what Lynch had done. He had been suspected of affiliation with the IRA long ago, his dossier made that clear. But it also made it clear that he had no direct involvement and that he was a good and conscientious doctor. He might have treated the odd gunshot wound and not reported it, but his sheet was clean. When a man who appeared to be clean made such enemies, something was wrong and Hedley could not afford not knowing what.

At any other time there would have been no rush. Militants in both the Catholic and the Protestant camps were always plotting against each other. Cold-blooded murder was a way of life in Ireland. But, with the approaching Royal Tour, all leads had to be run down. And that brought him to what he felt was a larger problem. Martin Burke had escaped. One of the most celebrated assassins in the North. Celebrated but not convicted. They had been caught up in interminable remands, trying to gather the necessary information. It was on his way from Long Kesh to appear for a remand that the van had been hijacked. The bastards had pointed a bazooka at the driver. A clean get-away, no leads. Not that he expected any on someone like that. Hedley secretly hoped that he was far from Ireland.

He looked again at the board. The lack of information on Lynch was unsettling. And now there was Stan Chalmers' body. What had Chalmers been doing at the train station in Belfast? An MI-5 man for fifteen years in England, retired and gone into personal security, working for the Free Presbyterians, Paisley's Church and now he was dead on Hedley's turf. His throat had been expertly cut. It was assumed that Lynch was the murderer from a description received and there had been signs of a physical confrontation. But why? In any event, Lynch must have taken the last train south and so the rumours of his planned crossing would be their best lead. The train stations had been alerted and extra troops had been put on the border patrol, including the SAS. And that meant Barton.

Hedley could tell Barton was getting itchy. He was reluctant to send him on an interception detail. He could wait and try to pick up the pieces when his supergrasses came up with something but that might be too late. Charles' visit was too important. And a rise in sectarian violence would do the Accord no good either. On the other hand, if Lynch tried to shoot it out with Colonel Cutthroat they would have to pick his brains with a pitchfork. Too many Argentinians had learned that the hard way. And a few Irishmen as well. He glanced at his watch. It was late, and it was time for a decision.

"Barton," Hedley intoned, taking his glasses off. Everyone jumped. Wilkes almost fell off his chair. He had drifted off into dreams of the paradise a great deal of money could buy. Barton stood, a military man at the ready. Hedley looked him directly in the eye. "I want no 'international incidents'. It is imperative that Lynch does not reach the South but I want him alive. Is that clear?"

Barton smiled. "As you order, sir."

THE BORDER, ARMAGH

5:00 am, 2 Meitheamh

Barton's chopper dropped onto the large pad at the base at Crossmaglen. Two other choppers were there, unloading everything necessary for maintaining the base. Barton was in 'bandit country' and the thought of it raised his blood-pressure. Northern Ireland, an armed forces base, and all supplies had to come in by helicopter because the IRA was so successful at mining the road and hi-jacking the convoys. He hadn't had this much trouble in the Falklands. If they would only replace the regular forces with the SAS and give them four unencumbered months, the terrorists would be wiped out, in the South as well as in the North.

Things hadn't even been as bad in Oman. He had seen his wildest action there, at Mirbat, in July of 1972. He and nine other SAS troopers and a handful of frightened locals armed with FN's had turned back over 300 rebels armed with AK-47's, mortars, rockets and more grenades than he cared to remember. That battle had turned the tide in Oman, and in his life. When Oman was finished in '76 he had remained in the SAS and his skill and loyalty had brought him rapid promotion. Before Mirbat he had planned to get out of the service. He had been in for eight years but he was still young enough to make his way as a civvy. What he learned and felt there, though, made him realise that he could not be happy in any other profession. He was a warrior.

Along with promotions had come Ireland. In the days of Elizabeth I, and from then on, Ireland had been a battleground which defeated even the most gifted of English generals. But it would not be that way for him. He promised himself that. Ten thousand regular troops couldn't do much but

400 roving SAS troopers made up for them. Still the nature of this exercise bothered him. Only one side was allowed to fight a total war. He constantly had to hold himself and his men back: Ireland was like a teasing slut, enticing his men to action, then denying them that action. And he treated the Irish as he would a slut, and with the same degree of respect. They were a bothersome race at best. At worst they were barely human.

When his call came for the Falklands it was seen, by him, as a vacation, and a time to prove to the War Office and to himself that he still had what it took. His brief respite in the 'Malvinas' had been pleasant. There he was more or less free to move with precision and weight. Here though, the troops were hamstrung by the civil authorities so most things had to be above board. While he was away one of his lads had even been convicted of murder. Ridiculous!

This time around, however, Hedley and Wilkes had released him from all that. Lynch was to be taken directly to MIHQ, Belfast. No muss or fuss with civil authorities. Just a black hood over his head, pop him in the chopper, and away. Barton relished the idea.

He had directed some of his men to cover the stations on the line down, but he was sure that Lynch would avoid them. Information was that he would cross between Crossmaglen and Killeen, probably in the woods to the west of Killeen. Barton had three special squads ready and he would command the patrol covering the most likely area. It would be a good hunt.

Barton entered HQ command post which was focussing on the twenty miles of border between Crossmaglen and Upper Fathom on Carlingford Lough. The other patrols were already deployed and his men were ready and waiting. He greeted them casually, then entered Cyclops — the electronic surveillance operations centre. The sergeant on duty reported to him immediately.

"Nothing on the border, sir. We've stepped up surveillance. Listening posts report nothing. Motion detectors are clear and urine detectors are negative."

Barton blinked. "Urine detectors?"

"Yes sir," the sergeant said, with a cocky air, "we took a trick from the Yanks. They had them in South East Asia. We've placed them just off any trails. Even the Provos are human. Picks up human urine within two metres, sir."

"Yes sergeant, and when the Cong figured out what they were, they pissed on them and the Yanks would go blasting off, expecting a yellow horde." The sergeant immediately went quiet. Barton strutted about the room for a moment. He felt hot today. "Sergeant, I'll be keeping my chopper at the ready during the operation."

"Yes sir."

As he was about to leave, something on one of the screens caught Barton's eye. "Sergeant, I thought you said the motion detectors read clear. What the hell is this?"

The sergeant moved quickly to the screen and grabbed the log. "Cows, sir. We've been picking them up since about 0400 this morning. It's pretty common but we sent a chopper in to confirm, SOP. They've strayed a bit, but we usually see them in that general area. We have detectors set in all the unexposed and partially exposed areas about 500 feet deep from the border, sir. In the exposed areas we just have them 100 yards deep. But those are cows, sir. Random pattern of movement, occasional strays returning to the herd, basically stationary, grazing. And as I mentioned we had visual confirmation at about 0430 from the regular chopper patrol, sir."

"And what sector are those cows in sergeant?"

"B patrol's area sir. I can give you the co-ordinates if you'd like sir."

"I'd like that sergeant. Give them to my navigator." Barton strode out and led his men into the chopper that would take them to the beginning of their sweep area. Cows my ass. Lynch would be crossing there. Odysseus outwitting Cyclops, he chuckled to himself as the chopper lifted off, these Paddies love the Greek myths.

Burke looked up at the sun then checked his watch. It was past six. He'd been busy for the last four hours, and he hoped it would pay off. He had positioned himself at the appointed crossing after completing a five mile run from the east. He'd moved early and planted a urine bottle connected to a timed spritzer set to go off at 6:35 near where he had been told he would find urine detectors, as a diversion. On his way back he'd seen a chopper hovering over the crossing zone then leaving, but, as he set up to wait for Lynch, he realized that they must have been checking out the cows that he had moved into the area with a trail of salt chunks and clover.

Things had certainly changed from his grandfather's day in the IRA. Vietnam and NASA had contributed. In the old days it had been a romantic struggle. Now it was technology and terrorism. The romance still existed in pockets to be sure, but though the game had changed the stakes were the same: get the British out of Ireland, for good. Now he only hoped that he could get himself out of Ireland for good; leave it to the new breed of fighters; make a new life and forget. Forget everything. Except Lynch. He was Burke's ticket.

Burke stood up and trained his binos on the cows nearly two miles away. He swung his M-16A2 to his side and scanned the entire area, planning a number of routes, just in case. He would be glad when it was over. He would ditch this ridiculous cammo and dump the rifle and Lynch in Sullivan's lap. He turned to see if he could catch a glimpse of the cottage where Sullivan and Feeney sat waiting. It was there, almost four miles across the fields, its white wattle walls shining in the early morning sun. He resumed his search for Lynch. The urine would be going off soon.

Lynch pedaled slowly along the country road. He had slept well and sound in the little shack and had awoke with a start, thinking he'd be late. The bicycle hadn't been too hard to find but it had taken him a while to get used to riding again. He only hoped that, if he ever was away from sex, it would come back to him easier.

He kept glancing around but there was no one in sight. It seemed this would be easier than he had expected. There was the transformer number on the electric company's pole — 3250. He was to proceed in a southerly direction from there to a stream, then head south through the trees and cross the border in a ravine where cattle would be grazing, all the while moving slowly and erratically — 'serpentine' Feeney had said. His contact would cover his crossing and take him to Feeney.

But what would they do about his information? It might be too big for them to handle. And yet, there was nowhere else to go.

Lynch slowed and got off the bike, hiding it in the bushes. It was 6:30. He headed off down the trail which hugged the stream.

Barton sat on a tree stump taking a drink of water from his canteen. The temperature was already up too high and his spirits were sagging. An hour of hunting and no sighting at all. In addition to that he was tired of having to move his men slowly in order to let the two Fusiliers keep up, but he couldn't very well leave the radio and the navigator behind, although he knew his men could move easily and effectively over this terrain. Co-operation. He had to co-operate with the regular forces a little.

The radio man had just given HQ a position check when he jumped up and called to Barton.

"Sir. HQ reports a urine detection in the sector approximately five miles east of our position."

Barton leapt up. Five miles east. Perhaps the cows had been a diversion. They would have to high-tail it to get to that sector in any reasonable time. "Check if C squad is nearer and if there's a chopper in the vicinity." The radio man inquired but the response from HQ was negative. They advised him to proceed there immediately. Barton burned at that. Reg Force suggesting that he do anything was an insult. Suddenly a thought struck him. "Sutherland, check with HQ for any movement north to south near the cows in this sector."

The reply was slow in coming. "Sir, they report an erratic movement north to south but it's a stray cow."

"Did they see the cow stray in the first place?"

Again Sutherland relayed the response. "They aren't sure sir. They were checking the urine detectors."

Barton slapped his hand on his thigh. "Let's move to that valley the cows are feeding in. Someone is pissing up the wrong tree." His men were up and following him at a quick trot while Sutherland and the Navigator scurried to gather their equipment and follow. Barton was smiling to himself as he ran.

Lynch found the walk pleasant. The sun broke through the trees along the brook and speckled the path with light. He paused every once in a while or moved off the path in order to try and follow directions but there seemed no use for them now. He'd passed the cows which were feeding on the other side of the bank and was following the path up to higher ground. There was still enough cover there and he was only about 200 yards from the border.

Suddenly the ground in front of him puffed three times in rapid succession. In the moment before the report of the rifle reached him he was at a loss to explain to himself what it might be. As the report struck home he turned and saw, in the distance, a troop of British soldiers. Panic struck. They were firing at him! He raced across the side of the hill following a zig-zag pattern so as not to afford a predictable target. He glanced behind and saw that they were in pursuit.

His breath became laboured now as he cleared the rise and emerged into the swath cut through the trees. Small, white stone markers were spaced through the centre of the cut. The border! A branch swatted him in the face and he fell, rolling up against an exposed root. His shoulder hurt like hell but he rose again and continued.

They were closing on him. He had to cross the border. More reports were heard and he dodged the bullets which had already missed him. He ran madly across the clearing.

Where was his contact? Make for the high ground, he thought. His contact would see him there. He tore off toward the hill to the right. He was in Eire but he didn't trust the patrol to respect the border.

Barton led his men swiftly through the trees. As he reached the border he stopped. The radio man panted up to him and dropped to the ground.

"I'll radio in sir. It's regulations. We're at the border."

"Sutherland, you make a sound and I'll ram this barrel up your arse. Billyboy, Handsome, Joe, Dobie; come with me. You two wait here in case this is a decoy. Sutherland. Call in my chopper. Use code 'Paddy Down' and give him the co-ordinates of that hill there."

"But sir. We have no authorization to cross."

"We're crossing on my authority. Now make that call Sutherland, and not another word." With that, Barton and his men dropped their kit, grabbed their H&Ks, checked their clips, and were off toward Lynch.

Burke watched from his vantage point as the drama unfolded a mile away from him. He was surprised enough to see the patrol and hear the shots following Lynch's appearance. He was even more concerned when he saw the squad of five men cross. It had to be SAS. He had little time. The squad had to know that Lynch wasn't armed. There were five men following so it was likely they were going to take him alive. Otherwise they would have dropped him in the open zone. It was not a kill action. Tactics? They would call in a chopper and try and circle him.

He checked with the binoculars again. The men weren't spreading. No one was on point. They must have thought Lynch was alone. Now he had a chance. He grabbed his rifle and sped off to try and intercept Lynch. If they knew Lynch was covered they might hang back. They had to know they had crossed over. That would limit the amount of time they had.

Burke dropped behind a tree and checked the squad again. They were about 200 yards behind Lynch but he was slowing. Suddenly the squad broke. Four men continued as one dropped to his knee. He took aim and fired. Lynch was still running. The bullet struck the ground to the right of Lynch and he deeked left. Burke knew what would happen next and it did, too fast for him to stop it. Lynch's leg erupted in red and he fell. There was no time now.

Using the trees as cover Burke laid a line of fire between Lynch and the squad. Instantly the squad dropped. He grabbed his binos and checked Lynch. He was moving. Alive. So far. He'd have to get to him soon or it'd be too late.

The squad was deploying two points and checking to see where the fire had come from. Burke moved into the trees to get a better position. Then he heard it. Over the trees to the north came a throbbing chopper, gun-bay open and manned. The squad was tensing, ready to make a dash for Lynch. Burke laid down another line of fire and they dropped again. He could see the squad leader waving directions to the chopper. No radio. The chopper moved toward him. He fired again, hitting one of the men on point, then raced through the woods, coming out behind the chopper. A quick burst caught the gunner in the leg and the chopper pulled away to the squad and prepared to set down for evac.

They were leaving. There was a time limit to crossing during an operation and remaining undetected by the Garda. Even now there would be trouble. From Dublin the Dail would scream at Parliament about another incursion, the Americans would curse and the British would swell with self-righteous pride, diplomatically claiming map-error.

He had to double back and secure Lynch. The squad was loading as he sped across the clearing. The chopper began to lift and he fired a burst. Specks of metal flew from around the engine cowling and it flamed as it continued its ascent.

Barton was screaming his ass off. Two men wounded and now the goddamn chopper was hit. They couldn't take any more chances. If they went down in the Republic there'd be hell to pay. "Take her back to base." As the chopper swung around, Barton's defeat stung even more. He glanced down at the figure zig-zagging toward Lynch and shooting short bursts at the chopper. The face sprang up at him. "Christ, it's Burke!" He pulled himself up and grabbed the heavy machine gun and poured bullets at Burke as the chopper headed north. He saw Burke roll out of the way and then he was lost from sight. "Son of a fuckin' bitch," he yelled and slammed the barrel against the side of the chopper. "Get us back to base."

Burke watched the chopper fade into the sky as he reached Lynch. There was too much blood. He had been hit by the last blast. Burke knelt by the man's side. "I'm from Sullivan and Feeney."

Lynch coughed and blood oozed out of his mouth. "Get to McHenry," was all he could say. The words bubbled through his lips. He dug his fingers into Burke's arm and a shudder ran through him. He stared into Burke's eyes. Burke stared back but the light was gone. Dr Lynch was dead.

He wasn't worried about the SAS now but he had to clear out before the Garda got to the scene. Someone would've heard the shooting and seen the chopper. He slung his binos and the M-16A2 over his shoulder, then bent down to pick up Lynch. He hoisted Dr Lynch onto his shoulder, sickened by the soft, damp feeling of the man's chest. He turned and headed for the farmhouse.

As Burke approached the white wattle cottage carrying the bloody body, Sullivan and Feeney burst out of the door. "What happened?"

Burke pushed through them and entered the cottage, dumping the body on the table in the centre of the room. "SAS followed him across. I think he's dead."

Feeney checked him over as Burke slumped into a chair beside the low window and rubbed his eyes with his index fingers. "He's dead alright."

Sullivan came over to Burke. "Did he tell you anything?"

"Just some name."

Feeney looked up. "The message was strictly verbal. What names?"

"Name. McHenry. He said 'Go to McHenry' that's all," Burke answered without opening his eyes.

Sullivan and Feeney paced back and forth in the small room, muttering to each other. They looked at Burke, then moved over to the doorway and continued their conversation. Burke's exhaustion was passing. He hadn't been this active in a long while and, in a strange way, it felt good. It felt good until he became aware again of the damp, red stain on his shoulder and chest. He looked over at Feeney and Sullivan as they spoke in hushed tones. Feeney had his hand up covering his mouth as if he was afraid Burke could lip-read.

Sullivan approached him, removing his glasses. Feeney stood behind. "Martin, we have a job for you to do." Burke just looked up at him. "We need you to go to Belfast and contact this McHenry. Dr Feeney thinks it's a man that Dr Lynch had mentioned before, a physician. I think we can find his address."

Burke shifted in his chair and clasped his hands together. "I'm sorry gentleman but I can't go. You know there's still a warrant out for me in the North. And with the Royal Tour, it'll be crawling with Brit intelligence and SAS. I'm sorry, no."

Feeney moved closer. "I don't think you understand Martin. We need you to go. Until we have the information that Dr Lynch was carrying we consider you still under contract. Should you breach our agreement both the Garda and the British authorities will be informed of your whereabouts. Lynch can be shown to be connected to you, not us. We have men in the Garda who will see to that. You will be deported and returned to Long Kesh for the rest of your life."

Burke turned in his chair to face Feeney. "Little man," he began, "I told you not to fuck with me and you're fucking with me. That can get you killed." He shut his eyes and leaned back in the chair. He sensed the two men moving away from him. They would be looking at each other, wondering what to do, he thought. But as much as he knew he shouldn't go to Belfast, he knew he would. His failure to bring Lynch across, though not his fault, had become a question of honour. And he had enjoyed this brief taste of action, though not its result. There were other things too that beckoned from Belfast. If he played his cards right he could up his fee. They were right about one thing. They needed him.

Sullivan spoke and Burke opened his eyes. Feeney was standing off in a corner. "Martin, I want you to reconsider. Dr Feeney has a tendency to over-react but the information that Dr Lynch was carrying is crucial. Absolutely crucial to the future of Ireland. We had no way of knowing the SAS would be involved. At least discuss the matter with us."

Burke knew he had them in a good position now. "I'll discuss things with you, but Feeney is out."

Sullivan paused for a moment, then nodded his head affirmatively. "Alright, but we have to go now. Dr Feeney will cover our tracks here." Sullivan limped outside and Burke followed him.

As they reached the truck Burke asked Sullivan to wait as he had forgotten something. He walked back inside and went up to Feeney. "I forgot to say good-bye." Without hesitation he slugged Feeney under the jaw, knowing from the feel that the jaw had not broken but had made direct contact with the skull, forcing Feeney's brain to slosh out of control. Feeney collapsed on the floor, unconscious. Burke paused to rub his hand. The truck horn sounded and he bent over to pat Feeney on the cheek. "Pleasant dreams." Satisfied, Burke rejoined Sullivan and they left.

MIHQ, BELFAST

11:45 am, 2 June

Barton entered Wilkes' outer office at MIHQ and stood with the grime and smell of battle still on him while the secretary went in. He had just arrived from Armagh. His men were in hospital and he had stayed with them as long as he could, but Wilkes had wanted to see him immediately after receiving the information by radio and Hedley would want a briefing at noon. There would be hell to pay. No one had told him Martin Burke would be there. Everyone assumed that he would be out of the country after his escape. He remembered interrogating the bastard after his arrest in 1984. He was an arrogant sonofabitch and he had killed two of Barton's men by that time. The courts still hadn't been able to prove it and the prosecutor had advised him that they probably never would, unless they could put the arm on an informer. But Burke had done it. There was no doubt in Barton's mind. And this morning he had had a chance to kill the bastard legitimately and had been unable to do so. Politics.

"He'll see you now."

Barton strode in, shut the door and stood in front of the desk. Wilkes was standing by the window. He turned and motioned to the chairs at the side of the room. "For Christ's sake Gerry, have a seat. How are the men?" he asked pouring a couple of scotches.

"They'll be fine Ken. They're good lads. But Dobie will be going home for awhile." SAS never used last names: it would be too dangerous in the field to reveal a family name; there was always the risk of retaliation. "Martin Burke was there." He took the scotch from Wilkes' hand and took a drink as Wilkes sat in the other chair.

Wilkes looked at his drink for a moment. "It's a hell of a thing when a man like that can move with impunity. A hell of a thing when our lads get shot up and we have to hand the offenders over to a civilian Irish court." There was no mistaking his tone when he said 'Irish'.

"Any trouble from the Dail?"

"No. Hedley's people called them immediately and reported that you had established contact on this side of the border and that they had crossed and fired on you. He thinks it may not even be reported."

"That's good," Barton replied, relieved that he was off the hook. "What about Lynch? We downed him and I think that we might have hit him with the last burst. If we did, he's dead. How important was it to bring him back, really."

"Not that important. In a way, it's better if you did kill him." Wilkes was silent for a moment. "Gerry, we've been friends for a long time, we've served together..."

"Anything you ask, Ken. You know that," Barton answered quickly.

"It's not as simple as that. I want you to consider carefully what I'm about to say. It's no secret that we've taken a beating here. England has taken a beating everywhere, usually trying to help others. We play a larger game than most people can deal with. But here, Northern Ireland is a place we can't pull out of. There are too many lives at stake. And I know men like you and I could rid Ireland and England of the IRA if we were given some room to manoeuvre." Barton nodded. "Then there's this business of the Accord. We have to recognize the United Ireland Policy of the South and they have to stay out unless there's a majority vote up here to join. But the Sinn Fein is taking seats in the Dail. Who knows how long before the IRA might be able to shift things even more in their favour. Our people here feel the Dual Mandate is a politically expedient solution to the problem. Basically we'll give up, in measured stages, and leave our strongest allies in the hands of those murdering bastards. And after we're gone, well, I don't have to tell you what happened in the other colonies when our politicians gave up, or what happened here after partition. Marxist insurgents, more killing, and before you know it we could have an even more deadly enemy sitting on our doorstep. I don't feel like being encircled."

Barton sat forward. "Well?"

"What if something happened, something terrible, which finally convinced the politicians that the Accord was the wrong way to go and that direct military intervention was the only sane approach to the Irish question?"

"I'd say it was the best damn thing to happen since Cromwell."

"It's interesting that you mentioned Cromwell. What if the IRA were to assassinate Prince Charles?"

"We've already been through that in strategy sessions for the visit. Hedley would be in contact with the Prime Minister, there'd be a meeting of COBRA, massive military aid to civilian authorities, arrests..."

"I know, I know," Wilkes interrupted, "but how would you feel?"

"Me personally? Well, I wouldn't lose any sleep over it. Charles isn't my cup of tea. He's a vegetarian. And he plays with ouija boards!" They both laughed. "Andrew's worth ten of him. But I'd enjoy the opportunity to put a bullet in Martin Burke's head, and a few others."

"I couldn't agree with you more." Wilkes paused and looked out the window. "And if you discovered that such an operation was being planned, perhaps financed, handsomely, by Protestants in Belfast, and that this group planned to fit Martin Burke up for it and to turn him and the assassins over to the authorities afterwards, how would you suggest we go about stopping them?"

Barton paused too. He had known Wilkes long enough not to grasp the weight of this question. They had participated in actions in other countries which involved such scenarios. He also knew that the discussion would go no further than this room, not just because they were SAS, though that was reason enough.

Wilkes' secretary buzzed on the intercom. "He's ready for the briefing, sir."

Wilkes put down his empty glass. "Just some speculation, Gerry. Perhaps we can have lunch after the briefing." He rose and opened the door. Barton stood, put his glass on the table and followed. He already knew what his answer would be. The motto of the SAS said it all. 'Who Dares Wins'.

BELFAST

4:30 pm, 2 Meitheamh

Burke sat on a bench in Central Station. The trip from Dublin to Belfast had been uneventful. Apparently the British were more interested in movement out of the North than into it. He had gotten in with some Protestants who had been down to Dublin daytripping and he simply went back with them, singing Apprentice Boys songs and Orange tunes. He knew them well; hatred was often a good aid to memory.

His plan was to contact Hennessey. He hadn't seen him since he went into prison but he had heard that he was doing well in the IRA financial wing and that he was still living in Divis Flats. The last word was that Hennessey had gone to America on some fund-raising but that had been over six months ago. By now he would be back. Lynch had no family and it would be too dangerous to try to check out his house. MI would be all over it. Sullivan had come up with an address for McHenry and, once he got settled in with Hen he would try and arrange a meeting. After retrieving the information, he was to return to Dublin and Sullivan would have everything arranged for him to leave. Four soldiers approached. He pulled the newspaper up in front of his face until they passed, then grabbed his bag and made for the exit.

As he walked through the streets near the station he thought how strange it was to walk along the streets he had known in the past and which, until recently, he had thought would remain memories. There had been no great changes, just a gradual decline in everything that was human and gentle. Everywhere there was the green of soldiers and the rumble of armoured cars. The barricades still existed, mesh cages protected store fronts, sandbags were piled around the guards at banks, and there were the vehicle control zones where parking or vehicular traffic was prohibited. He remembered one American who had parked his car there, expecting a ticket at worst. When he returned the area was cordoned off and the Brits had blown the car up with a small charge designed to detonate any explosives in the car. Words like "normal" and "common" had different meanings in Belfast. People still had to go through the turnstiles and body searches to get into the city centre, patrols wandered about the streets and random check points popped up, then disappeared before the IRA could get wind of their location. Usually.

And the children were the same. Burke saw it in their faces. Most of them had lived their entire lives in the midst of continuous guerilla activities. War was their wet nurse.

Burke headed for the Divis flats, a sprawling tenement complex in the Falls Road area of Belfast. As he walked along a street just off the Falls Road he spotted a British checkpoint ahead, manned by the 1st Battalion, Parachute Regiment. And perhaps worse, he thought he saw a video camera. He paused, not sure what to do. If they spotted him turning around they might pursue him. There were no sidestreets between him and the checkpoint. As he slowed his walk he saw one of the soldiers stop a mother pushing a pram. She was not pleased and told him so. He reached inside anyway and checked under the baby for weapons, his probing hands waking the child who started wailing. The mother pushed him aside to pick up the baby and another soldier leveled his rifle at her. Three women who had been standing by the door to a house immediately started hurling abuse at the soldiers. The young one that had initiated the search backed away and the others came over to the scene unfolding. Burke smiled at the women. They had no fear of the soldiers and no respect for them either. He pitied the poor boys from parts English who had been raised to treat women with respect and in return expected shrinking violets. Not in Belfast.

"Go ahead you stunned fucker. Put a bullet in her head and one in the baby's too why don't you," one of the women yelled at the top of her lungs. The mother had now joined the women, babe in arms, the pram between them and the soldiers. It provided little cover for the barrage of abuse. One of the women reached down and picked up the baby bottle which had fallen to the ground in the search. She hurled it at one of the soldiers and caught him square on the knee. "Dead on," another women yelled and tossed a coke bottle at the troops now pulling back from the pram and forming a defensive perimeter around the saracen. The officer commanding appeared and made a futile attempt to quiet the situation. He spoke to the women who yelled back, pointed at the soldiers in one instant, the mother and baby the next. The OC spoke a bit longer and one of the women dashed out and, crossing the no man's land, stood with her hands on her hips shouting expletives to make a sailor blush. The soldier who had been hit with the baby bottle took a step toward her and she lunged out and punched him in the stomach. He reacted with a defensive manoeuvre which sent the woman sprawling. The others surged forward and the OC returned to his own men. The crowd had grown to about forty people and was getting hot. The OC now directed the men inside the saracen to aim the water cannon at the crowd. He asked them to dispel. It might as well have been Canute ordering the tide to cease its flow. Burke seized his opportunity and doubled back. Reinforcements would probably arrive and he wanted to be far away when they did. As he moved away the water cannon spurted and some of the less fortunate onlookers tumbled in the blast of water. He knew that bullets would be next and the crowd would dispel. It really wasn't that serious an incident. Just another episode in the day-to-day life of Belfast.

It had been awhile since Burke had been to Divis Flats but it was still the ugliest housing development this side of Hades. This high rise ghetto was near enough to the Protestant Shankill to be exciting and a good base from which to stage operations. Fortress-like and clearly sympathetic to the IRA, it was avoided as much as possible by the Brits. When he got to Hennessey's section he half intended to ask one of the children if Hennessey was around but he knew at best he would receive a dumb stare. There was a strict code of silence exercised against anyone asking a question. As he stood by the apartment door he could hear a telly on inside but that probably meant that Hen was not at home. It was more often on when he was out than when he was in. He knocked anyway but there was no answer. He was sure Hennessey still lived there from the news he had received in Long Kesh. Taking out a pen and a matchbook, he wrote a note, telling Hen to meet him at the Green Briar, a bar they had frequented when they had worked together. He slipped it under the door and gave one more knock. As he headed for the stairs a young boy stuck his head out the door to see who had been knocking. "Tell Hennessey that an old friend was here looking for him." The boy slammed the door shut. Burke knew he would pass the news on.

Back on the street, he passed the scene of the battle of the pram. The British were gone and so was the pram. The area was deserted again except for a few people standing talking. Along the curb was a furrow of litter washed there by the water cannon and, as Burke walked past he noticed the top of a broken baby bottle, its nipple filled with grit.

He stopped at a phone box on Brannen Street and called the number Sullivan had provided. There was no one home. He had to kill some time. He searched the street for a pub and saw one at the corner. Grabbing his bag he sauntered inside. Time for a whiskey or two.

Three whiskeys later he tried again.

"Dr McHenry's residence."

Burke heard a slight echoing ping. The phone could have a tap on it. He had not expected this but he should have. It had been a while and he had forgotten so much. "Is the Doctor in?"

"I'm afraid not. Is there a message?"

Burke responded in the negative then hung up. He would call back later, after he'd had time to plan a contact point. There would be plenty of places around the Falls Road which would provide him with a high degree of safety and he was assured of sympathetic and non-inquisitive people. They understood.

By 8 o'clock Burke had decided on a pub a few streets away from the phone booth on Brannen Street. He checked a house number near the corner, then called McHenry.

"Dr McHenry. Can I help you?"

Burke threw on the thickest accent he could. "Doctor, I'm glad to get a hold of you. Feeney suggested I get in touch with you. Said he was an old friend. Our little girl has got one hell of a fever and we don't have a family doctor. I was hoping you might drop by and have a look at her. We're a little worried. Could you come?" Burke held his breath.

McHenry bit. "Feeney, the old bastard. I haven't seen him in awhile. Sure I will. Where are you?"

"Well we just moved. You know, bills and all. We're on Brannen Street now, 35 Brannen. I'm sorry if I've bothered you."

"No trouble. I'll be there in a little while. What's the name?"

"It's Kelly, Doctor. This'll put the missus' mind to rest."

That had been simple, Burke thought. He would wait across the street in the pub and watch for the doctor. He didn't know what McHenry looked like, but he would watch for a doctor's bag. He would ask for a light on the street and tell him where they would meet an hour later. The last thing Burke wanted was to be spotted by the authorities. He did not relish a return to Long Kesh. Bobby Sands and the others hadn't softened the British resolve. It was still hell to those who knew it.

Burke stood by the window of Alison's with a whiskey in his hand. There was pleasant music playing on the radio and inside it was warm and bright, if a bit smokey. As he watched, a man turned the corner carrying a black bag. Burke downed his whiskey and moved out into the street. He planned to reach him before he got to 35. There were apartments there and he could easily go in and wait on the second landing for a few minutes before leaving. He could tell it was McHenry, not only by the bag but by the way the man moved — carefully, trying but not succeeding to be inconspicuous — an amateur.

It was then that Burke noticed another man lounging across the corner. The stranger straightened from the wall and cut across the street, moving toward McHenry. Burke was struck by his distinctive look: shocking red hair, sallow complexion and an aquiline nose. Then Burke heard a familiar noise. In the distance the clanging of dustbin lids began. The watchful children had spotted one of the many British patrols on its nightly rounds, snaking through the streets, had seen that they were moving with more precision than was required to simply 'show the flag' and were sending out a warning to the people.

McHenry froze and looked at Burke. Burke held his right hand up to his ear as if he were holding a telephone receiver and McHenry understood. The stranger glanced at Burke then moved his hand inside the pocket of his leather coat. What happened next was bedlam. Five British soldiers entered the street and rushed McHenry. Four of them were featureless but the fifth had a face which leapt at Burke. It was Barton. Again. Burke pulled himself back into the shadows. McHenry ducked down an alley way, followed by the stranger. The soldiers were close behind. Burke had cased the area earlier and realised that the alley twisted through a block of tenements, then ended at a brick wall. The only way out was a fire escape to the roof. McHenry would have to make it up that ladder or he would be taken. Burke slipped back around the corner, avoiding notice by the soldiers and headed to the next corner. He jumped up and pulled down the fire escape ladder then climbed toward the roof. The ladder banged back into place below him.

Sean sat out on the fire escape which jutted into the alley. He had climbed up to wait for his friend Dezy then they planned to play across the roof tops and watch for troops. He had heard the clanging of the lids and was ready to get to the street and head out in the direction of the noise when a man turned into the alley way and raced for the ladder. Dezy was going to miss another good time. The man was followed closely by another man, then by five soldiers. Two of the soldiers dropped by the alley entrance to cover the field. They knew whose town they were in. God, Sean wished he had a gun: an easy kill was just sitting there. He stepped back into the shadows of the doorway to watch the action.

The first man was climbing the stairs. He could hear him puffing. The Brits were yelling halt. Now the second man was starting up and the first man was on the flight which lead to the landing Sean was hiding on. A Brit yelled again, calling the man by name, McHenry, for Sean noticed a break in stride. That would do it. The Brits fired and this McHenry stiffened. He clutched the rail and looked at Sean. The second man was getting closer. McHenry grabbed at the railing and pulled himself onto the landing beside Sean. There was a lot of blood. Sean knew he couldn't take another shot, might not even survive this one. The soldiers had paused, not sure if they had hit him, not sure if he was armed. The second man had paused too and was watching Sean and McHenry from the darkness below. McHenry mumbled something and Sean leaned closer to hear. It was unclear at first. He mentioned some names and tried to describe a place, in a valley north of Belfast, and roads leading to it. Sean's mind raced to memorise what he was being told. His experience assured him that a man didn't make such an effort to talk when wounded unless it was important. Sean saw that blood was coming from the corner of his mouth. McHenry shivered in pain and wrenched himself up. Sean saw his eyes just before the beam of light from a soldier's torch found him. Below him the soldiers' gaze followed the beam up and Sean saw the OC tap a kneeling soldier's shoulder, and point at McHenry. Another shot rang out and McHenry toppled headlong into the black where the soldiers waited. The second man had made the landing below Sean and through the iron slats, Sean looked down into his eyes.

"What did he say, boy. The message was for me."

The soldier shot at the second man and a bullet whizzed past Sean's head. Things were too hot for Sean to stick around, and he knew inside that the red-haired man was not an ally. He saw the man reaching into his jacket pocket. Sean jumped in through the door and disappeared into the bowels of the tenement. He was sure the soldiers had not seen him.

The stranger had to move fast. If he went toward the door the boy had used, he would expose himself to fire. It would have been chance enough to try and kill him. The shot would have drawn more fire. He'd have to get the kid later. He leapt up onto the railing and sprang for the wall closing off the alley. Clearing the broken bottles at the top and landing in an open garbage dumper, he climbed out and lost himself in the backstreets. He had cased the area too.

Burke waited by the corner of the roof for a head to appear above the top. Then came the shouting of McHenry's name and the two shots. He sat tight but no one appeared above the roof line. After a few moments he saw some movement in the street and watched as the soldiers carried a limp body and a doctor's bag out to the van that had arrived on the scene. One body. The stranger had gotten away. He would have to move on too. The area would be swarming soon and there'd probably be a house-to-house search. SOP. He had to think, to plan his next move. He was back in the jungle again, moving as an animal and was lost in the gathering dark. As he melted away he was seen by, but did not see, a small boy leaning in a doorway, his face flushed with the evening's excitement.

Burke fell into the cab that stopped for him. He was deathly tired. The night had drained him and he needed a drink.

"Where to?" The cabbie leaned over the back of the seat.

"The Green Briar."

The cabbie drove off into the night. Burke sat pensively in the back as the street lamps illumined the car in a slow strobe of moving beams. There wasn't much traffic. It was a quiet night.

A second man had died on the way to meet him. The thought bothered Burke. How could he get the information that Sullivan demanded if all the pigeons died before they could coo in his ear? He had followed SOP: set up a rendezvous to mask the communication of a second meeting place. He hadn't reckoned on the Brits showing up and it made no sense for them to kill? Why not arrest? The Yellow Card demanded civilian power over the troops. But Lynch had been shot. By the SAS. And that fucking Barton had been there, leading the troops. In the dusk he had not been spotted but it left him with an uncomfortable feeling. He knew the SAS were liable to aim for the centre of the body mass rather than wing someone, and their warning shots often came second but still, with the Royal Tour approaching it would stand to reason that arrest and questioning of any suspicious characters would be the overriding concern. Dead men don't talk.

And who was the stranger? He was obviously laying in wait for McHenry but was not with the soldiers. Think, Burke! Too soon to draw conclusions. What are the possibilities? Informer? MI? Maybe a junkie after the doctor's bag? That was inconsequential for the moment. It was enough for Burke to know that he should exercise extra care. His largest concern was to get the information that McHenry had had. He would have to find someone who had been close to McHenry. Perhaps by attending the funeral he might be able to find a girlfriend, a wife, a brother, someone who would know something. It was all he had at the moment.

The cabbie pulled up abruptly to The Green Briar. Burke paid him off and got out. Pushing his way through the crowd just inside the door, he ordered a whiskey at the counter then took his drink to an empty table in the corner, eyeing the place cautiously. No one looked even vaguely familiar. The decor was the same but not the faces. Even the bartenders were different. He and Hen had spent quite a bit of time in this place in the past. Burke checked his watch and wondered if Hen had gotten home yet. If he didn't get here soon they'd be closing and then he'd have to find somewhere to hole up for the night. And most of all, at that moment, he wanted the comfort of a friend and a safe place to sleep. His first few days of freedom had been trying. He ordered another whiskey and sat back to wait. Waiting was a skill he had honed in Long Kesh. After his arrest in 1984 for possession of firearms he had spent a year of remands at the Crum — Crumlin Road Jail — before being sentenced to 20 years. He took up residency at Long Kesh, known also as the Maze, H-Block or Dachau depending on who was speaking. Each wing of the blocks had 25 cells and most of the prisoners were under thirty. They marvelled at how he had gone so long without being arrested and they marvelled equally at how a man like Martin Burke had ever been arrested. The answer was simple — an informer, a 'supergrass' the Brits called them. In the Diplock Courts the uncorroborated testimony of an informer was all that was required to take away a man's freedom forever.

Martin had often thought of 'his' informer, especially in the first few months; of how he might somehow repay the man or woman the kindness someday in the future, but the future rolled farther away from him. The British wanted more of his life and had began proceedings for murder trials. He was facing the prospect of spending a few lifetimes as a guest of Her Majesty.

It had been one short week ago that he was being transported from the Maze to the Crumlin Road Gaol in Belfast to await trial. He had ridden that path uneventfully twice in the last year. As far as the police were concerned he had resigned himself to a life in jail. In fact he had. His early defiance, which had resulted in him being confined to his cell twenty-four hours a day, was at best an attempt at solidarity but it didn't reflect his true feelings. The beatings and other indignities suffered by all of them were just too harsh to be real and he slipped away from them, turning in on himself. There were fewer and fewer things that were of interest to him. The institution had a way of pushing its way into a prisoner's brain, crowding out all other thoughts and he had embraced the peace which it offered.

He took another drink of whiskey and thought of his last ride in the grey police van. It had been moving slowly along a narrow one-way street and the guard sitting opposite him was smiling silently. Burke remembered smelling the sweat and excrement of rough times in the wagon's walls and thinking that the guard had to be over sixty. He had looked out the small barred window to the sunny street. A milk van was following them in the early morning, making deliveries. Suddenly the brakes squealed and his guard fell to the floor, his rifle sliding to the back door. Burke had leapt on the man instinctively and pinned him. Another van had backed out in front of the police van. Its side door swung open to reveal two men aiming bazookas at the two constables in the driver's seat. The milk van pulled up to the rear and an SMG poked through the rear window.

As he sat now in the Green Briar he wondered if any of the men here had been involved. He hadn't recognized anyone that day and they operated without conversation, quickly, efficiently. They bound and gagged the police constables and drove their van into a scrap yard, then put him in the milk van and headed south. He had been left alone in the van the entire time and, though he knew he was out of the Maze, he had no idea what to expect next. He slept. When he awoke the van was parked with its door open in a large garage. It was then that he had met Sullivan. He had received good medical care and, more importantly, good food. British prison fare was bad enough, but the 'Fenian Diet' was murder, slow murder. And now he was back in Belfast. Back where it had all started.

A man walked out of the lavatory and took a space at the bar. There was something familiar about that walk, Burke thought. The hair was short, the clothes were different but the walk struck a responsive chord. He watched for a glimpse of the face but it was too dark. Now the man was putting a cigarette in his mouth. Again familiar movements. Burke waited for the flare of the match. The match struck and moved close to the face. Hennessey!

Burke stood and walked to the bar, sliding in beside him, and ordered a drink. "Nice ring you've got there," Hennessey said, pointing to the silver ring with a red celtic cross which Burke had always worn on his right hand. "Why don't you just carry a fuckin' placard that says 'I'm a Fenian Bastard'. It'd be a little less obvious." He grinned. Burke punched him on the shoulder and they returned to his table.

"I recognized you when you came in so I trotted off for a piss to let you get settled. You've got great timing Martin."

"It's good to see you."

"The feeling's mutual but what the fuck are you doin' here? This is the wrong time for a prodigal return. And who in hell got you out? I sure as hell didn't have anything to do with it. Who'd want you," Hennessey said with a grin.

Burke explained in hushed tones the events of the last few days leaving out nothing. Hennessey had heard only that Martin Burke had escaped. "In a daring daylight raid the news said. They made quite a fuss about it all. And the troops were everywhere."

Martin looked at his empty glass then over at the bartender but Hen stopped him. "Look, let's head back to my place. It's still safe here but it's better to be out of sight."

Burke could only agree.

The apartment was small but friendly, with enough whiskey and Guinness to keep both of them happy for a long time. It was as if Martin had been expected. Hennessey had never heard of Sullivan or Feeney or, for that matter, McHenry or Lynch and he had no idea what they might be involved in, but he agreed with Burke that the best route was to attend McHenry's funeral and work from there. They would check the morning paper for details. Hen also suggested that he check with some of his contacts. Tomorrow. This night was for celebration, and catching up.

After Burke had gone into Long Kesh, Hennessey and Finnerty had parted company. They'd avoided visits as it was unwise for cell-members to visit and expose themselves to the English. Finnerty had settled into a retirement of sorts. At least this was what Hennessey had heard about a year ago. He had heard nothing since then. He himself had been away doing fund-raising as Burke had heard and had spent the last six months in Canada and the United States visiting sympathizers. Small speaking engagements had been set up by Noraid, and Boston, New York, Toronto and Chicago had been generous. The West Coast had been a different story. In Los Angeles he had attended a lot of parties but people there were more interested in picking his brains for the thrills of real life than in contributing.

"You wouldn't believe how much sun they have there Martin," Hennessey slurred as he reached for the whiskey bottle, "but the city's a drug. There wasn't much money there and so I decided to take a side trip to Texas. I got a ride with this old fellow, boots, hat and all. We were crossing Nevada when he pulled a gun on me. Naturally I thought he wanted the money and I didn't even have a cheque book on me. He told me to take a bottle of whiskey out of the glove box and then he held the gun to my head and told me to drink half of it. We were as close to flying without leaving the ground as you could be and I wasn't about to upset the pilot so I did. Then he handed me the gun, flashed a big Texan smile and drawled, 'Okay now make me do the same thing.'" Hennessey rolled on the floor laughing, tears streaming down his face. Burke joined in. It was the first time he had laughed out loud in years. It would be good working with Hennessey again.

They sat now in the dark, looking out the windows at Belfast below them. In the distance, he knew, was Long Kesh. Many evenings he had watched Belfast light. Many dawns he had watched it darken. Often he wished he would see nothing more. An old Alan Stivell song, *Spered Hollvedel* — Universal Spirit, came on the radio, one that almost drew tears from Burke. It had been long since he'd heard that song while thinking of the city and its troubles but the thoughts returned to him easily. This had been the first imperial battleground for the British and it would be their last. Here they had built their factories and enslaved a land. Once through the yoke, not only were weapons discarded but also language, culture, destiny. The Earls had fled, the Wild Geese had flown, the poets were dead and *geasa* were on the land. The people remained, empty vessels filled with a hatred borne of and fueled by the malevolence of foreign minds, pawns in a game which spanned the centuries. But the Geese and the poets would return, the *geasa* would be lifted as dark cloud clears in the dawn wind. The people would rise to a destiny of their own. Ireland would be free. Burke lifted his eyes unto the whiskey glass from whence came his inspiration. He banged back a shot. Hennessey farted then turned to him.

"You looked a bit serious and I felt some gaseous levity might be appropriate. As you might well remember that is my metier. You must have learned by now that if you're going to do a lot of remembering you have to learn how to forget as well."

Burke stirred in his chair. He glanced over at the telly. The sound was off but the late news was on. He watched a clip of soldiers checking pedestrians on the streets and then he saw the confrontation between the young mother and the soldier which he had witnessed earlier. It was chilling in its silence and the border between reality and fantasy softened. He wanted to say something about what he was feeling but nothing came. He knew then that he had had too much whiskey to remain awake or conscious.

"Goodnight."

Tomorrow they would have a lot to do.

FALLS ROAD

2 pm, 3 Meitheamh

Sean sat on the roof of his old apartment building, warmed by the summer sun. His mother was off at work and his brother Tim was out with his Provo friends. Sean had spent most of his 11 years playing in the streets or on roof-tops. The apartments he'd lived in had been too small and dark for him. And the streets had a curious blend of excitement and danger. So he took refuge in the open expanses of the roof-top.

Tonight they were moving. Just down the street, but they were moving, though there was not much to move. They had packed up seven times as far as he could remember; four since his father had been murdered. He knew his mother would be angry tonight, or in tears. She always got that way when she thought of his father, and she thought of his father every time she packed up the house. There would be clothes that he had worn, pictures of them all together and that picture which Sean liked best, the one of his father with a big happy Christmas grin, which hung beside the picture of the Pope. His mother never left anything behind. But Tim would leave the pigeons here for awhile. That and the view would make Sean stay on this roof.

It wasn't a picturesque view but it was what Sean liked most. He enjoyed watching. Watching people walk, watching patrols move along, watching the sixers — the armoured cars the British used — go by, pelted with stones by the children in the street. But today he was wondering about McHenry. He had learned the man's name and address from the papers that morning: another picture of a dead Catholic, another funeral announcement. He had already decided to go to Milltown Cemetery the next day for the funeral because he was curious as to why the man had been chased and what the significance of his last words was. Why had a dying man told him those things? Who was the other man who had leapt over the wall? And who was the man who had faded away from the scene in such a professional and suspicious manner? A lot of questions to be answered. He would find out more about this Dr McHenry. It was like being a spy. He enjoyed the role. But he would enjoy it a lot more if he could get a gun. He would have to get one sometime soon. Almost all of the other kids had guns. Tim had one too, but he didn't keep it in the house. If their mother ever found it she'd give him a good trouncing. She was like all the rest of the mothers. They never wanted their sons or daughters to take up guns but there was nothing they could really do about it. Sean knew he would get his. He just hoped it was soon.

He reached in under the tin casement of the roof and extracted a metal box which held some of his prized possessions: shell casings, one live rifle round, a rubber bullet, a CS gas canister, a piece of mirror, a half pack of cigarettes, some matches and other assorted but related paraphernalia. He took out a cigarette and lit it. Two things his mother wanted him to avoid in life: smoking and joining the IRA, 'the Ra' she called it. But both were his destiny. She never mentioned drinking. That would have been foolish. Checking to see that no one was looking he closed the box and slid it under the tin.

He leaned against the edge of the roof and took a drag on the cigarette, trying unsuccessfully to blow a smoke ring. He sat, soaking in the intense heat of the roof-top, smelling the tarred stones, feeling them with his hand. Tomorrow he would go to McHenry's funeral and after he would see where the man lived. He had never had a dying man speak directly to him before, though he had witnessed many deaths. He was entranced. He had to know more.

Looking down to the street again he noticed a small boy being led by his parents. Their clothes were different. Probably from America visiting relatives. He wondered what America was like. He'd seen lots of pictures: big houses with grass in front of them, cars, bathrooms that sparkled and shone and had carpets in them. He'd never go there. He would never leave Ireland. He watched the boy for awhile and decided to go down to the street for a closer look. He enjoyed listening to Americans talk.

Sean had been following them for half an hour now as they walked along the Belfast streets. They had discussed the weather, the buildings, how poor the man's cousins were, how they had to go out in the backyard to go to the bathroom and how they had to take the dog with them because the soldiers were always walking through the back alleys. Then they started talking about whether or not they would buy a pony when they got back to Toronto. Sean thought they must be very wealthy to be able to have a horse in the city. The boy was older than Sean, maybe thirteen, and he had been silent the entire time. He had earphones stuck in his ears and Sean had glimpsed the expensive tape recorder sticking out of his pocket. Once he had been close enough to hear the hiss of the music playing. He wanted something like that. He wanted to be able to walk the streets or sit on the roof and see all that he enjoyed seeing with the background music of his choice. They stopped by a small shop and the mother wanted to go in for souvenirs. The father followed but the boy just leaned against the shop window, listening to his tape and gazing off down the street. Sean decided he would get himself a tape recorder.

He approached the boy and leaned up against the wall beside him. In no time at all they were engaged in a conversation about Toronto and Belfast and the relative merit of various bands and the workings of the tape recorder. All the time Sean was sizing him up. He was bigger but not stronger. Even his face was soft and bored. He asked the boy if he wanted to get some new tapes and the lad seemed excited at the prospect. Sean explained that the shop was over on the next street but that they could cut through the alley beside the shop.

When Sean emerged on the next street he turned the sound up loud and listened with a joyous expression on his face to the music of U2. It wasn't a gun, but it was pretty good just the same.

Tim was there when he got home and he raced into the bedroom to show him the tape recorder.

"Pretty nice, kid. But don't let Mum see it," he said, then rolled back onto the bed and put his arm over his eyes.

Sean figured he could keep it in their room safely. His mother hardly ever came in. She was afraid she might find something. He looked over at Tim. He was tired. He hadn't come home last night and Sean was dying to ask him what he'd been doing but he knew Tim wouldn't tell him. "Mum's off work for the next week."

"I know," Tim said without moving his arm. He was quiet for a moment. "Thanks for your help the other day."

Sean was pleased. "A man got shot here last night. On the fire escape."

Tim uncovered his eyes and sat up. "I heard that. Did you see anything?"

"I was right there. It was SAS that shot him. There was another man there too but he got away."

Tim looked out the window. "He wasn't a Provo, the fella that got shot. Just some doctor."

Sean was tempted to tell him about the third man but Tim didn't seem interested. "Mum wants you to take some boxes over to the other place."

Tim smiled at him and got up off the bed. "Want to give me a hand with them?" He took a cigarette out of his pack and lit it then, noticing Sean watching him, pushed the pack towards him. "Want one?"

"Sure." Sean put his recorder on the table between their beds and took a cigarette.

"Don't tell Mum," Tim said, as he lit it. Together they went into the kitchen. Mum had said she wanted them to start there.

ON THE TOWN

8:30 pm, 3 Meitheamh

Burke and Hennessey had been in the pub drinking and talking about old times for quite awhile. Martin was becoming accustomed to his freedom and enjoyed the opportunity to be a normal human being again. They had been careful to stay inside through the day, though it had not been difficult as they'd spent most of it sleeping off the effects of the whiskey.

"I ran into road-blocks in Toronto when I was there," Hennessey was saying.

Burke looked up incredulously. "Really?"

"Sure. The police just stop cars on the streets. They want to know if you've been drinking."

Burke coughed and a fine spray of whiskey shot out of his mouth. "You've got to be kidding."

Hennessey shook his head and grinned. "No shit. And if you haven't been, they just let you go."

"Christ, that'd be nice."

"And the strip bars ..."

"I don't want to hear about it," Burke said and downed his whiskey. "I'm not strong enough yet. Let's go for a walk. It's getting loud in here."

Hennessey finished his drink and they moved out into the streets. "You still going to the funeral tomorrow?"

"Ya. I can pay my respects and I should be able to get something from his wife."

"It's a little risky. I mean, he's not an Official or a Provo, but the Brits might be covering it. There won't be any demonstrations to amount to anything, but he was shot on the street."

"Beautiful job the papers did. Drug deal! Fuck."

"It keeps the IRA out. Nobody will touch drug dealing. People can handle postal robberies and hold-ups. And they don't mind the Ra running the cabs or snatching the odd Dunne or Ruebens. That's acceptable." They passed three young girls on the street and slowed as Hennessey turned to watch them. "You want to go this way, Martin?"

Burke pulled him by the arm. "No. C'mon." They turned down a quiet side street. "You were arrested after they got me, weren't you Hen?"

Hennessey was silent for a moment. "Ya. They picked me up on the street the next day. Took me to Castlereagh."

"Was it bad?"

"No worse than what you got probably. They stripped me and made me stand with my hands outstretched and lean against a wall. There was no light and they had a generator or something running in the room. Just that fuckin' hum and nothing else. Then they questioned me. And kicked the shit out of me. That went on every day for about two weeks. Piss poor food and not much sleep. No Mass, no confession, Virgin Mary's a whore. You know the shit."

Burke didn't say anything and they walked on for another block.

"They offered me money if I'd give Queen's evidence against you."

"How much?"

"Told me to name my figure."

"And relocation?"

Hennessey pulled Burke to a stop and faced him. "They offered me whatever I wanted. And it wasn't two weeks. It was six. And I was in the hospital for two weeks after I got out. They had to take out one of my balls. The IRA took their turn with me then and I was taken out of action and put on funding. But I didn't turn, Martin. I didn't inform. So if that's what you want to know, you can fuck off."

Burke put his hands on Hennessey's shoulders. Hen shoved his hands in his jacket pockets and turned his head to the side but Martin pulled it back, looking him in the eyes. "It had to be said. We've been avoiding it. I wanted to hear it from you. I didn't ask anybody else. And if that's it, that's the end of it. Ok?"

Hennessey put his arms on Burke's shoulders. "Sure." They both smiled and walked on.

Turning the next corner, they found themselves passing a Protestant pub. As they went by, one of the lads lounging at the door caught sight of the celtic cross on Burke's ring. He punched one of his friends in the arm. "A fuckin' fenian. C'mon." Two more joined them and the four began following Burke and Hennessey.

Martin realised before they were halfway down the block that they were being trailed. He didn't want to get involved in anything and run the risk of being lifted but he didn't like walking with his back to the four thugs. He let Hennessey know and they speeded up their pace. They spotted a patrol down the street and turned a corner, then another. The four Prods were still on their heels and were now hurling insults. At the next corner Burke pulled Hen to the wall and they waited. The Prods came around the corner at full tilt and Martin grabbed the first one by the arm and swung him head first into the wall. There was a loud crack and he collapsed on the pavement. The other three ringed them and one of them pulled a knife. Burke squared off against him, taking off his coat and wrapping it around his left hand.

The lad who first spotted them made a play for Hennessey and Hen jammed his boot into the man's groin. He clutched his crotch and sank to the pavement, making retching sounds. The one remaining jumped Hennessey and they rolled on the street, punching each other.

Burke tried to keep out of range of his attacker's blade and they circled each other.

"I'll slice your throat, you fuckin' fenian cunt," he said and lunged at Burke. Martin stepped aside slightly and let the knife slash into his jacket. Then he wrapped his right arm around the man's neck and twirled him around, throwing him off balance. Pulling his left hand out of the jacket, he grasped his attacker's wrist tightly, bringing the man's elbow down hard on his knee. There was a loud crack and the knife clattered on the road. The man yelled in pain and Burke let him drop. He grabbed his jacket and turned to lend Hen a hand but Hennessey was sitting on his assailant, banging his head on the pavement. Burke went over and pulled him off.

Hen's nose was bleeding and he put his hand to his side as they moved back out to the main street. "He got in a couple of good ones."

"Looks like you did too."

Hen grinned and wiped the blood away from his nose. "I could use another drink."

"You've earned it," Burke said and put his arm around Hennessey to steady him as they headed for a pub. "You really only have one nut?"

"Ya, but they stretched my prick, so it all came out even in the end."

NEW YORK

4:30 pm, 3 June

Magee had been waiting for fifteen minutes and he didn't like waiting. He'd made arrangements with Ransom to meet him at the coffee shop beside the Statler Hotel, across from Penn Station. He'd spent the afternoon walking around Times Square, had gone into the peep shows, watched passersby get swindled out of their money by the hawkers playing three card monte on the sidewalks. It was hot in New York in the summer. Hotter than it was in his childhood memories. The people sweated, the air conditioners hummed and dripped and the pavement steamed and shimmered. He knew Ransom would come through but he had a tight schedule and he wanted to keep it that way. Too often plans failed because equipment and men had arrived well in advance and had been found by the authorities. He had gotten where he had by arranging things with split-second accuracy and that called for associates who could be trusted to come through under pressure.

He heard a tapping on the window and looked out. Ransom was there, sunglasses on, a big smile on his face. He ducked in through the door and came over to the booth.

"It's all arranged. Didn't I tell you it'd be a cinch."

"And you knew you'd be up shit creek if you fucked me around."

"Nothing personal Mikey", Ransom said as he ducked his head almost down to table level, drumming the tabletop with his thumbs, "but it was the fear of losing all that money that was the gun in my back. Feel like going for a ride?"

"Where to?"

"I need a coke. Hey, darlin' bring me a coke will ya? Over to JFK. The stuff is in Plattsburgh, New York and I was afraid it might not get here in time for the military flight I'd been counting on to transport it. Too much paper work to expedite it. So my buddy Jake, he's a pilot for National, he's got a flight going out tonight to Plattsburgh to pick up some troops. Gonna ferry them over to Frankfurt. It's an exercise for troop movement in emergencies using commercial carriers. And he can guarantee us a stop in Northern Ireland. He's flying a 747, old 9666 and it's always got engine trouble. If your people can work with that, we're laughing."

"Sounds good. What's the ETA?"

The waitress brought Ransom's coke to the table. "Thanks. He figures about 2 tomorrow afternoon their time. Your guys just have to off-load six crates. I got you one of those new TOWs the Corps is using, the BILL, and some high explosive warheads with anti-personnel steel balls. Good for about two clicks and it'll blow fuck outa anything it hits. And there's some more of those M-16A2s, a couple small rockets, those M-136s in the Kevlar tubes, and some very sophisticated timing devices for the explosives. It's all top of the line US issue and I brought us in under budget. Bonus, right?"

"Sure. Whatever you can shave off the allocation. What about your buddy Jake?"

"He's ok. He was a Navy flyer in Lebanon when we were there. I met him just after you went home. A good guy."

"How much?"

"A pittance, my good man. Five grand. And he's heading for the Haj flights after this, so he'll be out of the way. Did I do good or did I do good?"

"You did good. What about me?"

"Oh ya. You are going along as military personnel. Jake will tell the crew that. And the CO in Bangor has the same story but nobody's gonna ask. You'll ride with the flight crew to the plane at JFK so there's no problem with airport security. Then you can just slip out when the crates are off-loaded."

"You did real good Ransom. Have we got time for some drinks?"

"Are you kiddin'. There's always time for some drinks. There's this new place I found. It's a touch bar. You gotta see it. They bring the girls in from Montreal. Their English isn't so shit hot, but the rest of them is."

Magee paid the bill and they went up to his room so he could phone in instructions, then they headed back uptown.

True to Ransom's word there was no trouble with Jake and the National flight. They arrived in Plattsburg and loaded the soldiers. 505 kids got on with their gear and the equipment was stowed, including Magee's six crates. The Commanding Officer with the troops was part of Ransom's operation but he had no knowledge that Magee was the recipient. Ransom was skilled at keeping contacts minimal. And the pilot had no idea what he was carrying. He didn't say much and the crew left him alone.

The troops had taken a long time to get settled. It seemed they all wanted to take pictures of the flight attendants holding their rifles and then there was the job of pushing their helmets and kit under their seats or in the overhead storage compartments. Finally they had all been strapped in, rifles in their hands, and the plane had taken off again.

As Magee watched the boy-soldiers sleeping in their seats he remembered his first trip overseas. But it wasn't a training exercise. Lebanon had been a bit hairier than that. Still, he had done well by his time in the service. He had intended to profit from the experience and Uncle Sam had not let him down. Arms dealing was a lucrative business and there were enough contracts going around that he could pick and choose. It was safer than working as a merc and the return was a hell of a lot better. Those guys always talked of the big score and retiring, but they spent most of their time either dreaming or dying. He didn't plan on retiring either. There were plans afoot for some larger smuggling operations in the new year and he could see himself weeding out the competition. He had also made enough contacts on the dark side of the US military and the intelligence service that he might shift over into their field of operations.

He watched one of the boys wake from a shallow sleep with his mouth open and strain to wet it sufficiently to be comfortable enough to drift off again. The flight attendants were upstairs talking to the COs and everyone on this deck seemed to be asleep. He would join them soon. He thought of how different they were from the lads he had recruited in Belfast. They were training in Libya at a terrorist camp and he had a guy there he could trust looking after them. Amin Ali. He was PLO and he was good. They had done some deals in Lebanon and they trusted each other as much as they needed too, which was a higher level of trust than he had for most people. The lads were perfect for the operation, young Catholics dissatisfied with the Accord, dissatisfied with the lack of action on the part of the Provisional IRA. They didn't want to see the Accord work. To them the Republican Government had sold out, as it had in 1922; a sell-out which resulted in Civil War. And so taking out the Prince was an attractive proposition. And when they heard that Martin Burke was heading it up and that they would help spring him from Long Kesh before the job, they almost wet their pants. They had been raised on stories about him.

He wondered how they would feel if they knew that the operation was funded by Protestants who wanted the Accord off and SAS brass pissed off about having to kowtow to civilian authorities in Ireland. How would they feel if they knew that the end result would likely be a military backlash which would decimate the IRA? The stupid bastards. Both sides were fucking peasants as far as he could see. They deserved each other. Turning the boys over to the Brits after was fine with him but he didn't relish turning Burke over. That was some guy. Sort of a comrade-at-arms in the business, but too narrow. He figured the business had to be cleaned out every once in awhile. It made room for new growth. Survival of the fittest. And he felt fit.

MILLTOWN CEMETERY

2 pm, 4 Meitheamh

Hennessey's black suit was a bit tight for Burke and he loosened the second button in the vest then stepped out of the cab. He could see the funeral party at the graveside but noticed no choppers in the air. He was glad he was not late. Hennessey had gone off early on some errand and Burke had slept in. He was finding it difficult to resume normal patterns after Long Kesh. It was strange to be able to move freely, to have a choice of what to eat, to have a comfortable bed, to not have a nagging fear of corporal punishment gnawing on his intestines. As he crossed the cemetery he could see the Father closing his book. Next would come the Holy water and the handfuls of dirt, then off McHenry would go, into the deep damp dark. He arrived at the graveside and instinctively checked if his fingernails were clean. It was an old habit borne of days in parochial school and every time he was near a priest the response was triggered.

The day was raw with the wind but clear and surprisingly sunny. A few clouds scudded over, blocking the sun sporadically. Of the many faces around the grave two stood out. Two women, veiled, in black, stood by the priest. One, a very old women, was holding an infant. Beside her a younger woman in weeds cried. The widow McHenry, her child held by her mother or mother-in-law, no doubt. Then from above came the expected pounding throb. The English would not miss sending a chopper to the funeral of a man possibly connected with the IRA. The photographs would later be analyzed in detail at MIHQ and more faces would be added to the surveillance lists. Burke hung his head. He hoped he would not be seen by the nitred eye. The eyes about the grave held no threat for him. There were only about forty people besides himself and the priest. A number that small could not harbour a spy. In the building across from the cemetery there might be cameras but one could only take so many precautions. When he left he would duck quickly into his waiting cab; that would be sufficient. He caught a suspicious glance from others at the graveside and realized that he was an unknown quantity to them. He was pleased they had not recognized him. He rubbed his left eye with the fingers of his right hand then held it, three fingers extended, over his heart for a moment, the three fingers of his left hand extended at his side. In his past that had been enough to identify someone of the Third Battalion, Belfast. It was discarded now, but, judging by the age of some in attendance, the sign would be recognized. The faces of the men relaxed and he felt much more comfortable.

The chopper had passed now, and the mourners began picking handfuls of dirt and tossing them onto the coffin which now lay at the bottom of the grave. The widow took her infant's hand, pressed some dirt into it and held it out over the grave. The tiny fingers opened, depositing a lump of clay into McHenry's last resting place. Burke felt his throat constrict. Another fatherless child, made so by the violence of Ulster, by the British. He hated the entire situation. It would go on forever. He would be better out of it. He had once tried to do something but had only contributed to the malaise. Now the death which followed him had struck this family. He decided he could not approach Mrs McHenry now. The graveside was not the proper place to discuss the business which had resulted in her husband's death, and yet time was crucial. He could not remain in Belfast longer than was necessary and risk entrapment. There would be a gathering at the McHenry home in the afternoon as was the custom and no doubt many neighbours would be calling. That would be the best time to see her.

Burke joined the procession and tossed his handful of earth then followed them out to the waiting cars. He did not notice the man with the red hair lounging on the corner across from the cemetery entrance. However, as he ducked into his car he did notice a young boy with blondish hair who leaned in the doorway across from his car. Both the man and the boy recognized Burke.

Donncha Cronin had known it was Burke after the grilling he had received from his superior, Sullivan, following the incident in the alley. Sullivan had banged Donncha's chair with his cane in anger as Donncha had explained how he had failed in getting to McHenry. Then Sullivan had thrown a photo in front of him and yelled, 'Burke?' Yes, it had been Burke. Curiously, Sullivan had seemed pleased that Burke had been on the scene. But it hadn't made him any more pleasant. And Cronin didn't want to face an angry Sullivan a second time. He did not suffer fools gladly.

Cronin stepped onto the sidewalk as Sean moved out of the doorway, intent on approaching Burke in his car. Sean looked at Cronin then to Burke's car as it pulled away. He sensed danger from the red-haired man with the hooked nose and he reacted immediately. He did not know this area well but it was a rabbit warren of alleyways similar to most of the poorer Catholic areas of Belfast. Sean saw Cronin move toward him and tore down the nearest alley with his pursuer hot on his heels.

As Sean ran he could hear the panting of this man behind him and it frightened him. They dodged from one alley to another, down alleys built in the jumbled haste of impoverished construction. Cronin was getting closer, his long legs eating up the head start Sean had on him. He reached into the pocket of his bomber jacket and felt his automatic fitted with a silencer. The boy would not escape.

Sean's mind was racing. With lightning speed he chose turns, trying to keep track of his directions so that he would eventually end up back on the main street. That was the strategy of the streets — run a jagged square, tire your pursuer, then burst into the open and escape. The panting was louder now and their feet slapped the pavement in grotesque rhythms. Sean's forehead was beaded with sweat. Suddenly a wall loomed in front of him — a blind alley. He had guessed wrong. Cronin turned the corner before he could escape. Sean took a deep breath and stood, waiting for Cronin to get close enough for him to duck between his legs and escape. Cronin advanced cautiously on the trapped boy. He had grown up in similar streets and knew the tricks. He would take no chances. He drew his automatic.

"Alright boy, we're gonna have a little chat, you and me."

Sean waited, like a caged animal, watching for some opportunity or some salvation. "I got nothing to say to you."

Cronin shot into the pile of refuse in the corner. The silence of the shot terrified Sean. He backed against the wall, uncertain of what to do, frozen. Cronin pushed the end of the silencer into Sean's ear and with his left hand slapped him up from the chin. Sean's head banged against the wall behind him and he fell. Cronin bent over and slammed the barrel of the silencer across Sean's face, ripping his cheek. Sean was dazed and still frightened, but as he tasted his own blood a deep anger rose in him. "When we get the Brits you'll go too, you fuckin' prod." Cronin chuckled and Sean seized his moment. With all his might he forced his foot up into Cronin's crotch. The man's face exploded in red and he fell to the side. It was enough. Sean got to his feet and raced away. He thought of the other man he had seen that night. He had been at the funeral and had to be a friend of McHenry's. He looked behind him but saw no sign of Cronin. It was a long way to McHenry's address.

The soldier stood 50 feet above the street in his concrete box, watching. Through his slots he could view the neighbourhood from all directions and the binoculars helped. For the darkness he had his light amplification night scope. The people living below in the houses and rows had long since grown accustomed to this towering intrusion into their privacy. Often they would leave their curtains open. Always he would watch. The power stimulated him. It was not the occasional sex or bare breast he glimpsed, but the little things, someone picking his nose, someone having trouble deciding which dress she would wear, that meant the most. Like Zeus on Olympus he could watch and, if need be, send lightning bolts to, strike fear and death amid his charges. Today he was especially watchful.

The wind whipped along the street and, even with the bright sun, Burke was forced to turn up his collar. He had not bargained for the observation post. There were many in Belfast in the troubled areas and on the fringes. It was surprising that a doctor would live in this part of Andersontown but then there were doctors who were not concerned with the class distinctions money and education could buy. There had been lawyers like that too.

Burke walked up to the door. Inside he could hear the murmur of voices. Not too many. It would be all right. He rang the bell. Footsteps approached; a woman's. The door opened and Burke was surprized to see the woman he believed to be Mrs McHenry. Without her veil she seemed much younger and less distraught.

"Mrs McHenry?"

"Oh hello. The men are down at the pub."

"Well, I'd like to see you for a moment. I'm sorry to be imposing on such a day but I had arranged to meet your husband the other night... Could I have a word with you alone?" Burke noticed that she had twitched when he mentioned that he was to have met her husband.

Mrs McHenry shut the door. "I was curious after I'd seen you at the funeral. I don't believe we've met."

"It's better that I don't tell you my name. I've been sent by a Mr Sullivan regarding Dr Lynch." Burke saw that she was nervous but she displayed nothing to the guests in the parlor, some of whom were now glancing curiously out into the foyer.

"Mum, could you take care of Jeremy for a moment." She led Burke into what was apparently the Doctor's study and closed the door. The clean smell of antiseptic hung in the air, and a smell that reminded him of bananas. "Dr Lynch disappeared five days ago. I had expected him at the funeral. What's wrong?"

"I'm afraid Dr Lynch is dead. He was shot crossing the border."

"My God." Mrs McHenry composed herself. "Did he have a chance to speak to Dr Feeney?"

Burke decided to level with her. After the recent events, she deserved to know. "He spoke to me before he died. Mentioned your husband's name and that was all. Sullivan sent me to track down the information. I contacted your husband but the soldiers took him before he could get to me."

"So he didn't give you the information?"

"What information?"

"The information you were looking for. Some secrets are better kept, even from wives. He and Charlie, Dr Lynch, had gotten involved in something but I don't know what."

Burke sensed she knew more than she was saying, but he didn't blame her for being cautious. Suddenly the air was filled with the clanging of dustbin lids. She stood. "The patrol. They might just be doing a house search. It happens at funerals. But you may have been spotted. Quickly, into the kitchen." She grabbed Burke's arm and pulled him through a door. "Get out through the back. There's an alley over that wall that'll take you to the side street. Hurry. They might have it covered already."

Burke could hear the roar of a Saracen as it screeched to a halt outside the front door and the screams of children as they pelted the armoured car with stones. "But I need to know."

"I don't know anymore than I told you. I'm sorry."

Burke stood in the doorway leading to the back of the house. Boots beat a path to the front door and a fist banged. Burke looked into her eyes. "I'm sorry too." She understood. He jumped down the stairs as the troops entered and the guests started berating them for searching a house at such a time. Those feisty women would hold off the search long enough. Burke hoisted himself over the brick wall and dropped into the alley on the other side. There was no sign of troops. He moved hurriedly out onto the side street. Glancing up towards the corner he saw the tail end of the sixer surrounded by the children of the street. They, too, would help him escape. Then his eyes met eyes he had seen before. It was the young boy who had been watching him when he left the cemetery. Burke turned and raced off down the street, rounded a corner and disappeared.

Sean wasn't really surprised to see the man again. His instincts told him that this was the man he should talk to. But right now he had to help him get away from the patrol. He rallied his friends and concentrated the attack.

BELFAST

7 pm, 4 Meitheamh

Burke heard the door slam and for a moment he thought he was back in the Maze, but the voice was calling him by name, not number.

"Get up, you lazy bastard. I've got some news." It was Hennessey. Burke sat up on the couch and pulled himself into a sitting position. He had fallen asleep fully clothed and, sometime during his fitful sleep, he had pulled the blanket off the back of the couch and wrapped it around him.

"Back on the blanket are you?" Hennessey said, walking into the kitchen. "I was talking to Finn," he said as he bent over to open the fridge and pulled out a quart of milk, drinking from the carton.

"Who," Burke asked, still groggy.

"Finn. Finnerty. You remember him don't you?"

The old man's face flashed through Burke's mind and he saw him standing at his father's graveside. In a land of old faces his had been older still.

"I haven't talked to him in over a year," Hennessey continued. "He's working a newspaper vending operation down in the centre of town. We're going to get together tomorrow. He says to give you a good kick in the ass. And he thinks that red-haired guy you were talking about might be a guy named Cronin, Donncha Cronin. He's a small timer who did a few jobs including blasting a barracks a little while back with some rockets. He was with INLA. Finn heard he got arrested on suspicion but was released, a little too quick he thinks. Some think he might have made a deal but he's kept his nose clean and he hasn't done anything lately. I've also set up a meeting for tonight with some lads who might have some information. I heard they know of McHenry at least, so I thought what the hell. And apparently there's a good looking girl with them." Hen took another swig of milk.

Burke was standing now, stretching. "Who is she?"

Hen smiled. "I thought that might perk you up. It's been awhile, has it?"

"When I first got out all I could think of was good food and a beer. Now my thoughts have turned to the finer things of life."

"Looking for a sweet valley to lay your weapon in?"

"Nothing so lyrical as that." Burke moved into the bathroom and pushed the door shut.

He stood in front of the mirror and began shaving off the beard he had worn ever since South Africa. Even in Long Kesh, he had kept it, though he often woke up with maggots in it in the morning. Now a clean-shaven face might keep him from being recognized too quickly. As he shaved he thought of Finnerty. Finn had been old for as long as Burke had known him. The white noise of the water running in the sink blotted out the street noise below.

He was alone now, with old Finn, at his father's grave. Overhead a British chopper hovered, watching the mourners, as a squad of soldiers stood guard in the distance. No doubt his father's murderer was in their number. Burke's blood burned in his veins, his knuckles white from anger, and he was ready to attack that squad, to feel the throat of his father's murderer crush in his hands, hear the crack of the windpipe and the death rattle, see the blue tongue and bulging eyes, know that he had avenged his father's death. Finn must have read his mind, or perhaps had travelled that road many times himself. He placed his hand on Burke's shoulder and whispered a story to him. It began softly.

"In time Martin, in time. This land has been millenia in growing. It is the centre. And in time the pain will cease. Choose your own time of vengeance for it is a sweeter victory when it is you who are in control. Think back to the Desmond Wars when the Captain of Desmond, Fitzmaurice, battled the English Lord President of Munster, Perrot. Time and time again the English smashed at Fitzmaurice, time and time again he rallied his forces, gaining back whatever he had lost. Finally the English commander had had enough. He challenged Fitzmaurice to single combat, hoping to solve his problems once and for all and satisfy the malcontents back in England. Fitzmaurice agreed and began a long correspondence with Perrot, regarding terms.

"First they spoke of a place and a field in a clearing in Kilmore Wood, not far from Kilmallock was agreed. But Fitzmaurice would not fight on English mounts and so Irish hobs were agreed to. Then Fitzmaurice, not caring for English armour, demanded that they both wear Irish battledress and fight with darts and Irish broadswords. Perrot, exasperated and under pressure from his army to settle the matter, sent the Irish messenger back with word of his agreement, not aware that the messenger was none other than Fitzmaurice himself, in disguise. On the appointed day Perrot awaited Fitzmaurice, in front of his entire army, wearing scarlet tights and a yellow robe, with his darts and sword, astride a low-slung Irish mount. The morning dawned clear and bright. Perrot waited as the day lengthened and a drizzle began. No one appeared.

"Finally, wet and humiliated, he cast his sword aside and was ready to leave when the Irish messenger with whom he had been parlaying, rode up with another note. Perrot took the piece of paper and read it as the 'messenger' waited, grinning triumphantly. 'If I do kill the great Sir John Perrot the Queen of England will send but another President into this province. I choose rather to fight your soldiers for they, being closer to men than to politics, closer to blood than ink, know the meaning of the war I wage. When they are gone you will be defeated without need of arms, as you are today.' Perrot wheeled his mount and rode away, alone in the rain, weeping."

Burke and Hennessey sauntered down the street towards Doherty's, a noisey bar where the people gathered to sing along to music provided by a man seated on a small stage playing an accordian. It was a quiet night and the fog was only now beginning to roll into the streets. Here and there people passed, their tones hushed; not with fear but with intimacy. It was a night that would make Belfast look its best and make a passerby forget the Troubles. Hennessey lit a Gauloise and the pungent odour pleased Burke. He had stopped smoking a long time ago but he still enjoyed the smell of exhaled tobacco smoke. Through the frosted windows of Doherty's shadowy heads bobbed, drinking, talking, singing. Inside, the pub was noisy and crowded. Burke and Hennessey stood at the bar and ordered some Strongbow, then surveyed the place. There seemed to be a very regular crowd.

Hennessey entered the darkened back room lounge to check for the girl who had been named as the contact. It was quieter and less smoky. Men and women sat together in dark booths talking and drinking, passing time. He spotted her by the description he had been given. She *was* beautiful. He walked over to the table and introduced himself. She then pointed to a table in the corner where three men sat drinking and told him to bring his friend there.

Burke was just getting up as Hennessey returned to the bar. "You seemed to be taking a long time so I figured I should come in. Where is she?"

Hennessey gestured to the table. "Over there, but don't get your ass in an uproar. She's more my age."

Burke smiled and pushed past him. "Thanks for the advice."

When they reached the table one of the seated men rose, extending his hand.

"I'm Michael O'Donnahue."

Burke shook his hand. O'Donnahue turned to his companions and introduced them. Burke could not take his eyes off the girl and Meagan did not take her eyes off him.

Burke felt numb as the small talk began. These people were nineteen twenty, twenty-one. He wondered if he was an old man foolishly involved in a young man's game. And this Meagan O'Farrell he had been introduced to, he looked at her and felt things he had not felt for a long time, and it was frightening. Fear was not an emotion he was accustomed to. Nor was this other emotion he felt. He heard O'Donnahue drone on about how much he and the others had heard of Martin Burke and he nodded as if they were talking about someone with whom he was only slightly acquainted, or someone dead. They were glad he was out. Some of them had been there too. Some at the same time as he. He didn't remember any of their faces. He heard Hennessey talk about Cronin and what they needed to know. He heard her speak, heard her say that she had heard information that Brit intelligence was convening emergency meetings to deal with his escape and possible presence in Belfast and that he was rumoured to have been involved in what they described as the "McHenry Incident". As she spoke he focussed on her lips — moist, red, full. Then, the vision melted away before some cold, hard realizations. This was important information.

"They're very concerned about your escape and the coming Royal visit," she was saying. "Over at MI they've pulled out your old dossier and you're the number one priority. You'll have to be careful."

Burke stirred. "You seem to have some excellent sources. I plan on being careful. But what about this McHenry and," he looked at Hen, "you've told them about Sullivan and Feeney."

Burke watched as she looked at O'Donnahue and he gestered for her to continue. "Feeney and McHenry seem to have known each other in the old days. There was a rumour that McHenry and a friend of his named Lynch were placed on a hit list by the UVF but we don't know, though I found out that Dr Lynch disappeared a couple of days ago, probably to go into hiding. But there's other talk that they might have been informing on IRA members. There's no confirmation but they both had treated some of the lads and the lads are always getting arrested. Maybe the heat was on and they got their British friends to plant the rumour."

"That doesn't sound right. I was talking with McHenry's widow and she didn't know anything about his death or what had happened to this Lynch fellow. But I'll talk to her again though, maybe tomorrow. I had to leave in a bit of a hurry yesterday."

"I heard about that," said O'Donnahue. "Supremo Hedley was not pleased that you turned down his invitation."

Hedley. The name rang in Burke's ears. He had met William Hedley in Rhodesia during his time there. Hedley had come to monitor a military operation and, in the light of a bonfire of insurgents killed in the recent fighting, they had drank and talked, far into the night. He had known that Hedley was rather high up in MI at the time and he had felt that Hedley had known a bit about him, but Ireland was too far away and out there, in the stench of burning flesh, they were all white and British. Now Hedley was in charge of intelligence in Northern Ireland. He was a man to be reckoned with.

"Hen mentioned that you knew something about Cronin, the one that was tailing McHenry?" Burke asked.

"Not much more than Hennessey already knows," O'Donnahue continued, "but I'll check. There was some talk he'd been involved in the job on the Household Cavalry in London a few years ago and I know he had something to do with that last rocket attack on the barracks. That got INLA some good funding, though more is coming through to us now that Sinn Fein is ready to sit in the Dail. I don't think MI knows he was in on it or they wouldn't have released him. But he was a pretty small actor in the INLA manoeuvres."

Burke found all of this darkly amusing. "You sound like a businessman running over a sales campaign."

"It is a business," a young man named McCreesh rejoined. "You only get support if you're doing something. Ask Hennessey about that. He was fund-raising, wasn't he? We're in for the duration but the people on the outside have the cash and they want their donations to bear some sort of fruit or else they feel ripped off. With the Accord the central finance committee that works through Noraid and the Irish Caucus in the U.S. has been having more and more trouble. And the Noraid funds get more and more tied up in defense funds every time the CIA or the FBI busts one of our US buyers. When things get too quiet we loose the publicity. Who wants to fund a war that they never hear about? That's why we had to increase local funding sources like the clubs, not *shebeens* but legit clubs, and the co-ops and taxis. We let the Prods have the security businesses because we aren't geared up for that, but they have to pay us a surcharge when they act as security at building sites in our areas. We can hold on and eventually we'll succeed. There's no way to break a cell structure like ours."

Burke wasn't surprized at the youthful confidence. He'd come up against it before. "What about the French in Algeria or the Canadians in Quebec? The cell structure crumbled there."

McCreesh smiled. "I could argue with you on both those counts, but those were different situations. We have a large, sympathetic populace, the South which unofficially harbours us and lets us mount quick offensives and inexpensively train new recruits, though that's been hurt with the Accord. We have strong support in the US and we have a military opposition which is not popular with either side here. Either they do too much or too little. We have a better chance at survival than the PLO and a much much better chance at succeeding. If the Protestants would just understand that we're fighting the British for them as well and quit supporting them we'd be on our way. But Britain won't last. It's going down the tubes. 20% unemployment, racial disputes, a developing rift with the U.S. And we help. Every year the Brits pour money in here to try and beat us and to keep the Plantation happy. Time is on our side. We'll always have more recruits; in that way it's like a tribal feud. All we have to do is raise hell every so often to keep a profile and wait for the vacuum when Britain collapses. It's inevitable."

Burke was drawn in and wanted to know just how these young men did feel. "Well what about the Accord? The Protestants are afraid of it because it leads, so they see it, to eventual British pullout, papacy and pogroms."

McCreesh's friend, a thin long-haired blond called Cahill, spoke up. "And the peace movement is solidly behind it, the fucking sheep. The Accord is a fraud. It buys the Brits time to try and crack us. But they won't. And we can use it to our advantage. We can't stop the campaign or the money would dry up. So we continue our strategy of crippling the economy. It brings things to a standstill. If we piss off the Protestants with a few actions here and there, and you know how easy that is with Paisley and them, they'll over react as usual and the Brits will take steps to maintain Peace, Order and Good Government. It's just more bad press for them and that much more support for us, here and abroad."

Burke looked at O'Donnahue. "And in the end, with the Brits gone?"

"There's no denying there'll be trouble. We're moving into legitimate political arenas all the time but it's "ballots *and* bullets". The Unionists have asked for it. But we only take action against the Brits and those Prods who have moved directly against us. We're not in the business of sectarian murders. That's a Prod game."

Burke had to give that point to O'Donnahue. He remembered the tales of butcher squads who would send people out on buses to watch who crossed themselves as the bus went by a church, then wait until an identified Catholic got off. Two men would follow him and blow his brains out at the first opportunity. Sectarian murders had been committed in the name of the IRA to be sure, but it was against official policy; Civil War was always a thing difficult to contain. "But if you want to run a good business, you've got press problems."

Cahill leaned forward with his elbows on the table. "We're operating in what should be recognized as a legitimate form of warfare. Through isolated acts we can cripple the occupation force with minimal carnage. We've had a war going on for nearly twenty years and the death toll is low when you look at it in those terms. Would people want open warfare between governments? And this way we have a people's army, not some machine under the control of the industrialists."

Burke leaned forward as well. "That's right. Nearly twenty years and no resolution. How effective is that?"

"And so we're back to the press problem. I agree with you. The Press doesn't know what they're talking about. In North America they label everything here or in Lebanon according to the religion of the faction, not the economic or political persuasion. And the battle here is economic and political. But world press is just one more big corporation. I don't see the difference between the Communist Party dictating copy to Pravda or the networks arranging its stories so that they and their smiling anchormen can win in ratings." Cahill sat back and looked at his friends.

Burke took a drink. It was often the case that these conversations ended like this. There was no real answer.

McCreesh and Cahill checked their watches and got up to leave, saying their goodbyes. O'Donnahue finished his beer. "We'll keep our ears open and if anything comes up we'll get in touch." He looked at his watch. "Meagan and I should leave now. You two can leave in a few minutes ..."

"O'Donnahue," Hennessey grunted, "we know the drill."

Meagan and O'Donnahue rose to leave and Hen and Burke accompanied them into the next room. Amid the singing and drinking crowd Burke and Meagan were separated from Hen and O'Donnahue. "We'll be drinking later at Hen's," Martin offerred. "He lives at Divis Flats if you and Michael would like to drop by."

"Well, I can't speak for Michael. I think he's busy. His wife just had another baby. But I'll drop by." Burke scribbled down the address for her and they left. Burke watched them out the door. He noticed that his palms were sweating.

Hen slapped him on the back. "Careful old man. I'll bet she's hot to the touch."

He just smiled at Hennessey. "Is there anything to drink at your place?"

"Yes."

"Well, I think we'll have a visitor later."

Hennessey pulled Martin over to the counter for another Strongbow. "I'm not crazy about them, you know."

"I noticed," Burke observed.

"I noticed that you didn't tell them anything about Lynch either."

"No need giving them too much. I don't like trusting anyone, though I wouldn't mind thrusting Meagan," Burke grinned.

"Meagan is good looking, no question, and at least she's cool and calm. But the lads," Hennessey said with a shake of his head, "they're a bit fundamental. They've been through shit, I know. McCreesh spent time in Long Kesh and it was pretty hard on him. Cahill, he was all set to be a priest but he was out with a friend one night and their car back-fired in front of an RUC roadblock. They blew the driver's head off and kept Cahill in Castlereagh on remands for about a year but never got him on anything."

"That'll do it," Burke said.

"They talk well about the Cause. But I always get nervous about how confident they are. They've never been out of Belfast except to train in the country. They really don't know what it's like."

"You're beginning to sound like an old man Hen," Burke said with a chuckle on the edge of his voice. He downed his pint and slid the glass along the counter. "Let's get going, but careful," he added, putting his finger aside his nose, "just like O'Donnahue said."

As Hen got up, a man they had seen lounging outside the entrance ran in shouting, "Patrol!" Hennessey could hardly contain himself. "I knew that asshole O'Donnahue would fuck up. He's useless as a nun's tit. He ..."

Burke clapped his hand over Hennessey's mouth. "James, just hold on for the next few minutes. Let's just watch."

The pub was menacingly quiet as the patrol entered. For the Brits to show the colours in a few pubs each night was routine but never pleasant. One of the regulars banged his glass on the table. "Why don't you bastards all just leave us alone and go home then!" The squad ignored the comments and continued their sweep. Burke and Hennessey backed up a bit, trying to hide their faces without being obvious about it. Suddenly one of the guys at the bar took a swing at one of the soldiers and the two at the door jumped into the quickly escalating melee. The man who took the first swing caught Burke's eye and winked. He must have been a Provo plant, placed there by O'Donnahue and Meagan for cover. Burke looked at Hennessey with a grin, "You were saying?"

Hennessey bowed back. "After you Martin." Then they picked their way through the brawl and scrambled out the door and down the street, turning corners and losing themselves in the fog.

The fog was everywhere, thick and cooling to the skin. It made lamps into lighthouses and people into whirlwinds. But here and there as they walked they came upon crossroads where the wind had swept the area clear. At one such spot they heard the clanging of dustbin lids in the distance. Hennessey pulled Burke into the nearest doorway with a little too much zeal and they banged the door hard. They listened, rubbing their shoulders, as the noise approached them. Out of the fog and into the clear ran some children who stopped at the next corner long enough to clang some lids, then were off. Almost immediately the stomp of the patrol broke the air and Burke saw, just on the edge of the fog, soldiers, cautiously advancing up the street towards them. Burke and Hennessey froze. The patrol was midpoint in the block when shots rang out from the roof. The squad scrambled for cover as a muzzleflash erupted again from the roof-line. Hennessey pushed himself further into the doorway, realizing they were caught in a fire-zone. The children who had been hiding on the edge of the fog moved cautiously. The soldiers were intent on the sniper and radioed in for some assistance. He fired again and one of the Brits caught him. A rifle clattered on the cobblestones below, followed by the soft swish of a body as it slid off the roof and the harder splat of a body as it hit the street. One of the small boys made a play for the rifle. Burke held his breath. The soldiers were checking the body over. Perhaps they would miss the kid. One of the soldiers heard the scuffle of the boy dragging the rifle, turned and fired. The boy crumpled without a sound. Burke drew a pistol from his coat pocket, stepped into the street and shot the soldier. His comrades scattered again.

Hennessey was beside himself. "Burke, what the fuck did you do that for?" He looked out and a bullet whizzed off the brick wall not two feet from his face. "This really takes it. You call this a night out?" Burke shared Hennessey's concern with the situation but couldn't have stopped himself. His reaction was automatic, borne of years of hatred.

He looked up and across the street. In another doorway opposite theirs stood the young boy he had seen before. Their eyes communicated a strategy grown from living in the streets of the North. Burke pushed Hennessey to the side and Sean scurried into an adjacent alley-way noisily, drawing the fire. Burke stepped into the street then crashed back into the door. It splintered open and Hennessey took off down the hallway. Burke hesitated for a moment, making sure the boy had got away safely, then he rejoined Hennessey and they ducked out the back of the building and into an alley. They climbed a stone wall, dropped to the ground on the other side and lost themselves in the swirling white.

The whiskey had smoothed over the night's excitement; Burke and Hen sat now at the table talking about nothing in particular. Burke was staring into the space beyond the wall, not seeing the photographs which Hennessey had taken and hung there. "Hen, did you see the face on that little bugger? I've seen him before you know, and he keeps turning up at the right times. But his eyes. They were old. And he couldn't be more than ten. Christ!" Burke shook his head and took a drink.

"You're not hearing a word I say are you, you drunk bastard."

Burke wasn't. His eyes had clouded over and he was trying to remember happier days. But there was another memory which crowded in.

The last time he had shared drinks with Hennessey had been the night before his arrest. The day was too clear in his mind. That morning he had stood at the corner watching his contacts walking down the lane toward him.

"Let's get on with it Burke. We haven't got all day now, do we," said Sandy, butting his cigarette. "Me 'n' Johnny'll check the merchandise then call in the money and our truck."

Burke had been troubled for a week but he wasn't sure why. This deal was going to get him out of Belfast. He hadn't told anyone, even Hennessey, but he had sunk every penny he had into it and after it was over he would be free.

He led them into a dilapidated warehouse and over to an old panel truck. They swung open the back door. Sandy jumped up into the truck and pried open one of the wooden crates with a pinch bar. SMG's, fresh, still with their shipping grease on them. He checked a smaller box and was satisfied with the ammo it contained. "This looks good Burke. Johnny, call in the money."

Suddenly the doors burst open. Pandemonium! British soldiers were pouring into the warehouse. Sandy got out "What the fuck is this?" before he bolted for the door. He was cut down before he got three strides. Johnny used the opportunity of Sandy's death and Burke's struggle with a large number of soldiers to slip out. The soldiers wrestled Burke into submission then led him outside. While they were escorting him down an alley they spied Johnny and gave chase. Burke smashed the two soldiers left holding him up against a brick wall. Dazed, they let him go long enough for him to throw himself through a high wooden fence and roll into an old lady's garden. Between her slashing at him with her rake and the soldiers taking pot shots at him he almost didn't make good his escape.

Burke ran blind through the backstreets. Something drove him on though he ached deep inside, deeper than the pain of the slug in his thigh could reach. Luckily it wasn't bleeding very much. He leaned against a wall, took a piece of string out of his pocket and tied it tight above the wound. He was thinking now more of his failure than of the danger from the British soldiers. The thought kept crashing through his head. He should have known. Someone had informed. And now he would not get out. He had gotten sloppy. And the sloppiness had pushed over into his professional life. He would pay dearly for his mistake. And he could not afford it. His mind tried to reconstruct the last few days' events, searching for a clue. And yet he knew there would be no answer. It always comes. Maybe it was best. Now, at least, it was finished. He was so tired. Tired of everything. He longed for a city with no war, for a life with peace. He wandered in a fog. With his hands in his pockets he walked the streets, turning corner after corner, feeling nothing now and caring less. The last corner he turned brought him face to face with a British patrol. He paid little attention as they surrounded him. He stood silent for a moment then the anger welled up inside of him and he lashed out at the nearest soldier, though not in an attempt to escape. Rapidly he was brought to the ground with rifle butts and boots. They picked him up, more broken inside than out, and tossed him into the back of a lorry. His face was blank as they took him away, and he was just as blank inside. Burke hadn't thought about that day for a long time. He didn't like remembering it because it was the day he had given himself up.

Hennessey was still talking. It was 2 o'clock. He wondered if she would show.

"You've got to be careful about women Martin, believe me I know. And you should too. Don't ever get to the point where you have to depend on them because ..."

Burke shook his head and smiled wryly. He knew what Hen was talking about. "You know, everytime I have a dream with you in it, you're mute. You should try it. That was a long time ago. Another age." There was a knock at the door. "And James, if you expound on your philosophy concerning relationships while she's here I'll rip your last ball off." Burke smiled and rubbed Hennessey's dark hair.

"Alright Martin, it's your funer ..."

"Ah, ah ah." Martin pointed his finger at Hennessey's groin and Hennessey grinned and shut his mouth.

There was a second knock. They both knew it was her. Burke went for the door. His stomach twinged and his palms were moistening but when he opened the door his face betrayed nothing more than a friendly smile.

She stood there, fresh, clean, inviting. "Hi."

"Hi." Burke replied. "Come in."

He led her to the table where she greeted Hennessey. Another glass was found and filled. The music continued and the conversation continued. At a certain point Hennessey felt his presence was relatively unnoticed and so made his way into the bedroom, offering pleasant goodnights. He lay there on his bed, listening in the dark to the conversation swaying in the kitchen. Meagan was from a little town in Tyrone and had come to the city to go to university. Her parents had since gone to the United States but she had no interest in joining them. He listened as both she and Burke traded stories, laughter and refills. But he could not sleep. Or if he did fall asleep, he didn't remember, but suddenly the chairs were sliding back and Meagan was getting ready to leave. 'Old Burke missed a hit', he mused. 'Poor fellow.' He wandered out into the kitchen, squinting in the light. He hadn't remembered it as being that bright. Meagan was standing by the open door.

"Good night James," she said, twisting around Burke's side to give him a wave. Hen shot a little wave back at her. He saw her motion to Martin to come out into the hall with her.

Martin nodded then turned to Hennessey. "Back in a minute." The door shut behind them.

As Hennessey listened to them walk down the hall, he shook his head. "When you're in love you're always sixteen, no matter how old you are. He'll learn, someday." He grinned broadly, more from the alcohol than anything else, picked up a glass he had deposited in the sink, filled it with whiskey and sat back down at the table.

Meagan was leaning against the wall at the end of the hall and Burke stood close to her, rocking slightly from the alcohol, his hands in his pockets.

"It was really nice, but I have to go."

Burke wanted her to stay but he had not been able to ask. He grinned. "You've got an open invitation."

"What about tomorrow night? I'm free then."

"I've got some business later in the evening but why don't you come by earlier. Maybe we can have something to eat."

"Ok," she said, smiling. She reached up and kissed him then went through the door into the stairwell.

Burke stood for a moment listening to her footfalls on the stairs, receding until everything was quiet once more. When he came in Hen was slumped unconscious on the table. He turned the lights out and curled up on the couch.

BELFAST
6 pm, 5 June

The place was darkened, deserted, scorched from the flames of some past conflict, now just an empty room in an empty shell. Cronin sat at a chair in front of the glassless window, through which came the only light illuminating the room. As he watched Sullivan approach he wiped from his brow the nervous sweat which was accumulating. Sullivan was in his fifties and over weight. He limped and used a cane for support, and, at times, as a weapon. The lub-click of his purposeful walk echoed ominously in the barren room. As he emerged from the shadows Cronin caught sight of his face. It was not friendly. But this man was paying the bills. Sullivan's companion was present but stayed in the shadows.

"Well Cronin, how did it go?"

Cronin cleared his throat. "I've had some trouble. You know how hard it is to get anybody to ever tell you anything. And that kid doesn't seem to be anywhere. I've checked the neighbourhood."

Sullivan shuffled about and his displeasure with Cronin began to show. "It would have been better if you'd done things right from the start."

"It wasn't my fault that the Brits showed up and I didn't know the kid would be there. It wasn't something I could plan for."

"Then you should have killed the boy then and there. It was your job to stick to McHenry, to see that he didn't get to tell Burke anything, and to kill him just as they met. The soldiers took care of that part for you. But we still have this boy out there."

"I figure we watch Burke. He'll be looking for the kid. We just ..."

"Since when are you supposed to think," Sullivan growled, banging his cane on the floor. "You let him slip through your fingers."

Cronin was sweating now. "Between my legs," he said, attempting a feeble joke which was not appreciated. "I'll find him. I promise."

Sullivan shook his head. "What about you? Burke will be looking for you, that's for sure, and we know MI has identified you." Sullivan turned to his companion and mumbled, "He'll have to go away," then began to walk to the door, "and you've got a job to do too."

Cronin stood, a frightened smile on his face. "I've got family in Liverpool."

"That's not far enough," said Sullivan without stopping, shuffling to the door, his cane beating a strange rhythm as he walked.

Cronin took another step. "New York then. I have a cousin in New York. It'd be no trouble."

Sullivan was at the door. He turned to Cronin and paused. "Maybe Donncha, maybe," he said, then looked at his companion for a moment before leaving. "We'll need a couple of hours," he said, then he left.

Cronin stood beside the chair now, holding the back of it, listening to the lub-lub-click of Sullivan as he went down the stairs. He reached for a cigarette and gazed out the window. "I don't know what's eating him. It'll all work." He took another drag and turned, smiling. "What d'you say we go for a ….." The word 'beer' froze on his lips and he stared in silence, eyes wide.

There was an abrupt hiss and his body jerked, then he crumpled to the ground. The cigarette dropped to the floor beside him. A dark figure stood over him, unscrewing the silencer from the pistol barrel, then left as Sullivan had left.

Cronin lay on the floor, half in shadow. A dark pool formed under his body. Eventually it spread to the cigarette and extinguished it.

AT HENNESSEY'S

7 pm, 5 Meitheamh

For a change of pace Burke had headed out and left Hennessey sleeping. He had wandered most of the day, enjoying the freedom and keeping his ears open but he had heard nothing. The few people he had known three years ago were either in jail or dead. You didn't stay active too long in Belfast. It just wasn't a big enough place. And there was always an informer, someone with a grudge and an idea that he could turn somebody in and escape the wrath of the Provos. The truth was a little different. At one pub he had overheard two men talking about an informer who had given the Brits information about the lads. Even his family had turned against him. The word was out that he and his wife had resettled in England, in Exeter. The odds were against him seeing July.

Burke let himself into the apartment with the extra key Hen had given him. There was no one around but he could hear the shower running. He stuck his head in the bathroom. "Hennessey ..."

The curtain pulled to and Meagan stuck her head out. "It's me Martin. Hen left quite awhile ago. Said he'd be back late tonight. I decided to wait for you and I was looking pretty brutal. You don't mind do you?"

He saw the wet shower curtain pressed against her breast, saw the bulge where her nipple pushed at it, enjoyed the seductive outline of her hip and thigh. "No, not at all. Want a drink?"

"No thanks, but you have one. I'm done. Just have to dry my hair and I'll be out."

He poured himself a whiskey and listened as the shower stopped and the hair dryer started. It had been a while since he'd seen a sight like that and it excited him. She kept on looking better and better. He had to admit to himself that he longed for her. But perhaps it had been too long. And happiness invariably led to pain, the sort of pain that could dull the senses. His business had conspired against such things in the past. He had a job to do.

He would go and see Mrs McHenry again. He was sure she knew more than she had let on and it was worth the risk. He jotted down his plans for the evening then put the note under the lamp, where he and Hen had always left messages, noticing there was no note there for him.

The door to the bathroom opened and Meagan emerged, wrapped in a towel too small for her, her hair dry and bright, lightly brushing her shoulders. There was a certain smell which was reserved for a girl fresh from the shower and it overcame him.

"I left my clothes in the bedroom," she said, heading for the door, then stopped and sat down on the couch. "I'll have that drink after all, if you don't mind the towel." Burke found himself blushing as he assured her that he did not and got her a whiskey. They talked about things inconsequential with the radio playing in the background and the whiskey in front of them until suddenly he found himself kissing her.

"Let's go into the bedroom," she said, pulling him in. She had unbuttoned his shirt and was starting to pull it off him when he stopped her. "What's wrong?"

Again he was embarassed. "I just want to turn the light out."

It was then that she noticed the red scars like stigmata, bright on his skin, which led around his side and disappeared to his back, promising horror. "Is that from Long Kesh?" He didn't answer. She went to the light and turned it out then shut the door. The scars melted away in an adrenalin dream.

Burke woke with a start. It was late, almost 10 o'clock, they had dozed off. Meagan stirred in her sleep beside him. He had to go to McHenry's house. He glanced down at her, half-clad in the bedsheets. She would sleep 'til he got back. He rose, gathered his clothes and softly went into the living room to dress. It would take him an hour to get there. He would have to change taxis a couple of times and go in cautiously. He did not want to draw heat on Mrs McHenry as he had the last time. That child had already lost a father, and she a husband. That was enough.

He knocked on the doorpost as he looked up at the windows. The house was dark except for a dim light in the livingroom, and quiet. He was about to knock again when he saw that the door wasn't shut. He glanced behind himself to see the shadow of the British watch tower then entered the dark, bat-black hallway. The door to the dimly lit livingroom was closed. He called to Mrs McHenry softly, at first, then louder, but there was no answer.

The door to the livingroom did not give until some weight was applied against it, then it opened with a crash. Inside it was as if a troop of Gurkhas had run amok. The chesterfield was upturned, the lamps broken, tables reduced to kindling. Pictures had been ripped from the walls and smashed on the floor. He moved into the kitchen but it was the same: broken crockery and furniture, drawers emptied, their contents randomly sown across the tile floor.

There was the sound of a baby crying coming from the second floor. He crept to the stairs and mounted them cautiously, afraid of what he might find at the top. On the landing a door opened to the right. A baby was stirring softly in a crib, while all about Burke was dishevelment. Across the room an old woman sat on the edge of the bed, dabbing Mrs McHenry's forehead with a damp cloth. She had been badly beaten. Her left eye was puffed closed and black, her lips bled and she was suffering a mixture of pain and shock. She saw that it was Burke and recognized him from his previous visit, with obvious relief.

"Thank God it's you Mr ..."

"Burke."

"Mr Burke. We thought they'd come back."

Burke righted a chair beside the bed and sat down, seething with an anger he had not felt for a long time. "Who did this?"

The old woman went to get a damp towel. Mrs McHenry spoke though it was painful to do so. "I don't know who they were. Two of them came to the door. Said they were friends of my husband. As soon as they were inside one of them dragged me upstairs. He was tall and blond and he spoke with an American accent, I think. He threw me in here and started beating me. He didn't even ask anything. I thought he was going to rape me and rob the house. I remember hoping mother wouldn't walk in. She was out shopping.

"I could hear the other one downstairs busting up the house, looking through everything. Then the blond one started asking me about my husband. What did he know? Who had he talked to? On and on and on. I told him I didn't know what he was talking about but he just kept on slapping and asking. I didn't have any strength left. Then he tied my hands and feet and tied me to the bed. He took his silenced pistol and held it point-blank at Jeremy's ear and told me he wasn't going to leave until he had answers. I swore that all I knew was that my husband had been worried about something and had gone out in a hurry after receiving a telephone call the night he was killed. He said he knew that but he wanted to know who he had talked to. I didn't know what to say.

"The other man came upstairs and started in on the other bedroom, tapping the walls, I guess to see if there was a safe or something. Then the blond one came over and hit me on the head. I passed out. When I came to they were gone. Everything was quiet but I could hear Jeremy crying. I was never so glad to hear that in all my life. Mum came home later and found me. I couldn't call the peelers. What good would it do."

Burke was seething with anger but outwardly he remained calm. "Did you see the other man? Was he Irish?"

Mrs McHenry shook her head. "I don't know and I don't care anymore. I'm tired of this. Adan — he's my sister's fiance — he was recruited to work on some assassination team. There was a lot of money involved and he was gonna meet my sister in New York after. She's a nanny there. He and some of them went right to Libya, to some training camp. There were some others who had a job to do here, then they went down too. He wanted out but he was afraid he'd be killed. When he told Sars what was happening he and Dr Lynch got worried and tried to contact a friend of theirs in the South."

"Sullivan?" Burke asked.

"No. I don't know the name. He was a dentist."

Burke just nodded and let her continue.

"They were too afraid to tell anyone else. They were gonna do Prince Charles. And William too if they got the chance. The bloody gits. Broken English they called it. They're always so clever coming up with names for this shit." She stared at Martin in silence and he saw that her eyes were dry and hard with anger. "And don't be askin' for details 'cause that's all I know. It's all so goddamn stupid. I don't want to be a part of this. I just want to leave."

Outside in an alley two houses over from the McHenry residence a van sat parked, its windows blacked out, its motor running. Inside, Sullivan and Michael Magee sat amid tape recorders with headphones, listening. They could hear Burke and Mrs McHenry talking by way of the bugs that had been planted in the house during their recent visit. They listened to Burke's footsteps as he paced the floor. They could hear her rise as well.

"I have to get out of here. I'm not enough of a fool to wait around for them to come back. We're leaving as soon as we can get things in order."

Burke walked a distance and a door opened. Street noises could be heard. "I'll be in touch," Burke said, "and I'll try to get to the bottom of this but in the meantime be careful. I'll see if I can get a couple of lads to watch your house."

Mrs McHenry said goodnight and closed the door. "I'm going to nurse Jeremy, mum."

"Alright dear. I'll clean up here."

Mrs McHenry went up the stairs, picked up the baby and sat in a rocking chair, nursing him and humming an old Irish lullaby of ships and harps and heroes.

Sullivan turned to Magee and removed his headset. "I think she was telling the truth. But Burke knows too much now. I don't know whether we can afford to let him go any longer. You get rid of this Adan."

Magee nodded. "At least he wasn't part of the team that I used to spring Burke."

"What about the sister."

"I doubt she knows anything but I'll get some friends in New York to track her down. It won't be that hard. And I still think we can hold onto Burke, for awhile anyway. If he gets any ideas, we'll know about it. You don't have to worry."

"I'm paid to worry. He wasn't supposed to be here tonight as soon as he was." Sullivan picked up a small remote control device. "Are you sure this will work?"

Magee nodded. "Guaranteed."

Sullivan pushed the button and the lullaby was cut short by a ripping explosion followed almost immediately by the piercing wail of the microphones melting in the flames.

Burke turned as the explosion blew a wall of fire through the roof of the house. No one would survive that. He stood in a silent rage, the blood vessels on his temples bulging, his jaw clenched, his knuckles white. Suddenly the night air echoed with sirens and screams of neighbours. He hurried off, down the street, dazed, into the darkness.

It was past midnight when Burke returned to Hennessey's apartment. He had wandered around, lost in the backstreets, blaming himself for his role, as he saw it, in the death of an entire family: mother, husband, wife, child. And he wasn't quite ready to deal with the news of Broken English. That was murder, not of Charles, but of every Catholic in the North. The fires would rage under the Orange banner this July. Stumbling along the dark streets he had realised that he would probably be identified at the scene of the explosion. The film footage from that watch tower would be gone over with a fine tooth comb and there would be a close questioning of the neighbours. It was not that the English cared so much for a Catholic family but rather they would care that someone had been able to get a hold of high explosives. That was military issue. Those responsible had connections.

He rattled his key at Hennessey's door, when it opened he saw Hennessey seated at seated at the table with an older man, drinking whiskey. It was Finnerty. His hair was shock-white and his round face was nothing but folds and wrinkles, his teeth were shadows but his eyes were the same — blue pools with flecks of brown swirled into a black hole.

"Well, well, well. The Prodigal returns, as always." He rose and gave Burke a bear-hug-hello then sat him down at the table and poured him a drink. "You look a little rough Martin. Get that inside of you."

It was obvious from the bottle-strewn table-top and from the demeanour of Finn and Hen that they had been drinking for some time, and heavily. It was just as obvious to Finn and Hen that Martin was submerged and needed air. Finn poured some Jameson's into Burke's glass, while Hennessey went for another bottle. "Hen told me what's been happening Martin, but you look as if you need some diversion, and drink is about the only diversion that I can afford and that my body can tolerate. Drink and talk."

Martin did. He recounted every detail of his association with the men from the South, with Broken English, with Lynch and the McHenry family. In doing so he took the edge off his anger and frustration, re-established his relationship with Finn and, within an hour, forced Hennessey to rise again for another bottle. There was a deep silence as Hen filled their glasses. He placed the bottle down, took a swig from his glass, then stared at the table, deep in thought. "We can't afford to go on drinking like this."

Burke and Finn looked at each other for a moment then burst out laughing. Hen looked up in dismay, nodding his head in support of his statement. "Sure, laugh all you want, but this is hard-earned money for the Cause. I had to bust my ass and worse for it, and here we are drinking it away."

Burke and Finn sat back expectantly.

"Money doesn't grow on trees, and we aren't on a government stipend like Buckingham Palace. We have no polo ponies to sell if times get tough." He paused for a moment, then seemed to come to some resolution. "We could use a royal family of our own. When we need money we could just marry one of them off or get another one pregnant and sell commemorative plates."

Burke and Finn broke into huge grins but Hennessey paid no attention to them. He was off.

"Laugh all you want but that's the solution. What makes a Royal Family so special? There's something about them that just lends itself to money-making, but they're just people. If you cut them they bleed."

Finn piped in. "But they bleed blue."

Hen waved him off. "You people don't appreciate the true commercial potential. Do you realise that I could raise as much money as I did busting my ass all over North America if I could get my hands on a pair of Diana's panties, authenticated of course. To the highest bidder. Those Californians would have been all over me with cheque books and charge cards. Jesus, that's what the IRA should be doing. The guy that wandered into Liz's bedroom asked for a cigarette. I would have demanded underwear!"

Burke smothered a laugh. He didn't want to encourage him, but Finn was doing enough of that, mouth propped open in a continuous guffaw.

"Remember that you heard it from me first — the terrorist of the future will deal not in bullets but in bloomers."

Finn was on the floor, on his back, red faced and short of breath as Hen finally sat down. Burke looked down at Finn on the floor, quiet now and still. "Looks like you've killed him."

Hennessey sprinkled some whiskey on the old man's face but Finn didn't budge. "Yup," he said, with a Texas drawl, "he's dead alright."

Burke shook his head and looking around saw pictures which Hennessey had taken and mounted on the wall. Many were of young females. One caught his eye, She had dark brown hair, beautiful eyes, and a strange, twisted, almost painful expression on her face. He pointed to her and swung Hennessey's fluid neck around so that he too faced the picture. "That one there, what's wrong with her?"

Hen shrugged his shoulders. "Couldn't tell you. She was Belgian, from Brussels."

Sotto voce, Finn spoke from the floor. "They never affect me that way. Make my urine smell funny maybe, but that's all."

Burke and Hen exploded in laughter and stomped to their feet, hugging each other and looking down at Finn. "As long as he's with the IRA," said Hen, "the English have nothing to fear."

Hennessey sat down and filled their glasses but Martin went to the tap for some water, to the accompaniment of hisses from Hen. The laugh had done him good, had taken his mind off the recent events, but there were still some things nagging at him and he needed a clear head. As he looked at the rest of the photos on the apartment walls, Hennessey spoke up. "You see Mairead there, my cousin." He pointed in the general direction of a dark-haired, large-chested beauty. "She's getting married tomorrow and we're going to the wedding, ok?" Burke figured it would be a good break and he might find out more information from the guests. It might also give him an excuse to see Meagan.

The rest of the evening swirled in discussion of the information that Burke had uncovered, and whiskey. Many times he played the litany over in his mind, searching for the inescapable conclusion which would guide him. Many times he felt close and some of the conclusions were clear and direct, but there was a gap in the logic somewhere and, for the life of him, he could not find it. There was an assassination team, supposedly IRA though no one had heard of it, and they were planning to take out Prince Charles and anyone else who was around him. McHenry and Lynch had got wind of it and were trying to get the information to the two characters in the South. Lynch, who was in some kind of trouble with the Protestants, probably wanted to exchange it for protection or relocation. Presumably he had not leaked it to the English because he'd be killed for turning in IRA personnel but he had hoped the Officials in the South might move to stop what was clearly an unauthorised and, as everyone would agree, suicidal operation.

Burke needed to know more and there was a growing realisation that he would have to act somehow to see that this operation was not carried out. He would be fingered as responsible and that was reason enough to stop it. But it would also destroy Ireland. Much as he wanted to leave, Ireland was still important, always would be.

SULLIVAN'S

12:30 am, 6 June

As Magee sat waiting for the meeting to start, he felt strange. It was the McHenry job. Not killing the McHenrys. That was business and he had learned long ago that nobody got killed if they kept their noses clean. They had brought it on themselves. No, it was listening to Burke's voice. He had studied the man from a distance relying on newspaper clippings and stories told to him by a variety of people, most drunk. Sullivan had been impressed with him, and there was a lot to be impressed about. He had operated in Belfast for a long time without being arrested and, in Belfast especially, that was hard to do. But the voice capped it. There was a quality to that voice that Magee admired. In the end Burke would lose, because Magee had every intention of winning. Still, if the Provos had hired him for a job he might have been working with Burke instead of against him.

He thought too of Adan. He had known there was something wrong with that guy but he thought he would be able to pull him through. Now he'd have to be snuffed. The others would do it. They'd taken an oath. There was nothing like an execution to steel lads for an operation. If he was going to collect all his money, they'd have to do their job well. And he'd get Ransom to look up the skirt in New York. She'd be making arrangements to come home for the funeral probably. Ransom had enough connections at the airports to track her down.

He looked over at Sullivan. He didn't like the fucker, didn't trust him. The old man had been IRA, tried and true, but he had sold out for money. Magee had never sold out. He had never been committed to anything but himself. That was the difference between them. But Sullivan had come up with a good plan for the red-necks and it would work just fine, thanks to some fine-tuning by Magee. The Catholics would catch shit and the brass would have just what they wanted. 'And me', Magee thought, 'I'll be sipping fine wine on some quiet beach, far away from this rat-assed town. Let them bury each other.'

Wilkes and Barton entered and Sullivan welcomed them with whiskey. They gathered around the dimly lit table and Sullivan moved through pleasantries to the heart of the matter.

"We have eight lads currently training in a camp in Libya and from those we'll select the best four for the mission. They're fanatics when it comes to getting the British out and I have their names here so that you can begin to pull their sheets as soon as necessary. Your men are to be commended for their assistance in getting the armaments into the country. We might as well let you know that it was necessary to use some of that equipment to plug a leak tonight, but this exercise has been useful, not just to test our equipment but also to implicate Burke. At least that's what I gather from our brief conversation," he said, looking at Wilkes.

"Yes, we had a report come in that he had been identified near the house immediately after the blast. Our main concern is that he not be arrested too soon, but I've had Barton step up his profile on the streets and I will be watching things at HQ. In the unlikely event that he is captured, we could arrange for his escape."

Sullivan put his hands together on the table and leaned forward. "Fine. Now my principals want to ensure a success to the operation and so we have arranged for a second attack, a failsafe position, outside of Belfast. I'll need some information in order to set this up. In the event that the team fails in Belfast, there will be a missile attack on the train. Our American contact will take charge of that operation personally."

Wilkes now took over the meeting. "I have already made it quite clear that you must limit your attack to Prince Charles. We will provide you with recommendations for any attack in Belfast. We have had confirmation that Prince Charles and Prince William will travel on the Royal Train to Londonderry. Diana and Harry will travel by air, and so we can authorise your fallback plan. But I must make it clear that we need to have all of the participants as well as Burke. What about the terrorists that you don't choose to use?"

Sullivan cleared his throat. "Provided they all survive the training, the other four will be in Belfast during the operation. You can arrange to arrest them after. I presume those actively involved will die in a hail of bullets."

"Most likely," added Barton. "And we'd like to have an opportunity to identify them before the operation to make things easier.

Sullivan glanced over at Magee and he nodded. He looked back at Wilkes and Barton. "That can be arranged. I was hoping that we might be able to co-operate on their re-entry into Belfast. I want to make sure nothing goes wrong."

"It appears that we should meet again in a day or two. We need to confirm the travel arrangements and troop allocations in Belfast and I can have Barton work with you on getting them in here safely. And Burke?"

Magee cleared his throat. "We can guarantee delivery."

Wilkes swirled the whiskey in his glass. "That leaves the financial arrangements."

Sullivan smiled. "That's all being taken care of. At the next meeting I want you to provide us with banking instructions. Anywhere in the world. And you can verify that the money has arrived before the plan is carried out." He pushed a packet across the table. "There is an advance here. It's what we had agreed to earlier. I am also assuming that you'll provide us with the banking arrangements for the others in your group at that time."

Wilkes nodded. "What about you and your American friend? Have you been able to arrange satisfactory travel to get out? When you spoke earlier, you thought you might like some help there."

"We'll be travelling separately. It would be helpful if you could arrange for me to get a military flight to Gibraltar, if that's possible."

"I'll have to see what flights are going out on the 12th, but we'll do the best we can. What about you?" Wilkes said, turning to Magee.

"No thanks," Magee answered. "I'll be going out under my own steam."

Wilkes shrugged his shoulders then he and Barton pushed themselves back from the table.

Sullivan went to the phone. "I'll call a car for you gentlemen," he said. "The streets aren't safe at this time of night."

MAIREAD AND JEFF

1:30 pm, 6 Meitheamh

The wedding had begun at 11 in the morning and now they were all in the church hall, a small, cheaply wood-panelled affair with a low stage and pictures of the Pope and Cardinals sprinkled around on the walls, lacquered onto wood slabs. Mairead had changed out of her wedding dress and the guests had finished their meals and were sitting in groups talking and drinking or dancing to the music supplied by a disc jockey. Meagan had been pleased when Burke had asked her to come along and she seemed to be having a good time. He watched her as she danced on the crowded dance floor with Hennessey. He had to admit that he was beginning to like her a lot. And that didn't please him. It was easier to live without attachments and less risky. It was hard enough for him to look after himself without worrying about somebody else. Not that she needed him to do that but he knew he would do it anyway. He would have promised himself he would not let himself feel that strongly about Meagan but he figured it was already too late. He was captivated with her. She was intelligent, beautiful, vigorous and she made him feel relaxed, whole again. He enjoyed being around her. Hen seemed to like her too.

He looked around. Everyone was having a good time. As he watched some of the old women dance he thought of the joke about the Pope giving a special dispensation to Irish women to wear their legs upside down. Nasty but with a sliver of truth. As he watched, he thought of their lives. These people all had their own stories of relatives, friends and lovers dead, missing or in jail. And today they had gathered to celebrate the marriage of Mairead and Jeff. Jeff was a quiet lad, a mechanic. Mairead was a school teacher, outspoken, fiery, a real Maeve. They danced past him and as he followed them with his eyes he caught sight of Finn across the church hall, sitting with a group of old men, talking. He was trying to find anyone who knew anything about Broken English. But so far they had found nothing. Some had known of McHenry and Lynch. One old fellow even thought he remembered Feeney from his younger days in the IRA. Nobody seemed to know of Sullivan and there was not a glimmer of recognition for Broken English, though even the phrase, without any explanation, had occasioned quite a few appreciative responses and more than one toast.

As he watched Finn and the old folks, he thought of the picture of his grandfather which was now lost to him. These men and women might have been his age and all had no doubt been involved in the Cause. These men and women had smuggled guns, attacked armouries, bombed, killed, rejoiced, mourned at the graves of friends. And now they sat, old and withered, the gleam of glory in their eyes when asked for a story or an opinion. But their struggle had borne small and bitter fruit. Their children, grandchildren and even great grandchildren had taken up the fight. They would not live to see it resolved.

The old folks around Finn took on a new meaning for Burke. He would be one of them soon enough. What future was there for an aging IRA member? There were no employment possibilities, not with a record. There were no old folks homes. The people tried to take care of their own but the resources to accomplish this were strained. The new identity promised by Sullivan had a special importance. He could get out, perhaps with Meagan, though he crossed that off his mind quickly. It was not wise to think such thoughts. He hadn't had much luck in his task and it seemed to be diverting from the one laid on his shoulders that day at the border. He wanted to stop Broken English, with or without Sullivan or Feeney. But if he could use it to get out of Ireland, so much the better.

"If I'd had a gun I would have put a bullet in his head." Burke heard an old woman who was sitting down the table from him say, and he turned his head automatically. The woman beside her shook her head. "That's a terrible thing to say about your own son."

"But I mean it, I do," the other woman replied.

Her husband joined in. "He's no son of mine, the fuckin' bastard. You don't inform on your own, and he's gone and done that. I don't care what the British were promising him, that's not the way he was taught. He's brought nothing but shame on us."

"What about Noreen and the baby?" the other woman asked.

"He sent word to her that she could join him. The police would take her to him," the mother answered, "but she's not going to go. That girl on the next block, remember her. She went to her husband and then she left a year later. She couldn't take it. Living in fear like that. No, Noreen's staying with us."

The father took a drink from his bottle. "The neighbours aren't too friendly and I can't say that I blame them. He's sent four lads to jail already. Took money for it, he did. And I know for a fact one of them had nothing to do with the Provos. I just can't understand it." He got up and headed toward the washroom.

Hennessey and Meagan crashed down into chairs beside Burke, rattling the bottles on the table. Meagan wrapped her arm around him. "Aren't you going to give me a dance?" He was about to answer when Finn plopped down at the table. "No news Martin. It seems you're on your own."

Burke hunched his shoulders forward and took a swig of Strongbow. "Hen, would you mind if I left. It's a nice day and I'd like to get out for awhile."

"Not at all, Martin. Finn and I can stick around and maybe I'll do a little more checking around town later."

Burke nodded and headed for the door. Meagan grabbed her coat and followed. "Like some company?"

They walked along the streets for a few blocks then boarded a bus and headed for Milltown Cemetery. Burke avoided the McHenry plot, though he noticed the grave diggers working at it. They ended up in the Republican section and stood looking at the memorial to the Hunger Strikers. Then they just wandered around, up and down the rows, enjoying the privacy. He sensed that Meagan was aware of what was on his mind from her silence. They stopped by a bench and she went over and sat down. Burke lit a cigarette and stretched.

"It's too bad all this is going on just now," he said finally.

"I don't know. If it wasn't, I wouldn't have had the chance to meet the great Martin Burke, would I?"

"I hate this shit though. Not knowing what's going on. One way or another, I'm not going to be staying in Belfast too long."

"I don't blame you. It isn't the nicest city in the world, not that I've seen much else."

"No, and there's nothing here for me." He noticed that Meagan smiled too quickly at that statement. "You know what I mean. I've been through this stuff too many times. And it never changes. So I've been thinking about emigrating."

"I think if I had the chance, I'd leave."

"You would? I was thinking of Canada. And I've got a deal arranged that would get me there with a new identity. What do you think of Canada?"

"I've had friends go there and they like it. My parents are in Oklahoma City and I sure as hell couldn't live there. But... I guess it depends on who's there."

"Yeah. I guess you're right."

Meagan pulled her coat around her. "I'd like to be in Tahiti or someplace like that. No past, no future, just the present. Christ, here you talk about yesterday and 1690 and 1916 as if they're the same thing."

"What about the future?"

"I'd like to go back to college, when I have the money."

"What would you do?"

"Psychology, I guess. I wanted to work with children. You know, too much violence on the TV, sexist stereotyping, that sort of thing. But I'd have to go somewhere where that was the main problem. It didn't make any sense studying that here. No point really. What did you study?"

"Law," Burke said with a smile.

Meg punched him playfully. "Suits you, it does."

"You want to walk some more?"

"It's kinda cool. Why don't we go back to my place?"

Burke nodded and they headed back towards the road. As they walked she linked her arm around his. "If you do go, I'll miss you. But I wouldn't mind being invited for a visit. Was it something like that on your mind?"

Burke grinned. "Something like that."

THE SHANKILL

4 pm, 6 Meitheamh

Sean walked down The Shankill with Dezy. They'd both given their mothers the shake and were enjoying the relative freedom and danger of the streets. The Shankill was a Prod stronghold but it carried a special message for Sean, far beyond the simple thrill of invading the enemy's territory. His father had been killed here. The British were often prone to picking people up on suspicion and questioning them roughly for hours on end. A special trick of theirs was to take the unlucky Catholic, at the end of the interrogation and let him out on the Shankill in the late night then blow their horns and shout, "There's another Fenian bastard." If the Catholic was lucky he might escape the gauntlet that usually formed with no more than a beating. Sean's father had not been so fortunate. There had been too many people on the streets. Like sharks to a bloodied dolphin, they surrounded and attacked his father. It was a closed casket at the wake. Sean thought of that now as he strolled defiantly, listening to the music streaming through his earphones.

Two armoured cars screamed by, louvres open and a man in the turret, followed by a jeep and a bomb truck. A second later two stripped-down land rovers whizzed past, loaded with paratroopers in their red berets, covering each other. Sean looked at Dezy and they were off like shots, following, joining the troop of children of both persuasions already in pursuit.

They ran about twelve blocks, twisting through alleys to try to keep up with the convoy, but they were stopped just short of a good vantage point by the Brit barricades. Sean spit at one of the soldiers, but the young guard remained impassive, so Sean shoved his little hands into his blue windbreaker's pockets and nudged Dezy.

"Let's get out of here."

Dezy kept on craning his neck to see, so Sean nudged him again and winked, "C'mon." He was still slow to move so Sean grabbed him by the arm and pulled him away from the crowd. They walked slowly around the corner, ducked down an alley, pulled a plank off a doorway and forced the door open then made their way through the burned-out building.

Barton stepped down from his jeep and walked over to the bomb truck. He turned to see that his men were in position. Two were on the roof-line and the rest were positioned in doorways and window wells and casements or hunched behind lampposts, getting as much cover as they could. He opened the door and stepped into the blue darkness, closing the door behind him. The boom operator sat in front of his video screen, watching the car before them which, it had been reported, contained a dangerous-looking parcel. He looked up at Barton. Barton slapped his baton against his leg.

"Get on with it, sergeant."

The boom operator began manipulating his controls. From the outside of the truck a long boom mounted with a video camera and a small detonation charge started inching toward the Vauxhall parked on the other side of the street. All the surrounding buildings were stone, so Barton had decided to detonate any possible explosive in the potentially rigged car rather than risk a man to poke and disarm. They had cleared the area and sealed it off. The arm was now nearly to the car and the operator rotated the camera. There was definitely something suspicious about the package in the back seat.

"Okay, we'll go in there sergeant." Barton opened the door and looked over to the private standing by with a pump-action shotgun. "Blow out the rear window."

The private moved midway between the car and the armoured truck, lowered his visor and pumped his shot gun. The blast and the shattering of the rear window were simultaneous, but there was no explosion. Back inside the truck Barton watched as the boom entered the car. It was like being in a bathyscape, exploring the surrounding environment through an electronic eye. The operator again looked to Barton and, receiving a nod, turned on the siren to warn of the coming blast.

Sean and Dezy peeked through a boarded-up doorway across the street from the car. They had a grand view of the scene. In front of the hoarding over the window of the building in which they hid, two paratroopers watched as well. Suddenly the car exploded, unbroken windows blowing out. It lifted slightly off the paving stones and a torn roof appeared, like a set of prehistoric dentures, through the blue veil of smoke. But there had been only one blast. Sean shook his head. Big deal, he thought. He had just turned to tell Dezy that they might as well go when the window casement in the next room exploded outward, killing the two soldiers there and hurling stone blocks and shattered boards at the others.

"Blood of Christ," Sean yelled, "let's get t'fuck out of here." They tore out the way they'd come in.

Barton had stepped down from the truck, cursing, when the window blew. He saw the two soldiers fly through the air, like rag dolls spilling their stuffing, and land in heaps in the middle of the street. The car had been a lure, a set-up. He quickly seized the situation, sending his men to check the building and instructing his driver, who had a bleeding gash on his forehead, to radio in some support and a chopper.

Sean rounded the corner ahead of Dezy and saw the soldiers coming at them, so they headed down the other way. The soldier in the lead fired one round but it went wild, whining off the stone wall beside the boys. Dezy screamed in pain and grabbed his cheek. A stone splinter had imbedded itself in his face. Blood spurted out through his fingers. Sean grabbed his hand and dragged him off down the alley.

Barton joined the hunt and had rounded a corner in the rabbit-warren when Sean and Dezy ran into him at full tilt. They tumbled to the ground and Barton grabbed firmly onto Dezy's ankle. He screamed to Sean for help. Sean got to his feet and planted his foot abruptly in Barton's groin. Barton retracted into a ball, releasing Dezy who ran off with Sean.

When the two soldiers who had fired on the boys got to Barton he was still bunched up on the ground, red-faced, and though he tried to tell them to get the kids, the two soldiers knew they had no chance of finding them in these alleys nor were they anxious to stray into hostile territory without more cover. They helped Barton back to the main street where they would regroup and wait for a sitrep and a QRF.

Up on the roof Dezy winced as Sean dabbed iodine into the cut on his cheek. Though his mother had moved he still kept his secret box there. It was a safe place, and, as long as Tim's pigeons were there, it felt like home.

"You've been blooded Dezy," he said jealously. "It was something, wasn't it."

"Sure it was," Dezy agreed. The pain was fading now but he would hold his head high in the days to come. If he'd had the chance he would have turned the other cheek as well. Not out of any Christian commitment. Two badges of courage would have been better then one. But this would be enough to raise his stock. Sean wasn't the only one who had experiences to brag about now.

The smell of fried pork hung thick in the air even though the meal had long been finished. Sean was in the bedroom he shared with his brother, listening to his tape player. The batteries had run down and so he had lifted a packet earlier, after Dezy had gone home. He remembered how his father had always gone for a smoke in the toilet when his mother had started raggin' and now he felt the same way. Tim hadn't come home for supper and she had gone on and on about what he was doing and how he was going to get himself killed and how he was this and that. And when Sean had said that he would take care of her she had cuffed him on the ear and said, "Yes, and you'll shit purple ink too."

He had meant it and she hadn't, and so it was ok. She had gone to sit in the front room and he had come here. The tape finished and he pulled the earphones out of his ears and lay on his back, looking at the ceiling. He could hear her singing softly and rocking in the rocking-chair. When he had been smaller and his dad was alive, there had been a piano, a big black piano, and she had played that. He remembered going into the room, though he couldn't remember which house, and squeezing in behind it. He had been small enough to stand inside a place in the back of the cabinet in the dark. She had always played with the lights off. He liked to feel the vibration of the music and listen as she sang. Sometimes she would forget the words and just hum.

Once, right after his father died — he remembered the house now — it had been such a sad song she was singing that he started to cry. She had heard him and come around to the back of the piano and hugged him. She had been crying too.

Now da' was gone and so was the piano.

He got up and went out into the front room and his mother stopped rocking. "I'm goin' out for awhile, ok mum?"

She looked away from him and was silent for a moment. He knew what she was thinking. Then she sighed. "Don't be late and don't get into any trouble."

He grabbed his windbreaker and left.

Sean watched the dark street below from his roof top. It was past 10 o'clock and he would have to go soon. He didn't want his mother to worry too much but he wanted to wait here for Tim just to let him know how their mother was. Other than lending a hand with the move, Tim hadn't had very much time for him or their mother since the day that Sean had dicked for him with those two paratroopers. Tim had a whole new set of friends and a whole new set of responsibilities. It was a full-time job trying to get in with the Provos. Sean could hardly wait until he was old enough to be with them, to do more than throw stones, or watch, or dick. There were larger things which loomed on his horizon. Of that he was sure.

He knew he could see his brother here, for Tim would never forget the pigeons. He seldom trusted Sean with the onerous responsibility of feeding them and caring for them. They belonged to Tim and Tim alone. He would as soon kill a person who messed with his pigeons as kill a Brit.

People strolled down the street in twos and threes, huddled together in the cool night air, moving from one island of light to the next, going here and there — and nowhere.

In the distance he could hear the sound of shouting and the tramp of boots echoing in the side streets and alleys. The troops were out in force after the bombing that afternoon, checking door-to-door in certain areas known to harbour Provos and Bradys. The Prods with their UDR were making all the racket with the boots though, for the Brits wore rubber-soled boots. It was easier to sneak about that way. And there would be, in the morning, the burned out remains of hastily constructed barricades, perhaps a car or two and the broken bottles and cobblestones of street-fights.

Two figures turned the corner and walked down the street toward the deserted apartment building. One looked like Tim. Sean was about to shout hello to him when around the other corner came six soldiers. Tim and his friend froze in their tracks. The soldiers noticed them and began running towards them. Tim's companion ducked down a convenient alley but Tim stood his ground and pulled a revolver out of his coat pocket. He didn't even get one round off. The two lead soldiers dropped to their bellies in the middle of the street and their FN's sparked and smoked. Tim let the gun drop from his hand, leaned against the wall beside him then slid to the ground in a heap. Sean let out a scream and one of the soldiers shone a torch in his direction but he was gone, down behind the casement, his head buried in his arms. He could hear them gather around his brother's body, heard two soldiers run off in pursuit of the fleeing friend, heard the others comment on the revolver on the ground and the apparent age of the fallen boy.

A crowd was beginning to gather and as he looked over the roof edge again he saw the flashing lights and heard the sirens of the approaching sixers. In the distance he could make out the sweep of a chopper search-light as it came in his direction. He looked closely at the two soldiers who had fired on Tim, burning their faces indelibly into his mind. And there too was the man he had kicked in the groin this afternoon. Then came the sound of his mother. She must have heard the commotion as she sat on the front steps of their apartment building with the other ladies. Like a banshee, her soft cry of concern grew to a hellish shrieking as she drew closer to the scene and realised who the fallen victim was. Sobbing, she threw herself through the throng of people and past the soldiers. She cradled Tim's head in her arms and began keening.

Sean rose and steadied himself. Tonight was not the night for revenge, that would come in due course. He would find that officer and the soldiers. The man named Martin Burke would have to take a back seat to that and the information that McHenry had given him could wait. Now it mattered only that he made his way to his mother and helped to comfort her. He went to the fire-escape and descended into the street. He would care for the pigeons later.

AT HENNESSEY'S

2:00 pm, 7 Meitheamh

Burke had spent the night at Meagan's and had experienced none of the discomfort he had felt on their first night together. He felt himself getting drawn deeper and deeper into her and it bothered him less and less. In the morning they had eaten a late breakfast, then strolled through the Sunday streets before making their way to Hennessey's.

When he opened the door he was struck with a sight he had witnessed many times but had forgotten. Hennessey and Finn sat across from each other at the kitchen table, with all the lights out in the apartment. There was coffee in front of both of them and two lit cigarettes leaning in the ashtray. But their faces told the story.

"Havin' trouble boys," Martin said as he let the door slam.

Finn turned and stared at Burke with blood-red eyes. "I'm seriously thinkin' of killin' you when I get my strength back."

Burke noticed that Hen was thinking of saying something but mid-way through the attempt he gave up. Martin and Meagan sat down at the table beside them and Burke helped himself to Hen's coffee. "No luck I suppose?"

"Nothing Martin," Finn said brushing his hair with his hands and straightening up in his chair. "And how are you two this morning?"

Meagan grinned back at him then got up to make herself a cup of tea. "Fine. What did you two do last night."

Hennessey groaned at the thought of it and Finn chuckled. "After the wedding a couple of Hen's relatives decided to go out on the town. We wandered around the pubs for awhile and Hen here figured he'd make some easy money and got into a little drinkin' bout. The rest is history."

"I'm glad to see nothing's changed while I've been away," Burke said.

"But there is something Martin," Finn continued. "There's going to be a march tomorrow on account of the McHenry's."

Meagan turned as she finished making her tea. "Where?"

"There's a burial at Milltown so there'll be a rally there, then I guess they'll march through the streets. The call's out for it to be a peaceful demonstration."

"I think I'll drop in on it then. Maybe I can get something."

Meagan sat down at the table. "You'll get yourself spotted, that's what you'll get."

"No, Hennessey will be there to protect me, won't you Hen?"

Hen was too deep into something for it to be just thought and so Martin tapped him on the arm. "Won't you Hen?"

Hennessey's eyes cleared for a moment and he nodded then, smiling at some private joke, he rested his chin in his hands to watch the goings-on more securely.

Meagan finished her tea. "I just dropped by to chaperon the boy home. I've got some things to do." She got up from the table and said her good-byes. Martin walked her to the door. "Are you going to come around tonight?"

Martin nodded. "Later on. I think I'll hang around here for awhile. See if I can resurrect Hennessey."

"Good luck." She kissed him and left.

When Burke got back to the table he noticed that Hennessey had pulled himself up and was drinking his coffee, with a newly-lit cigarette in his other hand. Finn was leaning against the counter. "You two are going down in the medical journals as the Lazarus twins."

"We found out something else Martin." There was a solemn air in Finn's voice.

"You were asking me some questions the other night about who might have informed on you," Hen said, then took a drink of his coffee. "Well, everybody had been checking around after you got lifted but nobody came up with anything. Then last night, while we were drinking I heard some things. You remember Dave Sheehan?"

Martin thought for a moment. "Can't say I do. Is he related to Pat Sheehan, the one that got killed over in Omagh in '79?"

"That was his brother. It was Dave that informed on you. They kept it quiet and he left about three months after you were arrested. Went to work in Liverpool. He came back about six months ago."

"Are you sure of this?"

"Double-checked, Martin," Finn said. "It's true."

Hen looked over at Burke. "What do you want to do?"

Martin struggled inside to find the anger he had felt before but it was not easy. "I don't know."

Hennessey hunched forward. "He turned you in. You've got to do something."

Burke glanced at Finnerty but the old man just shrugged. "It's your choice."

"Do you know where he is?"

Hennessey stood up from the table. "I'll take you there now."

As he followed Hennessey out the door, Burke's hand rested on the Smith & Wesson in his pocket.

A cold rain was falling as Martin and Hen stood watching the Sheehan house. The overhang they sheltered under didn't provide much protection. Hennessey tried unsuccessfully to light a cigarette. "Pat was a good lad. He was a good volunteer, but Dave, I didn't really know him. I didn't expect this from a Sheehan."

"How old is he?"

"Twenty-one, I think."

"Are you sure it was him?"

"Positive, Martin. There was just him and Pat and with Pat gone he had to look after the old folks. The story is that he got lifted for something small but that he had known one of the guys that was buying from you that day and so he gave it to the Brits and they promised him a job in England. It was safe for him because he didn't have to testify."

"The IRA doesn't know?"

"I doubt it. He'd be dead. It was just by luck that I got it. The old fellow didn't know who he was talking to. Probably didn't even know he was talking. He was drunker'n I was."

"Do you know what he looks like?"

"Unless he's changed a lot in three years. I worked a bit with Pat before he was killed."

They saw the door to the row house open and a young man in a wheel chair backed himself out into the rain and pulled the door shut.

"That's him," Hennessey said, hitting Burke on the arm, "let's go."

Martin pulled Hen back into the shadows. "He's in a wheel chair."

Hennessey wiped the rain from his face. "So what? He can still talk." He pulled himself loose and started walking along the sidewalk. Burke followed. Sheehan was in front of them about two blocks, pushing himself along in the rain on the other side of the street, shielded by a large plastic poncho. As they walked, the rain grew worse and a group of people who had been walking further down ran around a corner heading for cover. Burke and Hennessey were now alone on the street with Sheehan. They walked on silently for two more blocks and Martin could feel the rain soaking through his jacket. Mid-block Sheehan wheeled into a convenience store.

"He'll probably be coming back this way," Hennessey said, ducking into a doorway and lighting a cigarette.

Burke stood beside him out in the rain. "I'm not sure about this. With me just busted out there'd be no doubt in the Brits' minds that I pulled the trigger. There's no point in heating things up just now."

"Bullshit. If he was walking down that street, you wouldn't think twice about offing him."

"Maybe, but he's not walking."

"Don't confuse the issue with emotion, Martin. He's an informer. It doesn't matter why he did it or what he's doin' now. He has to pay the price. You let somebody like that get away and that's a signal to everybody else."

"And if I'd believed that you turned me in, I should have just put one in you?"

"If you were sure of it, you would have."

Burke knew he was right. Yet he was hesitating. Broken English was overshadowing everything else. That wasn't all of it though. In some twisted way he had been satisfied to be arrested. It had taken him out of something in which he had lost control. And now the man who had done it was crippled.

"What happened to him?"

"I heard it was some industrial accident. The Brits cut him loose but he gets a disability pension."

Burke didn't say anything for a moment, then his thoughts were interrupted by Dave Sheehan coming out of the store with a bundle under his poncho. He felt the pistol in his pocket and there was a sudden urge to finish the matter there and then, but caution interceded. "If I'm going to do it, I'll do it right. He's not going anywhere. Let's finish Broken English first. I'm not going to stand on the street like some kid and do the fellow."

Hennessey dropped his cigarette in a puddle. "Have it your way. I've done my bit. Let's go get dried off. The least you can do is buy me a drink."

"Sure, but just one. I'm going over to Meagan's."

"Careful, Martin. Next thing you know she'll be asking you to pick up a loaf of bread on your way home."

Burke and Hennessey left but Dave Sheehan didn't notice. He was having too much trouble getting his wheelchair over the curb.

LIBYA

7:00 am, 8 June

The sun had been up for quite awhile and still there was little sign of activity in the camp. There was only one sentry on duty at the gate on the entrance road and he seemed more interested in the book he was reading than in whether anyone was moving in or out of the perimeter wire. He would be reprimanded later. Mines had been located at strategic intervals around the camp except for the area behind the latrines — the quality of the food too often required this area to be put to use by the camp members — and they had a good radar station, but still one had to be vigilant.

Amin Ali sat outside his hut watching the barracks building to the south over which flew an Irish tricolour. He put down his field glasses and ate a slice of orange sprinkled with cinnamon. There seemed to be some activity at the barracks so he raised his glasses again. Adan McCracken came out the door and headed up to the practice range with an automatic pistol. Magee had alerted Ali by coded cable received late last night that this man was an informer and would have to be disposed of. Ali had decided to wait until he was out and have the other members of the squad do the deed. It was unwise to carry out summary executions against a man who had seven armed compatriots with him. Better to turn them on him and have them carry out the directions of their superior. It was a good lesson for them to learn.

He walked across the dusty compound and adjusted his red checkered burnoose, his Uzi slung over his shoulder. The camp was full with men of many different nationalities — Japanese, Basque, German, Italian, French, Palestinian. It was a United Nations of terrorists, interspersed here and there with Libyan hosts and Soviet and Cuban instructors.

He approached a group of seven Provos who had come out as he approached and were now sitting outside their barracks in the sun, looking groggy. They didn't notice him until he spoke, for many men had begun moving through the compound, dressed in the standard cammo fatigues. They were young, 19 and 20, and fresh from Ireland, their first trip away from home. But he had trained them as Magee had instructed and they would be ready.

"Where did McCracken go?"

"He's headed up to the target range," answered Kelly, who had emerged as the leader of the group. "Why?"

Ali took the cable out of his pocket and handed it to Kelly. The others gathered around to read it. It was in their code and had the proper signifiers. They looked up silently at Ali's face. He watched their eyes for a moment and was satisfied that they understood and would carry out the command. He turned and glanced up at the hilltop practice range. "Get your weapons."

McCracken paused in his target practice and looked back towards the camp where he saw a group of men heading his way. He checked with his field glasses. Ali and Kelly were leading the others and they were armed. His heart skipped a beat. It had been made clear to all of them when they agreed to join this operation that absolute secrecy was the drill and any leaks whatsoever would be dealt with by execution. It had also been made clear that once committed there was no backing out. He had wanted out and he had told his girlfriend. There had been conversations with her brother-in-law which he should not have had and he had had a feeling that it would come back on him. His only hope was that he could get back to Belfast and slip away. He wondered if somehow they had found out. Perhaps he was jumping to conclusions. He stood for a moment longer and waved to the lads. They waved back. Through the binoculars he could see that they were smiling and talking and he breathed a sigh of relief. It was just another training exercise. Ali had been working them hard.

Adan joined them at the crest of the hill and they gathered around Ali who knelt in the middle of them.

"You'll be going back soon. You've all done well, despite what I say about you. Today I want to take you out on a run, tire you out and then see if you can still hit a target. A man is no good unless he can work under pressure. And his aim is no good if he cannot control his body. Start." The nine men broke into a run, heading west, in the general direction of Zuara.

Ali noticed that the heat had drawn out a heavy sweat on the lads. He himself was wet with it. But he wanted to take them far from the camp in order to let them carry out their duty. It would be easier. It was a difficult thing to do and he didn't want to have this house-cleaning affect camp morale. McCracken was in the lead. He was a good man and would have been a credit to the squad. It was a waste but it was necessary. Ali glanced sideways to Kelly and the others and they slacked off a bit. As McCracken went over a rise and started down a gully, Kelly opened up on him.

Just seconds before Adan had noticed that he was in the lead and the hair rose on the back of his neck. His intuition had been right. They were going to hit him. As Kelly squeezed his trigger, Adan glanced back and confirmed his suspicions. He leapt and rolled to the bottom of the gully where there was scrub cover. Bullets whined around him and bit into the earth. He swung his pistol and took quick aim on Ali, thinking that if he could take him out he might be able to reason with the others. But his aim was not steady enough and the shot went wild. Not wild enough though. Thomas McLaughlin doubled over, gut-shot.

Ali rolled back behind the crest of the hill and the others followed his example. McCracken had just made the job easier by killing MacLaughlin. That would convince the other members of the team. And he wasn't worried about getting him. They had him out-gunned by a considerable margin. It would just take a little more work. He crawled over to Kelly. "You're in charge of this. Organize your men. He's into the scrub now. If he gets away it's on your head."

As McCracken sat by a rock getting his breath, a bullet sizzled by him, and he leapt to the side. His pistol fell to the ground and dropped into a crevice in the parched rocks. It took only one glance to see that it had dropped out of reach, and he had neither the time nor the cover to fish for it now. He scurried to a dip in the terrain, ducking down behind a large boulder which rose out of the ground like some prehistoric and badly-hewn monument. It gave him some cover, but he knew that soon a hunter would find his trail and would be on him. He whipped off his coat and positioned it behind a bush about ten yards past the rock then ran back. With his combat knife he cut two metal rings off his cammo pants, snapped about three feet of trip wire from his pouches and wrapped one end around each ring, fashioning a crude garotte, then waited. He had learned from his teachers.

Someone cautiously approached the left side of the rock. McCracken edged his way around the right side in a twisted parody of some vaudeville routine. Costello had stopped and was taking aim on Adan's jacket, while wedged behind an outcrop of rock which he thought afforded him some cover. As he heard McCracken, he tensed and his neck muscles twitched, but it was too late. Adan swung the garotte over his head and around his neck, crossed at the back for leverage. Costello dropped his rifle and it clattered on the rocks, then he clawed at the wire but it was sunk too far into his skin and his grasping and gasping were in vain. McCracken held the wire tight until his former comrade stopped moving, then supported the dead weight just a little bit longer, to be sure. He laid him down by the rock almost gently. It had been difficult to kill a friend, even when the friend was trying to kill him. Sometimes things were just unavoidable.

Ali had been watching the rocks and though he had not seen McCracken kill Costello he knew that too much time had passed. Kelly should have sent two men in. He would learn from his mistakes. Through that tactical error Kelly had given McCracken the opportunity to increase his firepower. Now he would be armed with Costello's M-16A2, the Marine's new assault rifle, an adaptation of the standard combat rifle to take a 70 grain 5.56 NATO round with a faster twist to the barrel, 1-in-7. The round tumbled when it exited the bore to give it that much more stopping power. The rifle was also equipped with a side-mounted, horizontal bayonet. Ali decided that he would give Kelly some advice. They had lost two men already and McCracken would make three. If he did not deliver at least four well-trained men to Magee, Magee would not be pleased.

He moved over to Kelly's position. "He's killed Costello."
"How do you know?"
"I know. We can't afford to lose anyone else. You come with me and we'll circle him. Have the others drive him on, but not too fast. They should just hang back and fire on him when he shows himself. It's a little different than street-fighting."

Kelly nodded and found the others, giving them their instructions, then returned to Ali. They watched as the other four fanned out in the scrub. Out in front of them they saw McCracken run out from behind a bush and zig-zag towards a rock outcrop. The men laid down a line of fire and drove him away from the rocks and forward. Ali slapped Kelly on the back. "Now they're doing it right. Let's go."

McCracken had not been able to spot anyone else for some time now though they had continued to fire on him when he showed himself. The heat was hitting him. He hoped it was hitting the others even more. A furrow appeared in front of him and beyond it, the land dipped away. A stream flowed through here and on to the sea. He had seen this on the recon maps, and figured he was a little less than ten clicks from Zuara. He entered the furrow and dropped in exhaustion beside the stream, stretching out on the ground beside it, face down, to dip his head in the refreshing water, and to drink. He did not know that Ali was there with Kelly. They approached McCracken silently and Ali placed his foot on the back of the informer's head and pushed it under water. McCracken flailed his arms, but to no avail. Ali counted to fifty then bent over and pulled him up, gasping for air and choking as his face cleared the surface of the water. Throwing him down on his back on the dusty bank, Ali kicked his weapon away. The others had now reached them and gathered around around their fallen comrade.

"Where's the fire Adan?"

"Why are you fuckers trying to kill me?"

Kelly stood over him and smiled. "That's no way to speak to your friends. This'll be a lot easier if you just co-operate. You've been doing some talking and our American cousin is concerned. Who have you been singing to?"

"I haven't said anything to anybody."

Kelly swung his rifle around and fired into the ground beside the boy's head.

"Fuck off!" McCracken said, squirming. "Alright, alright. I told the girlfriend but that's all. But she's in New York. You can't kill me for that?"

Kelly hunkered down beside him. "What makes you think we'll kill you, Adan. But I don't think we can take your word for this. And whoever you've told, they've caused a little trouble for us all. Now we can't let that go, can we." Kelly reached into McCracken's boot sheath and removed his combat knife. "Now let's think again about who you were talking to."

McCracken knew there wasn't much of a chance but he had to take it. He kicked and sent Kelly sprawling into the water, then lunged at Ali but Kelly got out of the water and drove the knife hilt-deep into McCracken's back. The lad screamed in pain and stood, grasping at his back with both hands in an attempt to extract the stinger. His former comrades watched the strange dance of death. Ali pushed his way forward and knocked McCracken to the ground. He lifted his Uzi and, with one clean shot through the heart, put an end to McCracken's struggle.

He looked at the lads gathered around him. "When you're told to kill, kill. Now bury him and forget him." He slung his machine gun and headed back to the camp.

ANDERSONTOWN

2:00 pm, 8 Meitheamh

The crowd gathered in Milltown Cemetery at the McHenry plot and not far from the cemetery, in vacant lots, the British waited with their sixers and land rovers. Two helicopters made sporadic forays over the crowd and the news cameras of many networks, hungering for a story, positioned themselves about the rally. Though they knew the authorities would cover the gathering, Burke and Hennessey decided that it would be important to go there. They were sure there would be information on McHenry and perhaps his contacts as well. Meagan had offered to attend with them but Burke convinced her to continue her inquiries among her contacts and she had gone off to a meeting with O'Donnahue. The meeting was set for a spot near Finn's so Martin arranged for them to meet her at a nearby pub after and together they would head for Hennessey's.

Whole families had come out in horror at the killing of Dr McHenry at the hands of the British followed by the murder of his mother, wife and child. After the interment, speakers proclaimed this as another act of British barbarism and sectarian murder by the Protestants. However, the speeches were tinged with some moderation as priests spoke not only of the fact that people who resorted to this sort of action could not be considered Christians but that vengeance should be left to the Lord and the legal authorities. Though it was not an IRA funeral, here and there in the crowd Burke spotted men and women in the IRA uniform, their heads covered with black balaclavas. The Republican flag lent its colour to the spectacle as well. In the Catholic areas the IRA provided protection and crowd control.

Burke checked the faces in the crowd, looking for someone who might be the sister Mrs McHenry had mentioned, but there was no one in the family section who seemed the right age. He looked too for the young boy he had seen so often in the last few days, but with no success. Burke knew, as he moved about, that some of those present had recognized him. He saw their expressions of surprise, of solidarity and of caution.

Hennessey came back to Burke. "The sister couldn't get a flight over in time. She telephoned her family. Hardly anybody's talking about McHenry though, other than to say that he didn't have anything to do with the IRA and that the newspaper stories are a crock of shit."

"It was worth a try," Burke said, digging into his pocket for a cigarette.

"There's a lot of people that have seen you, Martin. I heard them talking about you showing up here. And some of them were saying that you showed up at McHenry's funeral and they're wondering what's going on."

"Well, we'll have to stay until it's over. It wouldn't be advisable to try and get past the troops by ourselves. They'll march after it's finished and we can duck out then."

"I hope so. Gimme a smoke, will you."

Martin held out the pack. He stood and listened to the same speeches given with the same undying conviction he had heard for many years. Occasionally he glanced to the helicopters or the British troops and RUC men in the distance. That hadn't changed either.

Burke waited at the corner for Meagan. Darkness was falling and he hoped she would not be too late. The rally had dispersed peacefully and he and Hen had no trouble getting away without complications. A couple of men had come up and shaken his hand then melted back into the crowd but he had felt no need to be concerned. Hennessey had gone off to check one of the pubs where a lot of the participants would end up at and said he'd be back at the apartment before they got there.

Down the street he saw a grey RUC truck turn the corner and slowly begin a sweep up the street toward him. There were other people on the sidewalk and he fell in behind a group of five as they walked past and lowered his head when the truck went by. Satisfied that he had not been spotted, he stopped at a bench outside a pub and lit a cigarette. The three men standing by the pub door didn't pay him any attention and went on with their conversation which had to do with the physical attributes of a girl by the name of Lorraine.

Ten minutes later the same truck came back along the street. It was not unusual for the RUC to swing back over the same area twice in a patrol but Burke was taking no chances. As he saw it nose out from the side street he ducked inside the pub and waited until it had passed. Then he went back into the street and walked to the corner where he was to wait for Meagan. As he looked in the window of a camera store he noticed two men standing behind him in RUC uniform but before he could react they grabbed him by the arms. His face squashed against the shop window and the weight of the one man's body leaning against his back immobilised him. The one holding him drew his revolver and held it to his ear.

"Out for a little shopping Burke? Check his pockets Ian."

Ian reached into his jacket pocket and pulled out the Smith & Wesson. "Come on. Let's get the bastard to the truck."

As they pulled him away from the glass he tried to break away but the officer with the gun slammed it against his temple. "You try anything and I'll blow your fuckin' head off. My uncle was riding with you when you busted out and he's still in the hospital. You broke his ribs," he said jamming the gun into Burke's side to drive the point home, "and I'd enjoy doin' you right here and now."

They marched him to thto the corner of an alley. Halfway down Burke could see the grey truck, lights out, its motor running. Ian smashed him face first into the side of the truck as the other officer unlocked the backdoor.

"We better call this in."

"Do what you want," Ian said, "but I want some time with this cunt before we take him over to MI. He killed my mate." Ian cracked his baton across Burke's back. "Do you remember Jimmy Richmond, you fucker?"

Burke's back stung from the baton but he tried not to react. Inside he cursed. He had made it easy for them, waiting out in the open. He hadn't been thinking.

The other RUC officer called into MIHQ and identified himself. "Jackson, RUC. We've got Martin Burke. No need for back-up, he was alone and he's in custody. We're going to wait here a bit to see who he was waiting for and then we'll bring him in."

Burke listened as he gave the street co-ordinates to MIHQ and waited for confirmation. The thought that he wouldn't be taken to Castlereagh didn't make things any better. Instead of a beating there he would get one here. And he didn't intend to take any beating. He noticed that Jackson had holstered his revolver as he made the call and, as soon as he completed it, Burke sprang into action, pushing against the side of the truck with all his strength and driving Ian into the brick wall of the alley. Ian let go and sank down onto the pavement, dazed. Jackson rushed at him, drawing his revolver but Burke kicked it out of his hand. Nothing happened for a moment as Jackson stepped back unsure of what to do then he leapt at Burke, tackling him. They rolled on the pavement and against the wheels of the truck, fists flying. Martin didn't see Ian getting to his feet and retrieving his weapon. He didn't feel the second baton blow either.

Jackson got to his feet and rubbed his jaw, then kicked the unconscious Burke in the side. "Put him in the back. I want to see if anyone else comes along and then we're gonna give that fucker a headin'. They want him brought in alive, OK, but he's not gonna have any fuckin' teeth left." Together they hoisted the body into the back of the truck and locked the door, then went to the mouth of the alley to watch the street.

"I'll call you right back." Sullivan hung up the phone. He was glad Wilkes was on top of things, but he didn't have much time. He quickly dialed another number and waited as it rang. A voice answered. "The RUC just picked up Burke. They called in to MIHQ but Wilkes intercepted it. They're a couple of keen yarbos and they're waiting to see if there's a contact. Get over there and take care of it." Sullivan dictated the address then hung up. He called Wilkes on the direct line. "I've got my people on it."

"Will they get there in time?"

"Probably, but I want you to cover it if they bring him in. You'll have to arrange for him to get out."

"Or we could just hold him and he could be killed in an escape attempt."

"Don't start trying to change the plan now. You'll have him soon enough, but I want him on the street awhile longer. That's the deal. Can you clear any record of his arrest?"

"I've already taken the necessary steps. If your people are successful, there won't be any record of the call."

"Good. I'll confirm with you as soon as I have word." Sullivan hung up and poured himself a drink. As he did, he noticed that his hand was shaking. This operation was going to be the death of him.

Burke opened his eyes. It took him a moment to realise where he was, but the sound of the engine running reminded him. He rubbed his head and felt the blood-matted hair then became aware of the throbbing pain in his side. He got to his feet and went to the back of the truck. Looking out the small window he saw that they were still parked in the same alley. As he leaned against the door it gave way and swung open a crack. He waited but there was no sound other than the engine. He pushed the door farther open cautiously, mindful of the many prisoners shot while trying to escape. There seemed to be no one outside. With his foot, he gave the door a kick then waited in the shadow for a shot to ring out. Nothing. Gathering his strength he leapt from the truck and scrambled to the side of the alley. Still nothing. Not wanting to question providence, he headed down the alley away from the main street and turned a corner into a dark back alley. As he entered he tripped and fell, landing in a pile of rubbish. Instinctively, he rolled to the side then got on his feet and raced along in the darkness for a few steps but no one followed. Curious, he retraced his steps and crouched by the rubbish pile. He lit a match and looked to see what he had tripped over. The bodies of Ian and Jackson sat slumped against the wall, heads lolling forward, a bullet wound in the back of each skull. His pistol was on the ground beside them and he picked it up, stuffing it in his pocket. Martin stared at the two bodies until the match burned down to his fingers. He tossed it aside and rose to his feet, stumbling on into the dark alley. He had to make it to Hennessey's.

"Jesus Martin," Finn said as Burke opened the door at Hennessey's, "what the hell happened to you?"

Hen and Meagan grabbed him and led him to the couch. Meagan saw the blood on his head and went to the kitchen, returning with a cloth and a bowl of water.

"The RUC grabbed me while I was waiting for Meagan."

Meg dabbed at the cut in Martin's scalp and he winced. "When I got there I didn't see you so I waited for a bit then figured you might have come on over here so I did too."

Hennessey gave him a shot of whiskey. "How did you get away?"

Burke pulled Meagan's hand away from his head. "It'll be ok. They cracked me on the skull and threw me in their van. Said they were going to wait around to see if anybody came looking for me. You were lucky," he said glancing at Meagan. "When I came to, they weren't around. But I found them in the alley, shot in the head."

Hennessey shook his head. "That was luck. Somebody must have picked them off."

Martin reached in his pocket and pulled out his pistol, checking the clip. It was full. "Whoever it was left my gun there."

Finnerty got up and poured himself a drink. "This isn't good Martin. I don't like the sound of it. Anytime you have to depend on luck, you're in trouble."

"You shouldn't have been meeting me in the open like that," Meagan added. "Not with things the way they are."

"Could it have been somebody from the cemetery that set you up?" Hennessey asked.

"I don't see how. The RUC truck went by a couple of times. I didn't think they had spotted me but they must have. I was sloppy."

"Well you can't afford that, young fella," Finn said.

Burke took the cloth out of the bowl of water and washed the cut on his head. "I get the message. But we're just spinning our wheels. I don't have much more time."

Finn scratched his head. "You're right there Martin. I spent the day checking to see if anybody had wind of who might have brought in heavy explosives, for the McHenry job, you know. But no one's been doing anything. I even checked with Jack McCloskey. You remember him. He checked into it and said the lab reports came up blank. It wasn't Brit issue stuff. So it had to have been brought in from outside."

Burke rinsed the bloody cloth in the bowl. "Maybe that's the way we have to go. If I can find out where the explosives came from, we might be able to track things down."

"And how do you propose we do that?" Hen asked.

"If you guys can keep looking here I think I might go out of town for a couple days."

Meagan turned as she finished making her tea. "Where?"

"Amsterdam. If I want to get to the bottom of this I need to know more. I need names. The McHenry's are gone and the one lad they mentioned is in Libya. There's no way I can get to him. There is that little boy, Hen you know the one. He keeps on turning up. Maybe you could find him. But there's this arms dealer that I used to buy from in Amsterdam and she's well-connected internationally. She might be able to help."

Meagan perked up at the mention of a 'she'. "She? Who's this?"

Burke grinned. "Nothing like that. Gardia Koolwein. I haven't seen her in years. It's just business. She may be able to tell me who has been purchasing stuff lately. The explosion at McHenry's house had to be military explosives and I'd imagine anyone with that sort of firepower would leave a trail. It's just a chance, but it's all that I've got. Charles will be here in four days."

He paused and looked at his audience. Hennessey seemed deep in thought. "Are you following me Hen?"

Hennessey looked at Martin and he nodded.

Finn cleared his throat, squinted at Burke through one eye and spoke. "Sounds like a good idea Martin. But have you given any thought to how you're going to get there?"

Burke was slow to respond. He hadn't wanted to be involved in this from the beginning. And now he was too involved to leave it. Not only was the plan dangerous for Ireland but, if it was successful, he would be the prime suspect. Nor did he relish the new role he knew he would have to take. In stopping Broken English he was saving the life of a British Prince. It did not sit well with him. "I'll need a passport and money."

Finn smiled. "How would you feel about travelling as an old lady in weeds. I can arrange papers for that. I haven't lost all my talents yet, you know. We could do things up tonight. You could be going to the funeral of a nephew on the continent, working in Amsterdam."

"Sounds good," replied Burke, warming to the possibility. "Where can you get them?"

Finn chuckled. "There's an old girl I used to know. She's still sweet on me. But she's clean. She could report her papers missing after it's over."

"Good. But what about funding?"

Hennessey had been nodding in agreement and now joined in. "Don't worry about money. I've still got some of the money that was collected in the US. This seems like a worthy cause."

Burke glanced at Finn. The old man's eyes were speaking caution but confirming the need for action. He would have to make many arrangements and though he wanted to be with Meagan he realised that would have to wait. She seemed to be thinking the same thing. He wasn't even sure that Gardia was still in Amsterdam but he could get Hen to confirm that. It would be necessary to travel there in person. It was too easy for people to imitate voices and he was not sure she would remember his name from all the customers with whom she must have dealt. Besides, she was too cautious to ever give out any information over the phone. There was really no choice. "Okay. Let's get started."

They had spent the night busy at Hennessey's apartment but it looked as if they'd be ready for the first flight out in the morning. Burke was more surprised at Finn's knowledge of disguise than at his ability to pop out for a couple of hours and return with the necessary papers. Hennessey took the photos of Burke in makeup and he and Finn doctored the passport professionally. Mrs David Monteith of Belfast was on her way to Amsterdam to the wake of her nephew Andrew. Burke would have to pick up another passport in Amsterdam to get back, but that would be no trouble. A British passport could be had in Amsterdam for under £800. Finn had also provided the weeds for Burke and he and Meagan had spent a great deal of time getting things just so. There was the question of the money and where to hide it but Finn figured the bosom as the most secure place.

He had gone out as well to leak some information about Burke to an MI informer so that the British would be thrown off. Supposedly Burke had gone up to Derry to wait until things cooled off in Belfast. That would keep the heat off long enough to get Burke through the security at the airport.

Meagan had offered to pick up the tickets but Burke had asked Hen to take care of it. That way they had been able to have some time alone. Meagan's role in the plan would be to escort him to the airport, posing as a daughter-in-law, and act as a diversion. He hoped it would not be a long separation; he felt the need of her.

Through his financial contacts Hen had also been able to confirm that there was still an arm's dealer named Koolwein operating in Amsterdam. Burke would go to the whorehouse on Buiten Wier Ingenstraat which she used as a front. He recalled the many times they had sat there, completing a deal, drinking gin and talking.

Burke's reminiscences were interrupted by Hennessey returning. He walked in, caught sight of Martin and stopped dead in his tracks.

"Well, well. What a beauty," he said prancing around Burke with his hand on his hip. He lifted the skirt and Burke smashed him on the head with his purse. Hennessey backed off, laughing. "That's right Martin. If those nasty Brits bother you, just hit'em with your bag."

Finn sat at the table with a big grin on his face and a glass of whiskey in his hand. "A nice job though, considering what I had to work with."

Meagan grinned but Burke stood up and pointed a finger at her. "Don't you start too."

Hennessey came over and put his arm around Meagan. "I was able to get a car, so we can go to the airport in style."

With some last minute adjustments and last minute instructions on being a lady, courtesy of Meagan, a bereaved aunt left for the airport to take her first trip in a plane.

MIHQ, BELFAST
9:00 am, 9 June

The Supremo leaned back in his chair at MIHQ. He faced another long day. There had been no time for sleep in the last few weeks and the way things were going he would have no rest until Charles was safely out of Ireland. Even then he could not really relax but at least he wouldn't have to worry as much about the press. The room was filled with MI agents, some SAS officers, including Wilkes and Barton, as well as some members of the Royal Ulster Constabulary. Hedley noticed that Barton was in dirty fatigues again. There was too much action in the streets for Hedley's liking.

Ireland was not a place that he enjoyed. London was much more to his liking. There he could walk the streets safely without bodyguards, enjoy a weekend of leisure. Had there been a Mrs Hedley he would not have accepted the appointment. Had Charles not been adamant about visiting Belfast and Londonderry in support of the Accord, the appointment would not have been necessary. Members of the Royal Family had visited Ireland during the last 10 years and, with the exception of Lord Mountbatten, all had returned safely. But to visit now, before the place had sufficiently cooled from the Accord, with the Princes, one who would one day become King Billy? The Catholics would be hot under their Roman collars.

Yet not to visit would be taken as a betrayal of the Plantation. In the early 1600's James I had followed the lead of Elizabeth I and established a Protestant colony in Ulster province in order to subdue the Catholic mass. In return, the British Crown took the obligation of protecting the people who formed their vanguard. Since partition the Protestants had lived in fear of assimilation or, in their minds, extermination by the Catholic south. And the Catholics had lived in fear of a similar extermination should there be no Union. It was a fear which had often been fueled by the British in order to keep their vanguard loyal. Without the presence of the military either side could fall prey to their paranoias and all hell would break loose.

And so it fell to the Supremo to see that peace, order and good government were maintained, with the accent on order. After all, Protestant or Catholic, they were still Irish. Both sides were his enemy. Charles' visit was necessary, most necessary in Northern Ireland. Hedley's job was to make sure there would be no problems. Painstaking devotion to detail and anticipation was the order of the day. Every formula was worked and reworked. However a strange variable had cropped up. Martin Burke had escaped and was free in Ulster.

Hedley looked down at the photo of Burke: bearded, blue-eyed Burke. Barton had identified him as the man who had thwarted his capture of Lynch. Barton had interrogated Burke at The Maze following his arrest. Again Burke appeared, but this time in Belfast at McHenry's funeral and later at McHenry's house. Somehow he had escaped, but the fact remained — he was back. Burke's connection with McHenry and Lynch was puzzling. Was there also a contact between Burke and news they had heard about a team of new IRA recruits going abroad to train? There had been no more about that, but still Hedley wondered. What was Burke up to?

Hedley had first met Burke in 1973 at a town on the border between Rhodesia and Mozambique. The quiet Irishman had intrigued him. Hedley had been sent to Rhodesia by the Foreign Office on a fact-finding mission. He had accompanied a Rhodesian commando on a routine search and destroy and they had connected with Burke's group. When the killing was over and the burning of the dead blacks began, Burke had wandered off with a bottle. The smell of burning flesh had sickened Hedley and he followed the young man. Together they had shared intelligent conversation, a few jokes and a great deal of whiskey. It was only on his return to England that he learned of Burke's activities with the IRA. His respect for Burke had led him to the conclusion that this young man might someday be a formidable enemy. Silently, he wished that Burke would die in Africa. But this was not to be the case.

Burke returned to the North and there he earned a reputation for his meticulous murder of so many British soldiers. Hedley had studied in depth the files on Burke's endeavours as much as they could be pieced together. Barton's interrogation had garnered no further information. A soldier would be marked for death when he killed any Irishman. The sentence would not be carried out immediately and, it seemed, many were forgiven, forgotten, or the example of a failure by Burke. It had taken awhile for them to piece together that it was Burke but information from informers and some lucky breaks had allowed them to determine that it was him. Details of his exploits were not made public to avoid making him a folk hero, and were kept from the troops in order to avoid morale problems. But rumours abounded and he became a symbol to many Irishmen. Then suddenly, in 1982 Burke stopped killing. His betrayal at an arms sale in 1984 had ended his career but it puzzled Hedley that Burke had stopped before that.

The dossier was skimpy and, in fact, Burke had only been convicted of the arms sale. The murders were going to be a more difficult matter. Hedley had considered instituting an intense manhunt, but the unanswered question of Burke's relationship with Lynch and McHenry stayed that order. Perhaps Burke would lead them to a third or others. First they would have to get a good fix on Burke and begin the trace. Second Hedley would have to make sure Barton and his men did not kill. Two mistakes had been committed. A third could not be afforded and would not be tolerated.

Hedley skimmed the rest of the dossier on Burke's ancestry, his father's death, his activities in Africa, then closed the file. He stood with a pointer and pressed a button on the console at his desk. An image of Burke appeared on the screen, tired and haggard, bearded. Hedley paced the front of the room angrily. "This man has been making fools of all of you. For a week now he's been here and the body count is rising. Lynch was killed while he was trying to get him across the border, we have reliable information that when McHenry was killed he was trying to contact him, he may have been involved in the killing of a soldier in a recent street exchange and apparently he entered McHenry's house and successfully demolished it with explosives, killing the three occupants." The monitor now ran footage in slow motion from the barracks' cameras showing a shadowy figure of Burke, clean-shaven.

Wilkes noticed some of the MI agents trying to lean back into anonymous darkness.

"You're all to blame." Hedley pushed a button and the image changed. "Donncha Cronin, found dead. Execution. Presumably Burke. He had been spotted at the McHenry incident."

Wilkes looked over at Barton but he seemed to be holding up well. The man was trustworthy and would never desert the operation. But it still paid to be cautious.

Hedley carried on. "You still haven't even been able to get me any thing about McHenry or Lynch. I'm literally in the dark and you people are coming up with nothing. The 12th is fast approaching and you're letting a trained assassin slip through your fingers. We have been assured a ceasefire in our negotiations with the IRA and the Protestants but the Home Office is worried. And the difficulties are not just with Burke. The McHenry funeral was without incident but I've received a report of two constables found dead in an alley. We can't link it to Burke but it may well have been connected with the demonstration. COBRA is standing by because Burke is on the loose and because the number of incidents is on the rise. Gentlemen, I do not even want to begin to sketch out the calamity which may befall Britain and yourselves should you fail to get me Burke, alive, within the next three days. I have already alerted agents to the possibility that he may be in Londonderry. One of our supergrasses brought that in. I will have no more mistakes or excuses." Wilkes noticed that Hedley looked directly at Barton as he said this. "Burke will be taken alive after we can ascertain his other contacts, but in any event, within three days. There is no need for further discussion."

Barton butted his cigarette in aggressive acceptance amid the shuffle of chairs and feet as all hurried off to get to work. As he walked past Wilkes, Wilkes assured him silently that they would talk later. They had a meeting to go to with Sullivan and the Protestants who had financed Broken English and, as well, he wanted to assure Barton that everything was under control. Even with COBRA geared up the operation was still safe. The Cabinet Office Briefing Room was chaired by the Home Secretary and had representatives from the police, MI-5, the Ministry of Defence and the Ministry of Foreign Affairs. It would also most likely have someone from MI-6 as well. MI-6 and MI-5 did not always see eye to eye. But the crucial keystone for Wilkes was that there was always an SAS man present at COBRA and he knew this would be Windgate, and Windgate was with him. He would know anything that happened at COBRA as soon as or before Hedley got the word. And if all went well, he was sure that Windgate would swing COBRA into authorizing Operation Swift, a 'modest proposal' to retaliate for the murder of Prince Charles and Prince William at the hands of the IRA. He and Windgate had already drafted such an action and Windgate was currently re-drafting it to take account of current deployments and conditions in Ireland. The entire matter was well in hand. Hedley would have Burke, but not on his terms.

SULLIVAN'S

9:30 am, 9 June

Sullivan shook his head, then leaned back in the leather chair in his study. "That bastard is getting too close. I need this thing cleaned up or our support is going to run for cover."

Magee looked up at the ceiling. "I sent word to the camp at Libya for Amin to get rid of McCracken. He's confirmed that it was carried out so that'll take care of the leak. I was going to do it myself but I didn't have enough time to get down there and it had to be done there. I didn't want to take a chance on Adan getting back into Ireland. And my man in New York has located the girl. He'll find out if she's spoken to anyone and finish that end of it. What about Feeney?"

"He's too scared to tell anyone but I'm having someone pay him a visit just in case. I don't want anyone around that can put me with Martin Burke. Poor old Feeney, early retirement for him."

Magee sat up in the chair he'd been slouching in. "So there's just Burke. You've arranged for him to be covered. What's the problem?"

"I just got word that he's off to Amsterdam, and he's already left."

Magee leaned forward. "Amsterdam. Why?"

"He has a contact there. An arms dealer, some woman named Koolwein. He knows there's going to be a hit and he knows it'll call for special equipment, so he's going to see if she knows of any deals. Will she?"

Magee shook his head. "I can't see how but you're right. He's too inquisitive. What do you want me to do?"

"Get over to Amsterdam. Immediately. I want to know what he finds out. If he doesn't find out anything, make sure he gets back here in time. I don't care how. If he gets too much information you'll have to kill him. We can still claim he's involved. He'll just 'elude capture', but I don't want him on my tail. I'm not telling Wilkes about this until I have to. It was bad enough that he was almost brought in last night and thank God Wilkes had the presence of mind to deal with the matter at his end. Now they think he's gone off to Derry to lie low." Sullivan leaned forward. "If you have to kill him, do it right. I want photographs and his right hand to convince them."

"How about the ears and the tail?"

Sullivan ignored the comment. "Will you be able to locate this Koolwein woman?"

"I shouldn't have any trouble. I know some people there. I'll take care of it, don't worry."

Sullivan leaned back in his chair and tapped the top of his cane with his hand. "I'm getting sick of hearing that."

AMSTERDAM
11 am, 9 June

Mynheer Dobbe had been proprietor of Vanhout & Verhooven for seventeen years, and in his days of standing near his shop window peering past the mannequins at the passing and ever changing spectrum of females he had never quite seen anything like this. She might have been Italian — the severe face, the black dress and kerchief — but she was much too large for that. And her gait was decidedly unfeminine, even for her apparent age and infirmity. Yet there she was, browsing determinedly in his store, pushing suits to and fro on his racks. He hesitated to go over and offer his assistance because she was so intense and just as he felt obliged to do so, she obviously made some decision and came to him.

"How much?" she said, in a clearly masculine voice, in English.

Mynheer Dobbe looked into her face and realised she was a man. He controlled himself: Amsterdam was filled with strange people.

Burke changed in the store dressing room, removing the American dollars from the hidden pouches inside the black garments. The fact that he had no men's clothes with him had been unavoidable as it would have been very compromising for him to have opened his suitcase during a customs inspection in his guise as Zilla Monteith. He was glad now that he could again become a man.

Now he had to find Gardia Koolwein. She operated her arm's business at an address in the *Zeedijk*, the red-light district. The house of pleasure was a good front for the operation. A rhyme from the American army flashed through his head — 'this is my rifle this is my gun; one is for killing, the other for fun.' It had been three years but Hennessey had found that she was still operating and so this address was all he had to go on.

He went back into the store, handed the proprietor $400 and smiled. The man smiled back in an accommodating manner and managed a slight, polite bow. It was always a pleasure doing business with those who, from experience, he had learned not to question when curious situations exposed themselves.

"Shall I dispose of the ... clothes, Sir?" he asked, in an extremely good English.

Burke stuffed them into the battered suitcase, took out a $50 bill and gave it to the clothier, then shook his hand. "No thank you," he said, smiled, then left.

Mynheer Dobbe looked at the $450 American. The price of the clothes, even with a generous rate of exchange, should have been $360 American. A profitable transaction, and one to forget. Completely.

Burke wandered about the streets of Amsterdam, pleased with his clothes and the warm sun. He smiled to himself as he thought of the storekeeper. The Netherlands had always been the most open-minded area in Europe down through history, ready to allow individuals to go about their business, as long as it was good for business. The man had done his best to uphold the liberality for which Amsterdam was famous but Martin thought that he had pushed the man to the limit. He dropped the battered suitcase, with its weeds, into a dumpster in an alley and continued on his way. It had been quite awhile since he had been in this city but he remembered the streets which led to Gardia's 'office' in the Nieuwmarkt area. It was good to be out of Ireland, to leave the Troubles behind, even briefly. Here he was free to do whatever he wanted, to go wherever he might. Except that he now had no identification papers. He would have to rectify that as soon as he contacted Gardia.

As he turned the corner into Buiten Wier Ingenstraat he was struck with the way the street had changed. It was cleaner than he had remembered, though Amsterdam never really got dirty. And it was still early. The girls would not yet be sitting in the windows of their townhouses, bathed in coloured lights, dressed in their lace and rayons. Burke reached 13 Buiten Wier Ingenstraat with its blue stoop and twelve steps leading to a blue door with a huge brass knocker in the centre. He climbed slowly. The steps and door had been a different colour, the towering townhouse more rundown the last time he had been there. It looked almost too respectable. He placed his hand on the knocker.

The door opened. Before him was a girl of about 19 or 20, blonde, tall, well-dressed. "*Komt U binnen. Kan Ik U helpen?*"

Burke stuttered in English, fearing that the house had been converted to residential purposes, "I think maybe I've got the wrong place."

The girl smiled even more. "Oh, English. Good afternoon. I'm Katrina. You have the right place I think? Entertainment?"

Burke relaxed and entered the foyer. "Well, actually I'm looking for a certain woman."

Katrina closed the door behind him. They stood in the dark, warm foyer, flanked by padded benches. In front of him were frosted glass doors, closed, and beyond them he could hear music. "Yes, she may be here. We have women of all kinds."

Burke stopped and sat on the bench in the foyer. "I'm looking for a woman I knew once: Gardia Koolwein. She was here a few years ago."

The young girl sat on the bench on the other side of the foyer. "I don't know anyone by that name who works here."

Burke described Gardia, a short blonde, with large blue eyes, a broad smile.

Katrina smiled and shook her head. "Mynheer, you are in the Netherlands. I really don't know her but I've only been here for a year. If you'd like I could ask Mevrouw Van Kessel."

Burke agreed and followed Katrina in through the frosted glass doors. The place had changed quite a bit. When Burke last was there, it had been known as a place for young expatriate Americans and assorted adventurers and so it had had loud rock music and an American-style bar in the first room, where the girls and their clients would meet. Access to the rooms upstairs was controlled by an office at the foot of the stairs.

Now it obviously catered to those young Americans who could not beat the system and so had decided to buy it. Soft piano music was piped into the panelled lounge, tastefully decorated with Art Deco objects and furniture.

The Mevrouw came out with Katrina, looking the part of a successful bank manager. She sat beside Burke, who had seated himself on a black, camel-back sofa.

"I'm Mevrouw Van Kessel ... Mynheer ...?"

"Burke."

"Mynheer Burke. I wish I could help you but I took over this house about three years ago and I don't know this girl you are asking for. Her name?"

Katrina piped in, "Gardia Koolwein."

Mevrouw Van Kessel turned to her with a frown. "*Ga terug naar het kantoor! Ik zorg daar wel voor!*" and Katrina scurried away through some doors. "*Ik herinner haar niet* ... oh, I'm sorry ... I don't know her. However, if there is a certain requirement you have we will do our best to accommodate you," she said, smiling at him.

Burke flushed and it felt strange but pleasant, like the touch of a long-lost childhood friend. He stood and shook his head. "It's nothing like that. I was just looking for Gardia. She's an old friend. But thank you for your trouble." He stood and walked toward the door.

Mevrouw Van Kessel called after him, "As you wish. But, if we can be of any further assistance, don't hesitate to call." She rose majestically and mounted the staircase.

Burke let himself out.

The air was clear with just a hint of that pleasant sea-spice smell that is a part of Amsterdam. He spotted a street-vendor across the street, selling flavoured ices and crossed, as his throat was dry. As he waited he noticed Katrina peering out from behind thick curtains on the first floor, quizzically, and smiled to himself, remembering their willingness to "accommodate his requirements". He imagined himself a rogue Irishman with a penchant for being spanked with a cheese paddle while bagpipes were played in the background by nude midgets on shetland ponies, standing in huge bowls of peach jelly, and Mevrouw Van Kessel doing her best.

He bought an ice and walked off down the street, not quite sure what he would do next. No matter how he tried to straighten his mind he could not erase the feeling that he was playing hooky from school. In a foreign country, with no passport, looking for someone he had known years ago and not knowing where he might find her, he licked an ice and felt like a boy on vacation.

A busy man clutching a briefcase bumped into him and brought him back to reality. He would have to find some way to contact Gardia. Hen had been assured that she still operated but at what address? A telephone directory would be his first source. Perhaps Gardia would be listed there.

A car bumped by on the humpbacked wooden bridge over the *grachten* and he squeezed himself against the railing as it passed, for there was not much room on these narrow little bridges. They were built so that they could be swung out of the way to permit canal traffic to pass anywhere in the city. He walked on, deep in thought. Gardia Koolwein.

He realised that someone was shouting and running toward him from behind. He heard her feet clatter over the canal bridge and she was almost upon him when he realised that she was calling to him.

"Mr Burke." She paused for breath, her cheeks flushed, her extremely short hair still showing the damp sign of a very recent washing. She was barefoot and had obviously rushed to pull on her jeans and blue silk blouse without towelling dry, as the damp imprint of her breasts testified. Her eyes flashed to his and warmed. "I'm sorry to chase you down the street." She spoke with an English accent, somewhere from the South, near Salisbury. "Mevrouw Van Kessel was upstairs joking about a timid Scot searching for Gardia. Gardia doesn't live at the house anymore. She moved out when Van Kessel took over. But I still see her once in awhile so I called her. She said you were a friend of hers and to send you to her new place. Do you want the address?"

"Yes," Burke said, feeling as if the sun had broken through to warm him alone in all the world.

"She has a shop over on the edge of the tourist district. It's called Die Bazaar, on Kalverstraat. You can find her there."

Burke thanked her. She hesitated for a moment, then shrugged a 'you're welcome' to him and jogged back in the direction of the house.

The streets were bright and thronged, not at all like the dull streets he had left behind him in Belfast. Here no shoppers had to be submit themselves to a manual or an electronic search before entering a shopping area. Here no one had to expect to be stopped by 19-year-old soldiers at a spot checkpoint. Here mothers with prams did not have to expect their baby's sleep to be disturbed by the rough hands of some British soldier. There was not a pervading stress in the faces of the people he saw. Not that the people of Belfast displayed stress. At least it was not something they wore on their sleeves. Centuries of living under the domination of the English had taught them, first resignation, then acceptance with a degree of flair, and then a certain nonchalance when all about them was troubled.

The Irish peasant had learned that to improve one's land was to invite a rise in rent, to show intelligence was to strike resentment in the minds of the British lackeys, to demand rights was to tempt fate and call down swift retribution. Certainly, the problem was all but gone from the Republic but in the North the years of living under British rule and the fear in the hearts of the descendants of the Plantation had left its mark on the bodies and souls of the people. However, it was also, in part, responsible for the development of the colourful and sharply cynical Irish tongue, and for the ability of the Irish to face difficult situations with a confident smile.

It was with this confidence that Burke now approached Die Bazaar. As he crossed the street he noticed a woman, her long blond hair tied back in a ponytail, dressed in blue coveralls with a red turtleneck underneath, standing in the display window. She was arranging an assortment of scarves to look like tandem kites, festooning them, here and there, with Moroccan gold ornaments and jewellery. He pressed his face against the glass. She turned with a frown, obviously displeased with the leering attentions of this passerby. Suddenly her frown transformed into a warm, broad smile and she mouthed his name, pointed to the door of the shop, then leapt out of the window into the store and headed for the door.

She burst out into the street, elbowing pedestrians, and flung her arms around Burke's neck, drawing him close to her in an excited hug. She pulled back and held him at arms length, making sure that she had not mistaken his identity.

"Martin. It is you, isn't it?"

They sat in the office in the back of the store drinking white wine. Gardia filled Burke in on what had been happening in the business since he had gone to jail. She had left the whorehouse after a change in management and had been sad at the loss of the cover. But this new cover had proved even better. She could travel on buying trips and make deals at the same time. The only trouble was that the store was becoming so profitable that she had recently been considering whether or not to ease out of the arms business. Martin didn't say much about his time in the Maze and Gardia knew better than to ask. But he did give her enough information about the events of the last couple weeks to perk up her interest.

"That's the risk you run when you decentralize operations: it's much more difficult to do any great damage to the organization but you lose control. The explosives used on the house, was any analysis done?"

"All I could find out was that it was military and that it wasn't from a local source."

"But no chemical analysis."

"I couldn't get anything more than that. There was a guy there with an American accent. It might have come in through the United States."

"There's a lot of Ami ordnance moving through now."

"Gardia, I know that from the newspapers. I thought maybe you might know more, or know someone who did."

Gardia clasped her hands in front of her on the table. "You know I can tell you nothing of my clients, Martin. Would you deal with me again if I did. Priest, lawyer, arms broker: we all take our secrets to the grave. But we go back a long way so I will make an exception in this case and tell you everything that I know. I don't know anything. You were the only one I ever had dealings with in Ireland. Personally, I try to stay away from causes of which I might be fond. It would make it too difficult to deal with the other side and I'd hate to lose the business. My business contacts are too much like me to be of any use either. I wouldn't deal with them if they weren't. But I'll go further. There has been nothing moving from here to Ireland."

"Through you?"

"Through anyone that I know. But don't go out and try to verify that, just accept it."

Burke filled Gardia's glass from the wine bottle. "I do, don't worry. So it might have been direct from the United States."

"If it was from the US. But it could have come in direct from a hundred other places."

Martin shrugged. "It was worth a try. I had to get out of there anyway."

Gardia took the bottle and filled Martin's glass. "You're not out of luck. There is a lounge in the old neighbourhood, they have sex shows there. You might be able to get some information from a man called Wilson."

"I thought none of your contacts were the type."

"They aren't. I wouldn't ever do business with Wilson. He talks too much." She raised her glass and they both laughed. "You can see him there just about any time. It's his office. Anything that can be found out can usually be found out through him, for a price. I can arrange through the owner for an introduction for you. Just don't mention my name. Go and see him. You can stay at my place tonight and get back to Belfast on the first flight in the morning."

"I'll need a passport too. I came in as an old lady but I don't want to go back as one, in case they caught on."

"Shezad can get you one. I'll call ahead to arrange things. You can see him this afternoon then meet me at my place after you've seen Wilson." She took a key out of her pocket. "In case I'm out just use this key." She wrote the addresses on a piece of paper and handed it to him. "He'll charge you maybe £700, but that's a good price. He does a big business in fake EEC passports to get refugees to England but he'll be able to set you up with a proper British passport."

"Fix me up, I hope you mean."

Gardia laughed. "Ja, fix you up." Burke rose and headed back out into the store. Gardia gave some instructions to a girl at the cash register, then accompanied him out into the street. She made him take the first cab that stopped and gave him a peck on the cheek as he got in.

"See you later," she said, and waved as the taxi drove away.

Magee had arrived in Amsterdam on the next flight after Burke. He had immediately contacted the Van Koppen brothers, Erich and Fritz. They had been useful to him before and, though they sometimes reminded him of the Katzenjammer Kids, they would be useful again. They had known of Gardia Koolwein and had been able to take him directly to her store on Kalverstraat. They had sat in the Volvo and watched as Burke had entered the store. He had been inside with Gardia for almost an hour and now they watched him drive away in a taxi. Magee hit Fritz on the arm. "You keep an eye on her, and don't lose her. Erich and I'll tail Burke." Fritz rolled out of the car and positioned himself opposite the store as Gardia went back inside and the Volvo sped off after Burke's taxi.

As Erich followed the taxi through the streets Magee considered his options. He had hoped to be able to assure himself that Burke would find out nothing, and it was unlikely he would find out anything from Koolwein, but he would have to be sure. He knew that he would probably have to confront him. But if they had to lose him now it would not jeopardize the operation. Dead or alive they could use Burke for the fall guy. Perhaps better dead.

BELFAST

5:00 pm, 9 Meitheamh

Sean walked along the street, his hands pushed far into the pockets of his windbreaker, listening to music on his tape player. He had added some songs to U2 from the radio at home and the music made the city seem so much better, like a movie. Life needed background music. He was in the Protestant neighbourhood again, not just for the thrill of the risk this time. He had thought he had seen Barton the day before and had followed him into this area and had lost track of him. Now he was looking for him again. He wanted to know everything he could about the bastard because he was going to kill him, if he ever could find a way. His mother had been quiet and strong during the wake and the funeral but after, she had just sat by the window in the apartment, not speaking. She had returned to work — what choice did she have — but something had changed inside of her. There was no joy at all in her eyes. She was a shell. He wanted to avenge this murder as well. And somehow he would see that Barton paid for all the pain that had come to his family.

The streets were fairly quiet and no one really paid any attention to him all day. He could see that the troops were edgy and figured that was due to the coming Royal Tour. The trouble of the last few nights was what could be expected in Belfast in the summer.

Something made him stop and take the earphones out of his ears. There was a loud drumming sound somewhere in the vicinity and the noise frightened him but quickened his blood. It was different from the drumming on the tape and it came from down one of the alleys. He checked to see that the coast was clear and moved in, past a sandbagged barricade deep into enemy territory.

As he moved along the drumming became louder and louder. He pinpointed it now in behind a wall in the alley and he knew why it had interested him but why it had spelled fear. It was a Lambeg drum; the huge drums used by the Orangemen as they marched the length and breadth of Ulster with their banners and silly bowler hats, proclaiming "English we are and English we shall remain." The only thing which he found more frightening were radio speeches by Ian Paisley, denouncing the Pope as the Roman Whore and encouraging the Orange men to 'cut the croppies low'. He found a pile of crates and climbed up the wall and onto a roof. From there he was able to move in closer to the drumming and finally, after crossing a low rise in the roof he could see an enclosed courtyard. In the middle of it was a boy of his own age, drumming with abandon at the big drum, resting on the ground in front of him. The leather thongs about the sticks were cutting into his wrists and there were specks of blood on the drumhead but the boy kept on, trapped in some barbaric mind set, drumming all Catholics to Hell, drumming until they lay dead in a sea of red, marching with the Orange order through the Catholic ghettos, marching to the gates of Rome itself and throwing down the Pope who had fathered so many bastard priests, cutting off his horns and his tail and returning triumphant to an Ulster bathed in sunlight and ringed in soft white clouds.

Sean picked up a roof-slate and winged it at the boy, missing him slightly and bouncing off the round top of the drum. The drumming ceased. They looked at each other. They were about the same age and size and, in any other place they could have been friends.

"Come down off the roof you fucking fenian," cried the boy in the courtyard, making an uneducated guess.

Sean stood now proud, defiant. "Make me, asshole."

The boy stepped back from the drum and sang in a sing-song voice, "Teeter, totter, holy water, sprinkle the Catholics everyone. Take them to battle and kill them like cattle and make them come under the Protestant drum."

Sean threw another slate and the boy jumped sideways to miss it. He stood a moment longer, then turned and rushed into the house. Sean looked around and picked up another slate and backed up to the wall of a second roof level. He didn't have to wait long. A skylight opened and the boy emerged. Sean sized him up. He was smaller than he looked in the courtyard and puny too. Then a second pair of hands appeared on the edge of the skylight, and a third and a fourth. Four Protestants now stood in a row facing Sean. Two had long sticks. "Fuck," said Sean, "see Sean run," and he hoisted himself up to the next roof level and raced away. The Protestants were in hot pursuit. Sean was frightened. Four to one was a bad ratio and the roof didn't go on very long. On top of that the slates were slippery. The only reason he was able to put a distance between him and his pursuers was that falling was the least of his worries and the greatest of theirs. He reached the end of the roof and jumped down the fire escape and onto the street. One of the boys stopped on the roof, wrenched up a slate and heaved it, barely missing Sean. The others were down on the street in seconds.

Sean raced along the streets the earphones of tape player dangling down the front of him, banging into his legs with each stride. He crossed through one alley and into another street, crossed the street and kicked over a dustbin at the entrance to an alley then doubled back and into an alley heading back in the direction he had come but one alley over. His only hope was that they would naturally assume that he was trying to get as far away from the Protestant section as possible and would follow the lead of the knocked over dustbin.

He stopped in a doorway off the alley and waited. Suddenly three boys passed the mouth of the alley. He jerked his head back, listening, holding his breath. They seemed to be taking the bait. The he heard the fourth boy. He had obviously overshot the first alley and was now coming up this one to join his friends. Sean pushed back against the door and it gave way. He quickly jumped inside and closed the door just as the fourth boy went past. Safe, he thought, for the moment. He moved away from the door and the grimy windows. The room he was in had been burnt out in the past, like so many buildings in his neighbourhood. He moved through a doorway and into a second large empty room with equally grimy windows. There was another doorway but it was blocked with boards. As he approached the boards he heard voices, men talking.

He moved along the wall, listening as the voices grew louder. He came to a place where there was a space between the room containing the men and the next and slipped inside. Halfway down the space he stopped. The last speaker had called one of the men present by name and that name was Barton. Careful now, lest he give himself away, he crept silently to where light shone through a crack and peered in.

The men were seated around a rough rectangular table and some were up against the wall close to his vantage point where he could not see them, but he could make out Barton, seated almost opposite from him. The conversation was loud and clear, as if he were sitting at the table with them. He listened, holding his breath for fear he might be heard. It was clear they were talking about a hit of some kind and that the military was involved. There were also men who were obviously Protestants from the words they were using. He saw another man, off to the side, with a cane and he seemed to be acting almost as an intermediary, smoothing the waters between the two groups. The voices raised occasionally. Then he heard someone mention Martin Burke. It reminded him of the words spoken by the dying

McHenry and, sensing the importance of the conversation taking place, he turned on his tape recorder to record and held it up to the hole.

Sullivan tapped his cane in frustration. "Gentlemen, gentlemen. Please. This is not the time to get hot under the collar. We're all of us too far into this to let bickering split us. We have Martin Burke under surveillance. There's no need to worry, Wilkes. He will be there when it's time. His body will be delivered and you'll be able to take the rest of the men as well. They'll be coming in from Libya tomorrow. And Mr Smith, you and your associates have no need to worry. The papists have no idea that they're being financed by you. They have been recruited carefully by Magee, handpicked, and they have no doubt that this operation is sanctioned by the IRA and has Martin Burke at the helm."

Smith cleared his throat. "But Mr Sullivan, when we contracted with you and Mr Magee to carry this out, we were assured that there would be no leaks, that the information would stay bottled up. Lynch and McHenry were taken care of unwittingly by our British friends, and Mr Magee did a fine job of containing the spread of this information through the McHenry family,"

Sullivan cut in. "And the one problem was a leak in the team, but that has been taken care of, in Libya. We had the situation under control. There was no need for you to call in Chalmers and have him try to stop Lynch. And it was only due to over zealousness on the part of Barton that he was killed. I wanted to question him in the Republic. As it was we were able to stop things up through questioning the widow McHenry, but the interference caused by your group raised the heat at British Intelligence and has made it just that much more difficult for us to control Burke and keep the supremo out of our hair. You owe a great debt to Wilkes for containing the situation."

"Well, we're paying him enough," a friend of Smith's piped up.

Wilkes leaned forward. "Really, I must take exception to that. The funds allocated to my area of the operation have to cover a great many expenses. You forget that getting the equipment in through military channels is expensive. You forget that the average soldier must be compensated greatly for actions which could be seen by some as treasonous. There are those who would have us executed for what really amounts to plotting to assassinate our sovereign. The decision to take part in such a bold manoeuvre is not one that is entered into lightly and, I would venture to say gentlemen, with all due respect to Mr Sullivan and the absent Mr Magee, that without our assistance, this operation would not have been able to proceed. Most certainly Burke would still have been in custody if I hadn't notified Mr Sullivan and cleared the arrest record." Barton voiced his agreement.

Sullivan again banged his cane like a gavel. "Alright. The money has been spent, and we've received good measure for it. I don't want to hear any more. Jack, your contacts in the media are prepared for the response to the murder?"

Jack nodded in agreement. "They know nothing about the operation, but it is normal to play some wargames before tours like this and we've run through scenarios which, once the assassination occurs, will be implemented with the desired results. And the Reverend Paisley can be counted on."

"God, don't tell me he's aware of this!" Barton exclaimed.

Smith was quick with the response. "Certainly not. We have not told anyone outside of the circle. Jack's point is that he'll be in support of an indiscriminate action against the Catholics. Even if the matter is contained until the 12th of July it will certainly erupt then and both sides will be heaving everything they've got at each other. Britain will have no choice but to step in completely. This talk of gradual pullout will die a quick death."

Sullivan sighed. "Fine. Now Wilkes, you and Barton will have the last part to play. What do you need from us?"

Barton looked at Wilkes and Wilkes leaned back in his chair and clasped his hands across his stomach. "We'll need to know where the lads who are not involved in the actual hit will be holed up so that we can move in after and grab them. We'll cover that by placing them under surveillence. The first team will be allowed to carry out the manoeuvre, unless some of our men get too good at their job."

Sullivan interrupted again. "That is taken care of."

"Fine, fine," Wilkes continued. "You'll be having a meeting with them on the night before the operation. For final briefing. Barton and I will be there, in disguise in order to oversee things. It isn't that we don't trust you, but you can understand our position. I want to know their escape route and any rendezvous point which may be set up to convince them that they will be taken out of the country."

"They'll be at the warehouse at the end of Queen's Road on the Victoria Channel at about 1:30 on the morning of the 12th. We've stored their equipment there."

"Good. Now, what about Martin Burke?"

"As agreed, we will hand his body over to you. At the appropriate time he'll be shot and you will be called to the location. A shot will be fired as you pull up and you can open fire on the location. Our people will be out of the way. It will appear that one of your bullets killed him. You'll be able to work with that, I trust."

Smith now asked a question. "What if Wilkes' men are too good at their job, though? If Charles isn't killed, the whole thing goes down the tubes."

"We have made provision for that gentlemen. But I think you know enough already. Your guarantee is that we do not receive our full payment until the job is complete and while I support this operation and what it will mean politically, the sum of money lost to me should this operation fail is guarantee enough."

There was a great deal of laughter and shuffling of chair in the room. Sean pulled the tape recorder back from the wall and shut it off, then waited until the men had left. He waited longer, until there was no sound at all. He smiled to himself. The information he had recorded was definitely tied to what McHenry had whispered to him in his last moments on earth, and what Sullivan had not told the men assembled, he already knew. It had not been as clear before but now it was. Protestants, plotting to kill Prince Charles and blame the Catholics for it. It was chilling, even to a boy of 11. Perhaps especially to a boy of 11, for he realised that the horror of his life would be paradise compared to the wind which would blow after the 12th of June.

As he inched his way out of the space between the walls he thought of Burke. This was why McHenry had been trying so hard to get to Burke. The information was worth more than his life. That was clear. Now he would have to get to Burke. He looked out the doorway which opened into the alley and the way was clear. He headed off towards the Fall's Road. There was fog now in the dark streets and he raced through the empty alleys, in a flurry, like some dark comet with a diaphanous trail.

Hennessey noticed that a young boy was following when he left the Flats. He was headed over to Finn's to see how the old boy was doing and to get a free drink. This boy looked like the one who had been in the street when he and Martin had almost been cornered by the soldiers. And he was doing a half decent job of tailing him, but not good enough. He'll learn, thought Hennessey. As he got closer to Finn's house he turned a corner and ducked into an open shop then watched as Sean walked past. Satisfied that he'd lost the boy, he bought a pack of smokes and went back out and doubled back to Finn's. The old man welcomed him in and brought him into the dingy kitchen for a drink of whisky at the table. Finn lived in a small walk up with a fire-escape balcony and the general untidiness which attaches itself to old bachelors. He hadn't heard yet from Martin or Meagan and he had found out nothing more about Broken English. Hennessey had the same to report. There was a knock at the door. Finn rose and shuffled toward the door, mumbling 'Meagan' as he went. Hen trailed along after him, through the livingroom and paused at the corner of the dark hall which led to the door. When Finn opened it the young boy was standing there.

"I'm looking for Martin Burke," Sean said, noticing the look of surprise on Hennessey's face and nodded to him, smiling inwardly.

"Who isn't," said Hen. Finn turned to him. "You know this gos do you?"

Hennessey took a step forward and saw the boy retreat a pace. "Seen him before. He saw me with Martin. What's your name, son."

"Sean, Mr. Hennessey," Sean replied, "I have to talk to Martin Burke. It's important."

Finn spoke up. "Well, young lad, if you've been able to follow old fleet-of-foot Hennessey," he said, grinning back at Hen, "you should know that Martin Burke isn't here. But if there's something you'd like him to know maybe we could get the message to him."

Sean stepped back again into the dark hallway and looked each way. "No, I have to talk to him, him only. When can I see him?"

"There's no way of knowing lad. We'll get the message to him," Hen offered.

Sean headed down the hall. "No way. Tell him I'm looking for him. Got a message from McHenry and more. Tell him that. He'll know where to find me. But tell him to make it fast." And with that he bolted down the hall and down the stairs before Hen could get past Finn to give chase.

They both went back inside. "What the hell do you suppose that was all about?" Finn asked.

"Well, that kid's been around, maybe he does know something. Martin said he was seeing him everywhere. Better tell Martin as soon as he gets in touch." Hen finished his glass. "I'll have a look for him outside, but I imagine he's long gone." He pulled his jacket on. "I'm going down to Rumours."

"Tripping the light fantastic, are you?" Finn said grinning.

"Going to try to," answered Hen, opening the door, "I'll check with you tomorrow. Bye." He left.

Finn poured himself another glass and turned on the radio. He wondered where Martin was. The 12th was fast approaching.

DUBLIN

8 pm, 9 June

Feeney sat at his desk dictating a bill for Mrs Maxwell. As he spoke into the hand-held microphone he wished he could have convinced her to have root canal work done. It would have been worth a lot more than one simple extraction. But no, she could afford to lose the tooth, stupid old bitch. He switched off the tape recorder and looked at the small brass clock on his office desk. It was time for him to go. Margaret could type up the bills when she came in in the morning. He thought of trying Sullivan's number again but decided to wait until he got home. He had not been able to contact him for a couple of days and he was getting nervous. They had agreed not to say anything to anyone until Burke reported back but it had been awhile. The last time they had spoken, Sullivan had assured him that everything was alright and that he and Burke were working together in Belfast to get to the bottom of whatever was going on.

He pulled on his jacket, switched off the light and walked through the dark surgery. Something made him pause. He thought he heard a noise. He poked his head into the second surgery and a gun butt slammed into it.

The bright operating light was shining through the gauze covering his eyes when he came to. He struggled to rise but found that his hands and feet were tied tightly to the chair. Even his head was immoveable. The gauze which covered his eyes went around the headrest, encasing his head and neck completely, save for his nostrils, mouth and ears. It was as if some menacing spider had entangled him in a web, then spun a restraining coccoon around him. Someone walked into the room. Feeney ceased his struggle.

"Who's there?"

A stern voice replied, "Who have you been talking to about Broken English?"

"What?"

A hand slapped his face so hard that his ears rang. "I want to know who else you've talked to, now!"

"I don't know what you mean!" A fist slammed into his temple and he cried out in pain.

"Don't make it harder for yourself. You know you can't take it."

He remained silent. Then he heard a familiar sound — the hum of one of his drills.

"I've dreamed of doing this," his attacker said. "Putting the drill to a dentist."

The drill came closer and Feeney clenched his mouth tight. Suddenly the bit tore into his lips and he screamed in agony, only to scream louder and try to swing his head to the side when the heat from the drill spinning on his front tooth excited the nerve within to a frenzied level. "Please stop," he tried to say, but the drilling continued and the pain increased. Then it stopped. He sobbed from both the pain and the release from it.

His tormenter spoke again. "Now either you talk or I use the drill on your cock."

Feeney yelled no but he heard the ominous noise begin again. The drill began to pull at the crotch of his pants. "Alright, alright," he cried. "A man named Lynch, but he's dead. And then there's Sullivan and Burke. No one else. I don't know where Sullivan is but I think he's with Burke, Martin Burke, in Belfast."

"Don't give me that shit," he heard the intruder say and the drill started up again.

"I swear it's true. I swear. Please."

"Who else knows about Sullivan and Burke?"

"Not a soul," he cried, "I haven't said anything to anyone. I was told not too." The drill stopped. His mind raced trying to imagine who it might be. The intruder walked out of the room and was rummaging through his cabinet in the next room. Feeney struggled again but it was no use. The pain had sapped all his strength.

Footsteps approached. "I swear no one else has been talking to me and I've said nothing to no one. I don't need this trouble. I just tried to help a friend, that's all."

There was no reply. It was the last thing he didn't hear.

He let out a cry of surprise as a needle slammed into the vein in his right arm and released a massive dose of sodium pentathol. It took about two minutes for him to die.

AMSTERDAM

9:15 pm, 9 June

Burke was pleased with Shezad's handiwork. The passport showed him as Mr George Dunn of Belfast and it had an excellent Dutch entry stamp on it. The long wait had been worth it. He had to pay a little more than Gardia had suggested but it would get him back to Belfast without any difficulty. He passed a tobacconist and felt a sudden urge for a cigarette. He bought a package of Gauloise, lit one and sat on a bench on the grassy bank of a canal to smoke it. There were too many unanswered questions and too little information. If there was a plan by an IRA group to assassinate Charles, other cells should have known something. It was not irregular for people to know very little about the operations of other cells. In these times groups had to work in complete secrecy. But such an operation would call for experienced men and sophisticated weaponry. That meant money and high-level organization.

And what of Sullivan and Feeney. The promise of a new life that they held out was not now as important as finding out enough about Broken English to stop it. Such an act would have severe repercussions, both in Northern Ireland and in Eire. Though the Americans had been extremely critical of England's actions in the North and of her incursions into the South, it would be hard to stop the British from sending their troops across the border to wipe out suspected training centres and points of refuge in the shock wave which would follow such an act. The Israelis had done it in Lebanon. The Accord would die and with it all the aid which the Americans had promised on its signing, and perhaps as well the support of the Irish Caucus. They had run for cover when Mountbatten had been killed. It would be worse this time.

He butted his cigarette, checked his watch then hailed a taxi and headed off to meet Wilson. He didn't notice the Volvo which followed.

The doorman walked through the crowded establishment and Martin followed. The place had been designed like an amphitheatre with three levels. The first was a ring around the outside where single men might sit in relative darkness and talk to nude girls or watch them dance. A second level was filled with sofas and large mirrored coffee tables which formed the stages for performers. And at the bottom level was the main seating area filled with tables and chairs and a large central stage. The doorman headed for this area. Martin had some difficulty negotiating the stairs. There was flesh and fantasy everywhere. Belfast was decidedly drab by comparison. He noticed above him a large net which had pillows scattered over it. From the applause it was obvious that a show had just ended and he saw a man and a woman leaving the net through a small door high on the wall at the far end of the room. As Burke and the doorman continued in that direction two other girls came out of the same small door and moved to the centre of the net where they sprawled on the cushions. The doorman stopped at a table against the wall and just below where the performers had exited. Martin tipped him and sat down on the russet-coloured sofa. A nude girl appeared and took his order, returning quickly with a beer. She placed it on the table and put her tray down. As she bent over her breast swung around in Martin's face and before he could do anything she had slipped her hands inside his jacket over his crotch and down his legs. Without a word she picked up her tray and walked away, pausing briefly at another table to deposit another beer. The man at that table turned and smiled at Martin. From the description Gardia had given him he knew it was Wilson. The man approached his table. "Mind if I join you?"

Martin pointed to the other sofa opposite him. "Go ahead."

"Not everyday you get frisked like that is it. The name's Wilson, Burke," he said extending his hand. As Martin shook it his eyes were drawn away by two girls who walked past.

"A lot of beauties in here, but just to watch. You haven't been in town long."

"No," Martin said grinning.

"Well, must be quite a change from Ireland." The music was loud and so he leaned forward. "You don't have to worry in here. No one can hear you above this noise and they're more interested in the show."

Martin nodded and drank some beer.

"I've heard you might be interested in some info about some deals. Maybe I can help you, if the price is right."

"And what would that price be."

"Negotiable. I'm a reasonable business man. But I really can't do much for under a grand, American."

"There have been some arms shipments into Ireland recently and its ending up in Belfast. US military equipment probably. Explosives most likely."

"It wouldn't have come through here, not in the last while anyway. There've been some odd lots of US weapons but nothing in explosives. And all that's been going to Northern Ireland are some small lots of Armalites and AKS-47s. Nice ChiCom adaptation. I can let you have some if you're interested."

"I'm only interested in finding out who might be moving explosives into Belfast."

"American you say."

"All I know is that there was an American guy around, a big blond guy. And he roughed up a woman pretty badly before he blew up her and her baby."

"My, my. What is this world coming to. Women and children aren't safe in Belfast." Wilson noticed Burke jawline stiffen. "Relax Burke, I just might be able to help you. There was a guy nosing around New York a little while back, looking for transport for some military odds and ends. Ransom. And he used to do work for a sonofabitch named Magee. That bastard would enjoy stuff like that. And I heard he did some work in Ireland a little while ago."

"What do you know about him?"

"Not much more than that about Magee. Ransom's another matter. Ex-marine. Still has ordnance contacts in the corps. He was setting up support for the Contras down in Central America two years ago. CIA contract. Advising and running guns. Fucker hired me then stiffed me when things got a little hot. I had to find my own way out. So I'm not doin' any merc tours again. You ever do any of those?"

"A long time ago."

"Well I've had my fill. I figger there's more percentage being an arms broker, but it's not easy over here. Everything's so fuckin' corporate. All the big guys have got everything tied up. I just get the dregs. Mostly personal use and entrepreneurial stuff. But it's still a good place to do business."

"Anything else about Magee?"

"Not much. I met him once a few years ago. He was with the marines too. A real go-getter. Not the nicest guy around. Somebody told me he had cooperated with the CIA on a sting operation to get some Noraid dealers. So he could get some government work. Is he gunnin' for you?"

"I don't know. Magee helped the CIA?"

"Sure. He set up a bunch of guys. They were trying to ship a trawler-load of stuff into the Republic. It went down about three years ago.

"Look, if you can get confirmation that this Ransom was moving stuff into Belfast and who he was contracting with it'll be worth double your minimum, if you can get me the answer tonight.

"That's a little tight. But I could check around and meet you later. It'll cost extra though."

"Give me a phone number and a time and I'll call you."

"There is some information you might be interested in right now."

"What's that?"

"I could be mistaken, but I think Magee just walked in. You can reach me through this place. I'll tell them to forward your call." Martin felt him slip something under the table. He reached down with his hand and felt a switchblade. "Just in case. I want you around 'til I get paid," Wilson said then got up quickly and joined a group of people walking past the table. Martin stuffed the switchblade into his pocket and glanced across the room. A tall blond man was making his way to the table. His dark-haired companion turned and stopped the doorman, then slipped him a bill and turned him away. The blond stood at Martin's table.

"Mr. Burke, the name's Michael Magee. And this is my tour guide, Mr. Van Koppen. You don't know me but I was the one that got you out of that prison van in Belfast and took you down to Dublin to Sullivan." He paused.

"I guess I owe you a drink."

"Thanks." Magee sat down opposite Martin. Van Koppen, after realising there were no other chairs around, slid in beside Magee on the sofa. Magee leaned forward. "What brings you to Amsterdam?"

"Just visiting some friends. And things are a little warm in Belfast at the moment."

"I can appreciate that. And I'd like to have a little chat with you about Belfast. You've been asking a lot of questions and you're compromising the security of a very important operation. I'd like to try and set you straight on things. We should talk but I don't want to do it here. I want to clear this thing up so we can get on with our job and you can get on with yours."

Martin noticed that Van Koppen was sitting with his hand in his jacket pocket. Magee noticed the direction of Martin's gaze.

"It's just a precaution. Certainly you can understand that. Nothing personal."

"Nothing personal," Martin agreed. "But I hope you're not in any great rush. They tell me the show here is pretty good and it looks like there's one ready to start. Let me get you that beer." Martin signalled to the waitress. He was angry with himself. Sullivan and Magee and Broken English. Mrs McHenry had heard tapping and thought they were checking the walls. It had been Sullivan's cane. Why hadn't he realised that? It made sense now. Sullivan had used him to bring in Lynch because he wanted to make sure the man had told no one else. When Lynch was killed he needed to do the same with McHenry. The whole family had been silenced. Burke's blood boiled. He had been duped. And now he was being set up, that was clear. There was only one conclusion: Sullivan wanted him dead and Magee was the pistol.

As the waitress reached the table Martin nudged it with his legs and beer splashed out of his glass. She put her tray down and bent over to wipe it up. Burke saw that Magee and Van Koppen had their eyes on her. He stood and shoved her over on top of them then stepped up on the sofa and reached for the netting above his head. He grabbed it and swung himself up then crawled along and into the small doorway he had noticed earlier. Behind him he heard a great deal of commotion. Magee wouldn't use a gun in this place. Amsterdam was an open city but the police didn't like anyone causing trouble there. And the lounge owner was sure to have his own security.

He was now in a long corridor which lead to a fire escape. As he paused at the window he looked down the stairs and saw a bevy of naked women sitting in a lounge having coffee and cigarettes. A couple of the girls glanced up at him then smiled and waved. He opened the window and stepped out onto the fire escape then climbed down into the alley. Cautiously he emerged from the alley then crossed the street into a park. He reached the shadows just as Magee and Van Koppen came out the door but it wasn't soon enough. They spotted him and raced across the street and into the park after him. It was a long narrow park which ran along the edge of a canal and Martin hurried along then paused, realising that the far end of the park terminated at another canal. There was a stone wall along the street and a gate at the far end, bathed in light. He was hemmed in. He could dive into the canal and try to make the other side but there was too much light there and with two armed men looking for him, his chances would not be good. For the same reasons he could not make a break for the other entrance. His only option was to turn on them. He swung in behind a tree, then crouched and scampered low across the grass to another tree. They had not seen him and were still coming, advancing with about 10 metres between them. Van Koppen would be closest to him. He waited, his heart pounding, until Van Koppen reached the tree. Burke kicked the gun from his hand and flicked open the switchblade and held it to his throat.

"Don't," he said, pushing the blade tight to the skin and tugging it to draw a little blood. Van Koppen didn't move. "Magee," Burke called out.

Magee stopped and turned.

"Magee, I want to talk but I want to talk on terms which are a little more balanced."

Magee took a few steps toward Burke and Van Koppen then shook his head and opened fire. Martin leapt to the side as Van Koppen was spun around by three bullets. He rolled to the Ruger Van Koppen had been carrying and shot, hitting Magee full in the chest. Magee flew backwards and landed in the dark. Burke glanced over at Van Koppen but he wasn't moving. He took a look at Magee then noticed that he was getting to his feet. His shirt was torn open and Burke could see that he was wearing an armoured vest. Before he could do anything else he heard the sound of sirens in the distance. They had probably been called by the lounge owner when the trouble had first started. Magee was now to his feet. His weapon had obviously flown out of his hand when he had been hit. Martin tried for a head shot but Magee deeked, then vaulted over the railing, diving into the canal. Burke had no time and no choice. He tossed the gun into the canal then made his way quickly to the street and walked nonchalantly along as the police cars went by and screeched to a halt outside of the lounge. He stopped for a moment and watched as the lounge owner spoke to the officers and pointed in the direction of the park then hailed a taxi and headed for Gardia's house.

Burke sat in the dark apartment waiting. Gardia had not been home and so he had let himself in with the key. He was hungry but he didn't want to go out for anything and miss her but he didn't feel comfortable with helping himself to the food in the refrigerator. He wondered where Magee was, what Meagan might be doing and when Gardia would arrive. Most of all he wanted sleep but with the events of the night still fresh he had to remain alert. He heard someone approaching the door of the apartment and cautiously enter. He stood and slipped back against the wall waiting.

"Martin, are you here?" he heard Gardia ask.

He breathed a sigh of relief and walked out into the next room as she switched on the light. "I was wondering what was taking you so long."

"I had some business to attend to," Gardia said almost brusquely and made herself a drink. "Do you want something? A beer perhaps? There're some in the refrigerator."

Martin helped himself to one. "I got into a little trouble after I met with Wilson."

"I thought you might have. Magee and Van Koppen?"

"Right. Van Koppen's dead though. Magee tried to kill me and got him. How did you know about Magee."

"Van Koppen's brother started following me this afternoon after you left." She led Martin into the livingroom and they sat with their drinks. " I didn't notice until this evening about 8:30. He made a few mistakes and I spotted him. At first I thought he was with Interpol but he was too clumsy.

So I took him over to a warehouse that I keep for storage and grabbed him. I persuaded him to talk to me and he told me that his brother and Magee were following you."

"They got to me while I was talking to Wilson. Magee answered my questions. Most of them anyway. Where's your Van Koppen?"

"I'm afraid he's with his brother, the little *rotzak*. I can't have people like that interfering with me. More importantly, where is Magee?"

"Last that I saw of him he was swimming across a canal. I couldn't really wait for him."

"He's good Martin. He shouldn't have been able to get this close. I want you to come with me to a safe house tonight. I'll make arrangements for you to fly to Paris tomorrow morning and go back to Ireland from there. I've already asked some people to find Magee but he may slip through."

"I appreciate this."

"Nothing personal Martin. It's just business. I would hate to lose a customer," she said with a smile.

BELFAST

2:00 am, 10 Meitheamh

There was a knock on the door which woke Finn from his sleep on the couch. When he opened the door, Meagan was there.

"Meagan, come in, come in," he said, motioning to her.

"I guess I woke you up," she said as she stepped inside. "I just wanted to stop by to see if Martin had been in touch. Sorry it's so late but I saw the light on and thought that you and Hen might be up doin' damage to your selves again."

"No. I'm gonna take the pledge. He hasn't been in touch, not yet. But don't worry, he'll be along soon enough."

"I hope he's here soon enough," she answered.

"Oh, he will be. You can depend on Martin. By the way, if you see him first, tell him a lad named Sean is looking for him. Dropped by tonight and said he had some information from McHenry. I didn't get a chance to talk to him much but it's important. Said Martin would know where to find him."

Meagan was surprised. "Is that the one that Martin kept bumping into?"

"Hen said it was. The boy didn't say where he lives though. He just said Martin would know and that it had to do with McHenry." Finn brushed his fingers through his hair. "Do you want a drink?"

Meagan sat down on the sofa but kept her coat on. "Just a touch. Hen was here tonight?"

"Earlier," Finn said as he poured a small drink for her and a substantial one for himself. He handed Meagan her glass and sat in the chair beside the sofa. "He went off to Rumours he said. You can find him there if you want."

"I don't know. I might go over but I'm kinda tired." She finished her drink and put the glass on the end table. "I really have to get going. Can't miss my beauty sleep."

"Me neither," Finn chuckled raising his glass in a toast.

She stood and Finn walked her to the door. "Come and see me tomorrow night, ok."

Meagan nodded and gave him a hug.

"And don't you be worrying about Martin. He'll be back safe and sound," Finn said. She walked down the hall and he closed the door, then returned to his drink. He was worried about Martin too.

FALLS ROAD

3:00 am, 10 Meitheamh

Sean awoke from a deep sleep to the smell of smoke and the cries of "Fire." He rolled out of bed and onto the floor, then waited for his mind to clear and to ascertain the situation before moving. The cries of fire were coming from down the street. His building, for the moment, might be safe. He dressed hurriedly and ran into his mother's bedroom. She was still asleep. He shook her until she awoke and roused her from her one escape. Together they went down the stairs and into the street where most of their neighbours were gathered. The fire truck had not arrived and might not for some time. It was often this way when the Protestants started a burn out. The trucks would be held up by streets made impassable by quickly thrown up barricades: a couple of parked cars pulled out across the street, a burning bus. The people were gathering to try and contain the fire. He saw a man wrap a wet blanket around himself and rush though a smoking doorway. Someone was still inside. The last time they had been threatened with fire his mother had filled the tub with water and soaked the blankets. Then the fire had not come and they had to do without blankets while they dried.

Suddenly there was the sound of small arms fire and they scattered. Sean's mother grabbed him by the scruff of the neck and pulled him over to a building, shielding him with her body. The protective action embarassed him.

"It's okay Mum, it's just the roof slates."

She looked up and listened and saw that he was right. The heat from the fire had started to crack the slates and as they did they gave off a sound like a revolver or a small bore rifle. The others realised that it was safe and went back to putting out the fire. The man who had disappeared inside came back out with a little girl. She was crying, shouting about her puppy. The man had been able to bring only her.

Sean thought of two things and broke free from his mother and raced back into the apartment building. There was now smoke in the hallways. He could not determine whether the building was on fire or whether the smoke was just blowing in. But he had to get his tape recorder. He got into the apartment and it too was full of smoke. It was curling up from the baseboards along the wall. He didn't have much time. He rummaged in his room for the machine and jammed it in his jacket pocket, after checking to see that the tape was inside. He went to the livingroom and reached up for the picture of his father, on the wall beside the Pope. The wall was hot to the touch. The smoke stung his eyes and tears flowed down his cheeks. He pulled the apartment door shut behind him and went back down to the street. His mother was standing on the other side with a group of women, their arms crossed, staring at the flames. They had stopped trying to fight the fire; it was already too large. He handed the picture to his mother, then made for the old apartment building.

He scurried up the fire escape and onto the roof. Tim's pigeons were safe but he wanted to be sure that, if the fire grew it did not spread to them. He would wait the whole night if he had to. He sat on the edge of the roof and looked down to the people, their faces red from the fire. Flames were flaring out of a couple of windows in the upper storey and had broken through the roof. The fire trucks arrived and the firemen went to their task.

He thought now of the conversation he had overheard earlier in the day and of Martin Burke. If the assassination was successful there would be a great many fires in the days following, and there would be real gunfire. He knew also that all he could do was speak to Martin Burke. He would know what to do. He watched his pigeons and the fire, and he watched for Martin Burke.

It was then that he saw the man with the cane. Sullivan. He had been at the meeting. And now he was on Sean's street, near the fire, watching the crowd, looking for someone. Sean drew back from the edge of the roof. He had spoken to people who he thought were friends of Burke and it was too much of a coincidence that this man would appear on his street. Sullivan was looking for him. Someone had told him that Sean had come around. Someone close to Burke. He would have to be careful.

BELFAST

10 pm, 10 Meitheamh

Hennessey finished his glass of Guinness and stepped out of the Green Briar into the night. The streets were quiet and largely deserted. It was a pleasant evening but for the fact that no one had heard from Martin. He was overdue. Prince Charles would be arriving in two days and they still had nothing concrete to go on. If Martin didn't return soon with something it would be out of their hands.

As he passed a dark alleyway he heard a rustle behind him but before he could turn to investigate a hand was clamped over his mouth. He was jerked into the alley and thrown against the brick wall. It was too dark to make out his assailant's face but he had Hennessey pinned so that he couldn't move or utter a sound. Then a familiar voice whispered hello. It was Burke.

"Jesus, Martin, you scared the shit out of me. Where the hell have you been? We thought you were dead."

Martin smiled in the dim light. "Not dead. Close though." He pulled Hennessey deeper into the alley and away from the street. "Look, we all have to talk. Get Meagan and bring her to Finn's. I'm on my way there now. Take a cab but change a couple of times. Make sure you're not followed."

"No problem. When did you get back?"

"This afternoon," Burke said, glancing around. I guess they're not watching for me to come into Belfast."

"Oh but they're watching for you all right, boyo. They're combing the streets. And the Ra isn't happy either. They got word that you ordered the execution of a trainee in Libya, some guy named McCracken. And they're wondering why you've got trainees there in the first place. That's the Broken English team, right?"

"Yes. That must be the guy Mrs McHenry was talking about."

"The Ra is sore because they claim you're acting without authority. You know how touchy they are about executions."

"Well I haven't got time for that. You'd better make doublesure you aren't followed, by anyone, from either side."

Hennessey watched Martin as he fidgeted, looking over his shoulder and at the roof. "Martin, what did you find out?"

"Later James. We'll talk at Finn's. Now get moving."

Burke pushed him back into the light and when Hennessey turned again Burke was gone. He didn't even have a chance to tell him about the kid.

Finn answered the door. It was Burke.

The old man looked as if he'd just gotten out of bed; his shirt was only partially tucked into his brown pants and his hair was every which way. "Martin, welcome back, young fella," he said as Burke entered and he closed the door.

They went through the darkened livingroom and into the kitchen where Finn poured them both a drink. They stood leaning against the counter. Martin downed the whiskey and Finn poured him another. "I had some trouble in Amsterdam. They'll be looking for me here."

Finn gulped down half of the glass of whiskey. "Who?"

"A guy named Michael Magee. He's the hub of Broken English. And that fucking Sullivan. He was in on it from the start. They used me to set up Lynch and the McHenry's. They were the ones who roughed up Mrs McHenry and bombed the place."

"Michael Magee, you say. I seem to remember somebody mentioning him last autumn. He came over from the States, if it's the same fellow. Did a couple of hits for some Mafia clients, but things got a little warm for him over there so he came over here on a contract with the Protestants. Slipped away before anybody could get him."

"He was blond, a young guy, well-built."

"I wouldn't know what he looks like, Martin, so I can't help you there. All I know is that there was some talk about a Magee fella. But I do remember them saying he was an ex-soldier and that he was very good with explosives."

"So he would have been able to do the McHenry job. He worked for the Protestants? That's interesting."

"I agree," Finn said. "Martin, remember back a few years when the SAS were running Mobile Recon Forces?"

"The 'Freds'," Martin acknowledged.

"Right. Well, in '72 an MRF squad shot up Andersontown with submachine guns. They were dressed as civilians and they just drove in and sprayed the area. A lot of people figured they were just trying to drum up some retaliation, to bring out the Provos. Well ..."

Burke completed the sentence. "So the same thing's happening now, only in reverse."

Finn nodded. "The boy wins a prize. Get some new lads, put Martin Burke in the background — they'd have to bust you out — and hire Magee to play your part. Maybe they had a guardian angel watching over you when the RUCs picked you up."

"They're playing for high stakes, taking out Charles."

"Exactly." Finn paused dramatically and filled his glass. "And we'd catch the shit. Charles arrives on Wolfe Tone's birthday. What better time?"

"And by the time the marching season is over, ..."

"You mentioned Sullivan," said Finn. "I just heard today that a dentist by the name of Feeney was found murdered in his office in Dublin. Would that be your Feeney?"

Burke nodded. "Got to be. Can't say I'll lose any sleep over him. They must be covering their tracks for the hit. Anything else?"

"Dry as a nun's tit, Martin. There's talk about you though. MI wants you something fierce and the Provisionals aren't happy with you either."

"Yes, Hen told me. Seems I am the mastermind behind this operation."

"Say, there is one thing. A gos came by, Sean, a little guy, 10 maybe."

"Him. I keep seeing him all over."

"I told Hen and Meagan. Didn't Hen tell you."

"No. I guess he didn't have a chance. I sent him to get Meagan and bring her here."

"Anyway, the lad said he had a message for you from McHenry. Said you'd know where to meet him."

"What? I don't even know where he lives. A message from McHenry? Maybe he was a runner for McHenry, or was there when he died." Martin tried to recall the places where he'd seen the boy.

"Anyway, if that's all you've got to go on, it isn't much. You know, my boy, I don't often give advice, ..."

Martin chuckled. "But you're going to break the habit."

"Laugh all you want, but you're in need of some. The point is we're running out of time. Especially you. If this goes down, you're likely to go down with it."

"And a hell of a lot of other people," Burke added.

"That's true." Finn paused. "So it has to be stopped. If the Brits have any wind of it at all, they'll probably be pissing up the wrong rope. Have we got a hope in hell of doing anything about it?"

Martin opened a bread bag and took out a slice of bread. "To tell you the truth Finn, I don't know." He opened the knife drawer and pulled out an Browning with a silencer attached. "Aren't you the bold Fenian lad," he said, grinning at Finn and twirling the revolver.

Finn grabbed the pistol from him and put it on the counter. "There's no time left for jokin'. Butter's in the cupboard."

Burke buttered his bread. "Maybe this Sean knows something. I'll try and find him. I figure my best bet is to let Magee find me. He's gunning for me now. And maybe put the word out on the street."

"I wouldn't be too sure that the Provos would try that hard to stop it, even if we're right that it isn't a Provo plan."

"So what's your advice?"

Finn leaned back on the counter. "What about making a deal with Hedley. You put MI in the know and they lay off you."

Martin stared at Finn. "I never thought I'd hear the words come out of your mouth. Go to the Brits! Isn't it bad enough that we're working to save the life of a British Prince?"

"Martin, we don't have much choice. If you join forces there might be a better chance of stopping this and nailing Magee."

"Chance for a knee-capping. That's collaboration with the enemy. Might even get me executed, if it got out," Burke said with a grin. "No, I want Magee to myself."

"If they've got you named in this operation, you won't live long enough."

Burke thought for a moment. "Jesus Christ Finn, I can't. I'd be a fuckin' informer. The Brits would take those lads in Libya. I'd have them on my conscience. And the only way I'd stay alive is with the Brits sending me somewhere. I don't want to live like that."

"It isn't just you I'm thinkin' about. You don't have to tell me what it means to inform. I know the policy. Christ, I've killed some of the bastards myself in my time. But this is different."

There was a knock at the door. Finn put his glass down and began to shuffle toward the door. "It must be Hen and the hen. I'll get it. But mind my words Martin. You may get Magee, but will Charles be dead before you do?" He went on down the hall.

Martin stood at the counter, considering Finn's advice. There wasn't much time. This Sean might know something but would it be enough? He heard the door open followed by a heavy thud on the floor and running footsteps in the hall. He reached back and picked up the pistol on the counter. There was a moan from the hall and the sound of struggling. He could see from the mirror on the livingroom wall that Finn was on the floor kicking at the door to close it. Martin leapt to the hallway and a bullet whizzed past his head, imbedding itself in the wall beside him. Someone was on the fire-escape shooting through the open window. He rolled past the hall and into the small bathroom. Finn forced the door shut and lay in the darkness.

Burke peered around the corner and saw the outline of the man outside the window. It was Magee and there was another with him. He cursed himself. They must have followed him here. He thought he had been careful, but obviously he hadn't. And now Finn was down. Burke fired through the window, shattering glass. There was a muffled scream and a shadow lurched. Magee blasted back at Burke with a silenced automatic and pictures fell from the walls, the mirror cracked. It was madness. There was no sound of firing, just the sounds of things breaking and of pain.

Finn moaned again and Burke moved. He stood, fired, and ran toward the shattered windows. He busted through the sash, taking the curtains with him, and landed against the outer rail of the fire escape. No one was there. They had gone up to the roof. Cautiously he climbed the stairs and peered over the top, aware that he had only two rounds left. No one. He heard the scuffle of boots about two roofs over but he could see nothing.

Finn!

He hurried back to the man, dying on the floor of the hallway, in that dark, dingy apartment, and knelt by his side. He had taken two bullets in the chest and there was much blood.

Martin lifted Finn's head. It was only a matter of time. He propped him up against the wall and knelt beside him, carefully opening his shirt. Finn pushed his hands away. He mouthed strong words, but they came out whispers and gasps.

"I should get one o' them peep holes in my door, Martin. It's a hell of a thing, it is."

"Just shut up Finn. I'll get a doctor."

"Don't be a fool Martin."

Burke knew he was right. "I'll get them Finn. I'll get Magee."

"Sure you will, but mind what I said about Hedley."

Burke nodded his head and moved to open Finn's shirt but again he pushed his hands away.

"Don't be fussin' with my shirt. It's not that bad. It doesn't hurt much. I just sure as hell hope my life doesn't flash before my eyes Martin, 'cause there's some ugly faces in my past." He tried to laugh but it came out as a weak gurgle.

Burke was silent. He watched Finn's face. It seemed to grow a little more peaceful. He knew that numbing death was closing in.

"When I was young Martin, in Mayo, my parents died and I was taken in by a sin eater. You know sin eaters?"

Burke nodded.

"Course you do. I ate his sins when he died, you know. Don't be telling the Fathers that. Always worried that I'd die out in the field with all them sins on my soul. It's a terrible thing. But you forget after awhile. And when you got no family, no children, well, it's hard to find anyone."

Finn paused for a moment and Martin thought he was slipping away.

"I always thought of you as a son, Martin," Finn said, looking into Burke's eyes and holding his wrist tightly. "Do you think the same way about me, lad."

Burke knew what he was asking. "Don't worry about it Finn."

Finn relaxed his grip and rasped a chuckle then coughed more blood. There was a shudder as Finn took a careful breath but it pained him and a wracking cough pushed him closer to the edge.

"*Tabhair dúinn dhá ghloine fuiscí?*"

Burke went to the kitchen and got the two glasses of whiskey then returned to Finn's side.

"Are you sure Martin?" Finn said, taking a sip of whiskey and coughing, "I won't be forcing a *geas* on you."

"It's done Finn, don't worry."

"That it is, Martin." He grabbed Burke's arm for a moment, then relaxed his grip and shut his eyes. "*Dia's Muire dhuit a Mháirtín de Búrca.*"

"God and Mary to you Seamus Finnerty," Burke answered softly.

"*Is glas iad na cnoic i bhfad uainn.*" This was the last that Finn spoke.

The next half hour was a blur. Somehow Martin carried the old man into the bathroom, removed his clothes and bathed him. It was a gentle bathing, Burke, at one point, becoming aware that he could not remember a time in the recent past where he had acted with such compassion and care. It was a strange time and his mind raced at the speed of light. At times he felt faint, due not to the recent events, but to the velocity of his thought. The body was heavy and lifeless, like some pliant statue. And the wounds. His eyes stayed away from the wounds. He had not seen his father's body.

He had promised to eat Finn's sins and the thought made him shudder. What sins would he be taking into his body? And who else's sins would come along? Had they been accumulating since pre-Christian times? It was like some sort of pagan apostolic succession with the laying on of hands replaced by the laying on of a table 'in the presence of my enemies? Yea, though I walk through the valley of the shadow of death'. The psalm came to him now and both frightened and comforted him.

How many men's murders would be on his head? How many acts of violence? And how many insignificant acts upon which the Church had imposed the onerous title of sin? Would he ever find someone to eat his and their sins or would he carry them with him into the hereafter? He thought now of the men he had killed, the acts of violence he had perpetrated.

Were they sins? Was it a sin to wage war on 'my enemies'? Who would God or History side with?

And there were sins of omission. Not emission, which the good Fathers spent so much time concerning themselves with, but the omission to do certain acts. Burke's soul was heavy with the weight of those sins. In the last two weeks how many of those sins had he committed? All about him a string of deaths had blossomed and continued to grow, to stretch on like an endless string of knotted scarves pulled from some twisted magician's hat.

But he would act now. He would do that much for the man who had inhabited this shell now before him. He would seek out the assassin. He would kill Magee, not to save his English enemy but for revenge. And he would do it himself.

Suddenly he was finished. Finnerty, or what remained of Finnerty, was dry, dressed and on the bed. Burke retreated to the darkened livingroom.

He sat in the dark with a full clip and a glass of whiskey. There was a knock. "Come in. It's open," he yelled. Hennessey and Meagan entered and rounded the corner of the hallway into the livingroom where he sat.

"Where the fuck were you?" he said, looking at them. They stood, looking at him, puzzled.

Hennessey saw the broken glass. "What happened?"

"Magee hit us. Finn's dead."

Meagan sat down beside Burke and put her arms around him while Hennessey got up and began to pace. "Where is he?" she asked.

Without looking at either her or Hennessey he replied in a monotone, "He's in the bedroom. I've prepared him. Washed him."

Meagan sat back confused and Hennessey stared.

"I don't want to talk right now," Martin said forcefully. "He was a traditional man and he'll have a wake here. Meagan, you'll prepare some food." He looked at Meagan with detached eyes. She stood and went quietly into the kitchen.

Hennessey came over to him. "Martin, there's no time. We have to move now."

"After it's over James. I want you to arrange a death certificate and a burial. I don't want any post mortem or the likes. You have the contacts. You've done it before. We'll wake him this night and bury him in the morning. Take care of it."

"But what about Broken English?"

"Fuck 'em. Right now we take care of our own."

Meagan came back from the kitchen, white-faced and sat in between Burke and Hennessey who had just finished phoning around to make the necessary arrangements. She didn't even look at Martin. "The food's almost ready."

Her words roused Martin from his thoughts. "Finn told me that Sean had come here. You didn't say anything about that," he said to Hen.

Hen looked up at him. "You didn't give me a chance. The kid came around, followed me here, and wanted to see you. He knows something about McHenry by the sounds of it. Do you know where here to find him?"

"I've got some ideas, but we can all look for him and for Magee. We'll talk about that later." He glanced back to Meagan. "You can bring the food." She nodded and went to get the feast.

As she returned to the kitchen, Burke, with Hennessey's assistance, moved the kitchen table into the livingroom and laid a white sheet over it. Then they carefully carried Finnerty from the bedroom, laid him on the table with a copper over each eye and draped another white sheet over him.

"Martin, if you don't mind, what the fuck is it that you are planning to do?"

"Eat his sins," Burke said, matter-of-factly. "As a young man in the west he ate the sins of others. It's an old custom. The sin-eater eats a banquet from the table on which the dead man has been laid out. The dead man's sins go into the food and the sin eater consumes them, for the good of the dear departed and the people around him. There's no trouble as long as he finds someone to eat his sins when he dies. I'm doing it for him."

"And what happens if somebody offs you before you make the same arrangements?" Hennessey asked.

Burke stared at him. "I burn in hell. Forever."

Meagan laid out the pork and potatoes and two bottles of whiskey then went back into the kitchen and sat there alone. The old man's death had touched her and brought memories of the death of her grandfather in Tyrone. She cried softly in the dark.

It was keening enough for Burke. Hennessey sat on the sofa, watching and drinking, and Burke sat stiffly at the table, head bowed. His lips moved in some near-forgotten prayer then stopped. He began to eat.

Burke finished and looked up at Hennessey who was well into the bottle of whiskey he held between his legs. He grabbed the bottle half-empty before him on the table and moved over to the sofa beside Hen. Meagan came out from the kitchen and reaching for the bottle in Burke's hands, took a long drink. She blinked water from her eyes and coughed. They looked at each other and began to laugh.

"The old bastard's going to miss this drinking, that's for sure," Hennessey said with a large grin.

"He is at that," Burke replied.

Through the night they sat, talked of Finnerty and drank. They all seemed to have tales, some true, some invented. It was a last gathering of the four who, in these last days, had become so close. He would be missed, but not forgotten. It was only when the dawn wind rustled the curtains at the broken windows and the light of the new day began to spill in that they realised it was time for the burial.

Hennessey had arranged for a sympathetic doctor to fill out a death certificate listing heart failure as the cause of death, and for an undertaker who had acted before for the organization to have a grave ready on the outskirts of Belfast. They drove to the site, with Finnerty, in an old truck and there were met by Father Gillies, a priest who was always ready to say the proper words regardless of the circumstances of death. As they filled the grave and said their thank-yous to those who had offered assistance they themselves were filled with a great calm. Finnerty was gone, the ritual was complete, and now they would finish the job.

Back at Hennessey's they sat around the kitchen table. "I want Magee dead," was how Burke opened. He had tried to make a sketch but, after aesthetic objections from both Hen and Meagan, he had given up. He described him as best he could but what they really needed was to find someone who knew where he might be found. And that would be difficult if he worked for the Protestants. "I have to find Sean, too, but we have to get him within twenty-four hours."

"That's not going to be easy," Hennessey replied.

"We don't have much choice. Finn remembered hearing about Magee before. He'd worked for the Protestants. Finn thought maybe this Broken English might be a Prod operation that the Catholics would be blamed for. It'll draw fire on them."

"Draw fire, it'd be a fuckin' demonic *jihad*," Hen added. "Britain will pump up military authority and the Dual Mandate will be out the window. That'd make the Prods happy."

"Some Provos too," Meagan said.

Hen and Burke nodded. "I've got some places I want to check," Burke continued. "I suggest we split up, but be careful. Meagan, you see if you can get your friends to put things right with the Provos. I don't want them on my back, but stay with Hen. The heat's on and I don't want anything to happen to you."

"What about me?" Hen asked.

"Fuck you," Martin said with a smile. "We'll meet at the Green Briar around 10 and compare notes. And be careful." Meagan gave him a hug and they set out on the search for Magee and Sean.

FALLS ROAD

9 pm, 11 Meitheamh

Burke walked past Alison's Pub and along the street to the alley McHenry had ducked into just a few days ago. He had spent the afternoon walking the streets, looking for Magee and Sean, and had picked up more ammunition for Finn's Browning which he now carried in his coat pocket. He had been to each place where he'd seen the boy but to no avail. Now, with an hour before he was to meet with Hen and Meagan, he had come here. He recalled McHenry looking frightened as the troops approached before ducking down the alley. It had led him to his death. If Sean had a message from McHenry, he might have got it here.

The alley was cool, dark and damp with litter and urine. Bricks lay strewn about, weapons for children to attack the sixers with. Once he had seen a young lad of ten throw a brick with such skill that it hit the driver and the Saracen overturned, killing five soldiers inside. That boy had been a hero for weeks. He looked up to the rooftop. From there, too, the children threw bricks, but more often on soldiers than on the armoured cars. They were all one could expect to grow in the poisoned garden of Belfast, with its empty windows bricked up to leave less room for snipers, its Protestant and Catholic areas barricaded and spread with rolls of barbed wire. Children weren't supposed to have death and destruction baked into their daily bread. But in Belfast and Derry, as in too many other places, it was heaped on their plates; it was in their bottles, in their mothers' milk, in their parents' love-making.

Around the first corner in the alley Burke saw, at the far end of the alley, the wall which made it into a dead end. As he paced along he overturned stones and kicked aside papers. Finn's advice was heavy on his mind. He could go to Hedley. He wanted to repay Magee and Sullivan himself but the odds were against him finding them now. And there was only one day left. Less. Tomorrow Prince Charles arrived in Ulster. And he still had no idea where they'd hit him.

He went to the end of the alley and checked the wall blocking it off. There were no doors. McHenry had come this way, and Cronin too. The wall was too high to be scaled, but then he noticed the fire escape. They must have gone up. From there Cronin could have jumped to the top of the wall and gotten away. And McHenry, there he must have died. Burke had waited on the roof that night and no one had made it to the top. If Sean had been there, he had been on that fire escape.

Burke began to climb. The doors and windows he passed were dark and deserted. The building was probably empty; not an uncommon thing in Belfast. When a building lost its critical mass of people it wasn't long before everyone left. There was safety in neighbours. Still, he was careful and quiet; he didn't want to be seen.

He reached the roof, climbed over the top and stood on the gravel looking out over the city. In the distance he heard the sounds of a Belfast night: some gunfire, small arms, followed by a heavier machine gun, probably a Sterling mounted on a Saracen. Someone was taking shots at the British and the British were returning the fire.

There were pigeon coops on the roof and Burke walked over and watched the birds inside, nestling against each other, cooing. The water trough was empty but there was a water can nearby and so he picked up the can and began filling the troughs.

A door opened from below and a person stepped out quietly and professionally into the shadows on the roof. He saw Burke off to the side with a watering can in his hands. Stepping into the shadows he headed toward Burke, careful to stay low and in the dark.

As Burke poured the water he sensed that someone was approaching him. He couldn't see anything in his periphery and there was only the faintest sound. He was not going to be killed, at least not at a distance, or he would have been dead already. No, the person was approaching stealthily, getting closer, within range.

Suddenly Burke flung the watering can back and sprang sideways, rolling on his shoulder, whipping out his Browning, and ending up supine on the roof, pointing the Browning at the shadow which had screamed softly in surprise as the can slid past. "Nice and easy now. Into the light." Burke kept his pistol trained on the slowly moving shadow. "This'll blow a pretty big hole in you," he added, just to be clear.

Sean stepped out of the shadows. Burke hesitated for a moment, but the boy was unarmed and he recognized him from the funeral of McHenry, from McHenry's house and from that night, which seemed so long ago, when he had shot the soldier in the fog-bound street. He relaxed his aim and stood up. "What are you doing here?"

"Those are my pigeons that you were messing with. This roof is mine. Why did you sight on me?"

Burke was amused at the boy's guts. "Just trying to help. I didn't know who was there. I don't like taking chances. I know you, don't I?"

"You've seen me around. My name is Sean Fitzpatrick." The boy held out his hand.

Burke took it. "Martin Burke. I saw you at McHenry's. Did you know him?"

Sean shook his head. He walked to the coop and checked that the door was shut tight. "Have to watch that the rats don't get in," he said matter-of-factly. "I saw him die."

Burke sat beside Sean. "You were here when he died?"

"So were you. You used those stairs over there," he said, pointing with his small hand.

"And Cronin, the red-head, did you see him?"

"Fuckin' right I did. Bastard gave me a headin'"

"Why?"

"He wanted to know what McHenry told me before he died."

Burke felt his heart beat faster. Just a few moments before he'd been feeling as if the search was hopeless, but now there was hope. "Did you tell him?"

"No. The message was for you. You have to honour a dead man's wishes."

Burke looked him up and down. "How old are you Sean?"

Sean drew himself up. "I'll be 12 this autumn," he said proudly.

Burke thought for a moment of how old he had been when he was twelve, then looked into Sean's eyes. Not as old as this lad was. "I need that message now. It's important."

"How important?"

Burke nodded. "Very important. The lives of a lot of Catholics depend on it getting into the right hands."

Sean pursed his lips. "A lot has happened since that night. There's been other killings and a fire. I've got more information now. About you. About a couple of guys called Magee and Sullivan. They're going to kill Prince Charles. And they're going to kill you."

Burke was speechless. The boy knew it all.

"After I went to your friend's place Sullivan came looking for me. I think he started a fire in the building we moved to, the bastard. Somebody must have told him."

"Or they were watching Finn's place and saw you go there." Burke felt a great weight lifting from his conscience. Perhaps that was it. They might not have followed him there after all. Then it slammed back down. If they had been watching Finn it was only because the old man was his friend.

Sean got up from the casement and went nearer to the fire escape. "If the information is so important, I guess it's worth something."

The kid was no fool, Burke thought, and he found himself liking this boy. A man had just drawn a gun on him and now he was bargaining with the gun-man for a fee for information. But the kid was sharp. He had not given much information, just enough to whet Burke's appetite. "What'll it cost me?"

"Your gun," Sean said calmly, his face half-black in the roof shadows.

"What on earth do you want my gun for?"

Sean moved and Burke could see clearly the mixture of pain and hatred in his eyes. "The English killed my father five years ago. My brother was killed three days ago. They tried to burn us out. Now there's just me and my mother. I want the gun for protection."

Burke ran his fingers through his hair and stood. This child had stood at the graveside twice for his blood, had hated the English all of his short life, and now he wanted a weapon of destruction. But he was not even 12. Not even 12! He had heard him say protection but he knew it meant revenge. "I can't give you a gun. You're too young."

"Am I? I've been fightin' and dickin' as long as I can remember. There are other guys no older than me that have guns. Not Brownings though. But they have guns. If you won't give me the gun I can't give you the info." Sean turned his back, faced the street, then half-turned to glare back at Burke. "And you won't be able to make me either."

Burke believed him, but he knew what would happen if he gave him the gun. "Sean, that information, it can kill or save lives."

"Like your pistol. Mister, I'm not going to wait forever. If you kill me you won't find out."

"I won't kill you!"

Sean turned to face him. "I don't know that for a fact, do I now."

"I need to know more. You could be stringing me along. I'm not going to take a pig in a poke."

Sean hesitated a moment then came toward him. He held out a tape recorder with earphones dangling from it and went behind Burke. "Stay facing away from me and put these in your ears." He put an earphone over each of Burke's shoulders and Burke placed the soft foam balls in each ear. He heard a click and music played. It was an old U2 song, 'Bloody Sunday', ending. The Clash came on with 'Should I Stay or Should I Go'. He waited. What was the boy up to? Then the music stopped abruptly and he heard the hiss of poorly recorded voices. It was Sullivan talking; he knew the voice well. A man named Wilkes was mentioned. He had heard that name before, from Meagan when she was talking about MI. Wilkes was SAS. And they were going to deliver his body to close the deal with the Protestants. Finn had been right. Hedley didn't know about it. The voices stopped and the earphones were pulled from his ears. He turned and Sean was over near the fire escape.

"Is that enough to convince you?" Sean asked.

Burke paused. "You've heard it. Does it tell where the hit is going to be?"

"It tells everything you need to know to stop it."

Burke watched Sean. Enough to stop it; stop Broken English but not the Troubles. There was too much hatred, there had been too many deaths. And there were too many men and women who lived for the battle, who would continue to fight, even if the British were gone.

He looked at Sean leaning by the fire escape. If he gave this boy the Browning it was like releasing more death into the world. Either he would kill others, or, more than likely, he would himself be killed. But the tape. He could go on arguing his case but he already knew he had to give Sean the gun. There was no other way.

Sean sensed he had come to a decision. It was that resigned look on Burke's face and the slump apparent in his shoulders and back. "Is it a deal?"

"What will you do with a gun?"

"What I have to."

"It won't do you any good. You're smart enough to know that."

"It did you good. You're a hero. Nobody puts you down."

"Burke said nothing.

"It's a deal then, your gun for the tape and the player. Do I have your word?"

Burke stared at him. "Yes."

Sean spit in his hand, extended it and walked to Burke. Burke did likewise and they shook. Sean gave him the tape player and took the Browning from his hand then returned to the fire escape. He stopped and looked at Burke, happy now. "McHenry, when he was dying, he said to tell you that they planned the hit for Belfast, he didn't know where. But they had a second spot in case it failed. Up past Ballymena. They were going to blow the train with a rocket. McHenry said to go north on the A26 then take the B64 west to the B16, past Dunloy then turn off right then left. There's a hill there."

Burke nodded.

"Mr Burke? From when I was little I heard stories about you. You paid the bastards back, measure for measure. I'm glad I met you. Thanks." And with that he was gone, down into the darkness. He had traded his childhood for a Browning.

Burke shook his head. He had not been that old at 11. Not by a long shot.

Burke sat on the casement and listened to the tape. The plan was good. The men behind it, 'Smith' and 'Jack' had done well. They had Magee, the SAS, the Catholic lads. And they had Burke. They were promised delivery of his body. They sounded sure of that. 'Do this for us; we'll return the favour. You could say you owe us one already' Sullivan had said. Burke and Hen would make an appearance at their little meeting tonight. That would show the bastards. He'd settle the score and then he'd leave the others and the tape for Hedley. It was almost over. Time to head for the Green Briar.

He got out of the cab two blocks from the Green Briar just to be safe. The streets were quiet, dark and cool. As he looked toward the Briar he noticed a car parked across the street with three men in it and two pairs of men standing talking on either side of the pub's entrance. At that moment Hen and Meagan came around the corner on the other side of the pub and made for the door. The men leapt to action. One pair shoved Hen's face up against the wall and the other held Meagan. The men in the car got out and crossed the street. One had a radio. Before Burke could think of what to do, a police car pulled out of an alley and screeched to a stop. Hen and Meagan were hustled into the back seat and that car sped away followed by the other.

Burke stepped back into the shadows as the police car pulled up and now, after they had passed him by, he stepped back into the street. Meagan and Hennessey had been lifted. Had he believed in God he would have rained down curses to make St Patrick's relics quiver. Instead he turned and headed off down a side street. They had been watching the pub; there might be others around and this was not the time to be taken in. He turned another corner and entered a street dark from the lack of street lamps. The city complained that they were always being dismantled to construct switches for bombs, and seldom replaced them in the Catholic neighbourhoods. He had been hoping that together they could finish this thing and get away. There were identities to be purchased in Amsterdam. Hen would not have left but Meagan might, with him. Now they were both in the hands of the British. Ahead at the next corner a car turned, heading away from him, its headlights casting eerie illumination on the old buildings. The lights caught a patrol of four soldiers. Immediately, one dropped to his knee and sighted on the driver while the others pushed into the walls, looking for cover. Too often patrols were lit abruptly for snipers. The driver of the car screeched to a halt and flicked off his lights. Burke could make out the soldiers surrounding the car and the dome light came on. God, he hated Belfast. He turned and headed the other way.

He thought of the tape. The meeting would not be held until 1:00 am and he knew the dock area they had spoken of. It could only be one warehouse up at the end of the Queen's Road in Victoria Channel that they would be meeting in. The tape could now serve another purpose. He could use it to spring Meagan and Hennessey. For them, he would trade the pleasure of killing Magee. He would have to contact Hedley.

Hedley sat in his office at MIHQ. Another long night, and this was only the beginning. Prince Charles et al would arrive tomorrow and from that moment until they left this blasted isle he would get no sleep. There was no higher priority than their safety.

With his appointment as Supremo, his task had been to keep peace, order and good government under the accord and to make sure the Royal Visit was a success. Everything had been fine until Martin Burke had escaped. From then it had been one thing after another. Not only was the barometer rising in the city but Burke, and the trouble associated with him, was gaining momentum, rolling like some ever-enlarging black snowball on a collision course with His Royal Highness. But now there was a respite of sorts. He had cast his nets widely, 'pulled all the stops' as they say, and his men had arrested the Hennessey fellow and a female companion, Meagan O'Farrell. He didn't know what link O'Farrell had with Burke but Hennessey was worth something. They were being questioned now.

He placed a call to Wilkes but he had signed out. The same was true for Barton. "Out for a drink," their men had said. Damn the SAS, Hedley thought. Probably part of their ritual to gather and toast the coming days' duties.

The telephone rang and he picked it up. It was the night receptionist. "A call for you, sir. Mr Burke?"

"Put it through and get a trace on this line immediately." He placed his hand over the receiver. Martin Burke. This was providential. He heard the sound of the outside line. "Hedley here."

"Hedley, this is Martin Burke. You know who I am."

"I know who Martin Burke is, but I doubt he'd be calling me."

"Cut the shit Hedley. We met in Rhodesia in 1973. Shared a drink. There was a bad smell in the air. Alright?"

It was Martin Burke. No one else knew about that. "Well, well, Burke. To what do I owe this pleasure?"

"You've nicked James Hennessey and Meagan O'Farrell. I want to discuss a trade."

"I've arrested whom?" said Hedley, stalling for time. He needed that trace. He pushed a buzzer for security.

"Listen Hedley, don't fuck about. You have them, I want them and I have something you need. It concerns the continued good health of a Prince of the realm. I will call back shortly and I want to hear just your voice — no one else — or I hang up. Don't have anyone listening in, especially Wilkes and Barton. Your security has been breached."

"Wait a minute. I'll give you a direct line." He recited the number to Burke. "That will get you to my office. Now, what's this all about?"

"Just be there."

"Wild horses couldn't dra ..." The line went dead. Hedley knew there hadn't been enough time to get a trace. Burke would be switching phones. What did he mean 'security breached'. And what the hell did he mean about Wilkes and Barton. Two security officers were standing in his doorway. "Two prisoners, O'Farrell and Hennessey, are being questioned downstairs. I want them brought up here and placed in the next two offices under guard. Keep them separate and continue the interrogation. And put the Headquarters on a security alert." The officers left and he dialed the night receptionist.

"I'm sorry sir, we weren't able to ..."

"Never mind. That was Martin Burke. I want every possible agent out on the streets. He's using phone boxes. Keep the trace set up for my direct line. And find Wilkes and Barton." He hung up and opened Martin Burke's file on the desk in front of him. He reached for a cigarette and lit it. This would definitely be a long night. The phone rang and he grabbed it immediately. "Hedley speaking."

"Good work Hedley. How are James and Meagan?"

"They're fine, Burke," Hedley replied. "I've had them brought up to my office."

"Don't worry. This isn't a bombing."

"I just ..."

"Look, I want them out. There's a hit planned on Charles. It isn't the IRA but it's set up to look that way. Some Protestant faction has brought in a pro from the states named Magee but it's to look like I set it up. They busted me out for it. And Wilkes and Barton know about it. I assume they're not with you now."

"This is preposterous. I don't know what it is you think you can achieve but ..."

"Just listen Hedley."

Hedley paused and there was a click on the line. Then he heard the sound of voices. It took him a moment to adjust his ears and then he heard what sounded like Wilkes' voice and a conspiratorial discussion. The voices stopped and Burke came back on the phone. "Interested?"

"Burke, what do you take me for. Tapes can be altered."

"You know it's him. And Hedley, check your logs. I was arrested by those two RUC lads that were found dead. They called it in but I'll bet you won't find it on any record. They clubbed me unconscious and when I woke up they were dead. All I had to do was walk away. I want Meagan and James in your office when I call back. Let Meagan answer the phone." He hung up.

Hedley was slow to replace the receiver. The voice had definitely sounded like Wilkes. Goddamnit, he thought, it *was* Wilkes. He got up and opened the office door. The two security guards snapped to attention. "Bring those two in." He went back to his chair and sat down. His eyes fell on Burke's file. There was no record of an arrest. He could have been lying about that. But then there was the voice on the tape. He had been through that dossier countless times in the last few days, trying to get into the man's mind. What was he up to now?

The door opened and the two officers brought in O'Farrell and Hennessey. Hedley noticed that Hennessey's face was bloodied and he seemed to favour his right leg. No doubt the arrest report would indicate that he had resisted. He pointed to two chairs in front of his desk. The guards stood behind them. "Miss O'Farrell, Martin Burke has telephoned me and has asked that you answer the phone when he next calls."

Meagan looked at James and he shrugged his shoulders. The phone rang and Hedley looked at her, then pointed to the receiver. "Please." She picked it up and said hello.

Burke heard her voice and felt a mixture of relief and anger. "Meagan, it's me. Are you ok?"

"Martin, what is this?"

"It's ok, they don't have me. I'm working on getting you out."

"How?"

"It's not important right now. Are you alright? Did they hurt you?"

"No, I'm fine. James got the treatment but he's ok."

"Good. Let me talk to him."

Hennessey's voice came on the line. "Martin, old boy, you're missing one hell of a time. Can't make the party?"

"I guess you're all right. Look, I'm going to do a trade of the info I got from the kid for you two."

"Is it that good?"

"It's everything. Finn was right about the Prods. So sit tight."

"Well, if you insist."

"Get Hedley back on the phone." Burke waited.

"Yes Martin?"

Burke looked at his watch. "We have to talk. Do you want to hear more?"

"Please."

Burke turned on the tape recorder and watched as the LED's on the phone changed, indicating the money value left. He didn't have a lot of time left. He stopped the tape. "Well?"

Hedley sighed, then paused. "What do you suggest?"

"Meagan and James stay in your office so I can phone them. Take a car to the Green Briar then send it away. Wait for a cab, alone, and take the first one to the Ulster Museum. Sit in it until you see another car facing you flash its lights. Walk to that car and you'll be frisked. They'll bring you to me. Do you agree?"

"Fine. But if there's any trouble, your friends will be considered accomplices.

"Just be there." Burke hung up. He had work to do.

Hedley replaced the receiver and looked at the guards. "Hold them here until you hear from me and put an extra detail on outside." He turned to Meagan and James. "Apparently your friend values your friendship. If he should call again you may speak to him." He left the office and went to the briefing room. While he was waiting for the staff to assemble he considered the taped conversation he had listened to. He had little doubt that it was authentic. But he was nervous about meeting with Burke. It was a bit like putting one's head in a lion's mouth, he thought. But there was something about Burke. He had felt it the first time he had met him and he had retained that impression; the man was a warrior for the cause and, misguided as that cause might be, he was a man to be trusted. In the end the information was too important to pass up; Charles' safety was more important than his. And if he played his cards right, he just might bag a trophy. He checked the files for Magee. There was a record of him but he had been ranked a low priority, an ODC — ordinary decent criminal. The file had been designated inactive; signature: Wilkes. The pieces seemed to fit.

The staff had assembled. Hedley began. "I've arranged for a meeting with Martin Burke. Keep a tap on my direct line and trace any calls. Act on whatever information comes through there. I want undercover agents, the best, in the vicinity of the Green Briar and near the Ulster Museum. Get me a vest and a wire. I also want a pistol strapped to my stomach and a homing device. Keep well back from any cars and use at least three in tailing us, then switch them for the next car I go in. On my command or if anything goes down move in immediately," he paused and looked around the room, "and try not to hit me." The staff smiled and he continued with the briefing.

Hedley's driver let him off at the Green Briar. The bar was closed and the streets were deserted. He looked around for his men trusting he would not see them. He didn't and felt relieved. The three pounds of armour felt good on his chest but the tape holding the wire and the revolver was a bit tight. A taxi approached and he hailed it. As it stopped, he checked the back seat to make sure no one was hiding there. It looked clear so he got in. "Take me to the Ulster Museum."

The driver nodded and punched the fare box. As they drove, Hedley saw the man raise his left arm slowly. Wires ran from his hand around the side of the seat to a package on the floor. Hedley looked at the hand again and saw that the man's thumb was holding a button depressed. He glanced at the driver's eyes in the rear view mirror. It was Burke.

"Hello Hedley. You realise the package will blow if the pressure is taken off this button or if you touch the wires."

Hedley nodded. "It'll take you too."

"I don't care," Burke replied. "I assume you're wired. There's a tape in the recorder on the seat beside me. Reach over, carefully, and get it. Listen to the tape through the earphones."

Hedley did as Burke directed. The bastard had set up elaborate directions to throw him off, and it had worked. He placed the earphones in his ears and turned the tape on. There was some loud music and then the voices began. He listened, and the more he listened the more he realised that this was the truth. When it was finished he turned it off.

Burke looked in the mirror. "We have to talk privately. Dump the wire." Hedley sighed and opened his coat. "I'm removing the wire. Take no action. I repeat, I'm removing the wire. Stand by." He pulled the microphone out of his vest, wincing as it ripped the hairs on his chest, and disconnected it from the transmitter. He held it up where Burke could see it. "Satisfied?"

"Look, you know how valuable that information is. I don't want anyone hearing who might tip them off. You probably also have a gun."

"It's taped under the goddamn vest, Burke. Have a heart."

Burke smiled and shook his head. "Take it out and place it on the seat beside me. It's your own fault for being so fucking suspicious."

It took Hedley a couple of minutes and quite a few stomach hairs to remove the tape. When the gun slid to the seat beside Burke, Burke smiled. "Now, what do you think of the tape?"

"Where'd you get it?"

"Not important. What do you think?"

"For Christ's sake Burke, you know what I think. I have to stop this. If I don't the whole bloody place will go up."

"And is it worth a trade?"

"There isn't much time. It has to be stopped first."

"And I want to help."

"Then get me back to HQ. I need some men."

"And how do you know who to trust?"

Hedley thought about that. Burke was right. Barton and Wilkes were implicated and there had been a reference to someone in London. He couldn't even risk contacting COBRA. The SAS were there and that meant that Wilkes had a direct line.

Burke continued. "I want those bastards as much as you do. I don't give a damn about the Windsors but I can't let this go down, and I want Magee and Sullivan badly."

"So what are you suggesting?"

"A deal. We take them out."

"No offense to you Martin, but I fear we'd be outnumbered and out gunned."

"We can use Meagan and James."

"What assurances do I have that they can be trusted?"

"My word."

"Your word. What assurance is that?"

"It's not just the word, Hedley, it's who you give it to."

They were both silent for a moment, then Burke continued. "I want your word that James and Meagan will be in the clear — pardons, whatever. And I want to be relocated with Meagan. James too, if he wants to go. What do you say?"

"And if I say no?"

"There isn't another copy of this tape. There's nothing else to stop them."

Hedley considered the situation. Pardons were not out of the question in return for important information on terrorist activities. And the saving of Prince Charles and the family as well as the future of Northern Ireland would sit well with the powers that be, not to mention ferreting out the rats in the system. It might even be the sort of action which could result in a knighthood. "We have a witness relocation programme. I could set it up. I'm sure a pardon would be in order for this service. You could move to British Columbia with your ladyfriend. It's not too cold there." He thought of the poor chap he had sent to Tuktoyuktuk.

"I'll need to get away if I help you. The word will get out and I'll be marked by the Provos as well as the Prods."

"But you're doing them a service."

"Hedley, I know full well what I'm doing. This is contrary to every IRA regulation and I'm not going to be turned by being convinced that I'm doing them a service by collaborating with you. You seem to forget there's a war on."

Hedley knew he was right. "It's a deal then Martin."

"Not so fast," Burke said. "This has to be the extent of the deal. No other information, from me or the others."

Hedley nodded. "You have my word."

"Your word," Burke said with a grin, "that's all?" He tossed the button back to Hedley. Hedley squirmed to avoid it then lifted his feet from beside the package and jumped as far away from it as he could get. Nothing happened.

Burke looked into the rear view mirror and smiled. "Just joking."

Hedley relaxed. "Son of a bitch," he said. "Let's get moving."

THE DOCKS

1:00 am, 12 Meitheamh

Burke shuffled about in the dark warehouse, peering occasionally through the muddied, cracked windows out into the street. All along the other side of the block stretched a mammoth sign depicting a house on fire and a member of the Royal Ulster Constabulary. 'Stop the destruction', it read. 'If you have information on Terrorism call 999.' Burke was pleased to see that someone had painted raccoon eyes and a mustache on the policeman's face, but it still did not lessen the oppressive, dwarfing effect which the sign had on anyone looking at it.

They had stopped on the way to the warehouse and Hedley had called his office, directing them to release Hennessey and Meagan. In Irish, Burke had explained to Hennessey that he was to meet them at the warehouse and to come armed. Hedley had dropped Burke off at the warehouse to case it and had gone to park the car. The building was old and deserted, though it still held a large number of crates of various sizes. Along the rear of the building there was a second storage floor, open with a railing along the front of it and a circular iron staircase leading up. This area was also crammed with discarded wooden boxes and old ropes. The entire warehouse had the feeling of a structure which had long since outlived its usefulness and remained only due to lack of interest. On one side there was an adjoining door to another storage shed which held lumber but Burke was able to see that no one was there either. As he came back into the main building he came upon evidence that someone had been around earlier; there was a coke can on the floor near the front doors but the coke in it was flat. He also found some M-16A2s in a case stamped USMC. He took one and slapped a magazine into place. Standing by the door he saw Hedley walking down the street, stepped out and waved him in.

"It's all clear, but there was somebody here earlier. It won't be long now. The meeting was set for 1:30."

Hedley held up the radio transmitter and the detached microphone. "I brought this along. I can snap it back into place to call in some reinforcements if we need them. How long before your friends get here?"

"Any minute," Burke answered and handed Hedley a rifle and a couple of clips, then led him to the staircase and up to the second level. They moved in behind some crates and shifted them until they had a clear view. "Stay here. I'm going to wait for them downstairs. If anything happens, I'll get in there." He pointed to a pile of boxes beside the doors at the front of the warehouse in the corner opposite to where they were. As Burke was going down the staircase he saw two heads outside the windows and recognized that it was Hennessey and Meagan. He dropped to the floor and ran over to the door, opening it a crack. "Hey, you two, get in here." He pulled the door shut behind them and hugged Meagan, then took a good look at her. "You're ok then?"

"Sure."

He looked at Hennessey and put his hand under his jaw, turning his head into the light. "Not bad," he said looking at the bruises which ran down the side of his face and his half-closed eye. "Did you do that shaving?"

Hennessey smiled and nodded. "What's the plan?"

"Me and Hedley are up there," he said pointing to the rear of the warehouse. "I want you and Meagan in this corner here. Sean taped a meeting of Sullivan with Wilkes and Barton from the SAS and some Protestant bigwigs. They set up the deal to legitimize a military reaction against the IRA. Magee recruited some Catholic lads and set me up as the ringleader. They'll be meeting here. Hedley needs to hear enough to sink them and then we'll take them. You just stay low and cover them." Meagan and Hen nodded.

Hennessey reached into his pocket. "All I could find was this Smith & Wesson. You didn't give me much time."

"We don't have much time."

"Can you trust Hedley?" Meagan asked.

"I didn't have much choice. He's agreed to pardons and relocation."

Hennessey grinned nervously. "And life insurance with him as the beneficiary too, probably."

Burke led them to the cases against the wall and they each took a rifle then he and Hennessey dragged the box of ammo and clips over to the corner and pulled it in behind the crates there.

The lights of a car bounced against the doors of the building and startled them. Meagan and Hennessey nodded and knelt down in the darkness while Burke raced across the floor and up the stairs. He landed beside

Hedley as the doors were pushed open. Barton waved the car in and it parked off to the side. Sullivan and Wilkes got out and went to the centre of the floor while Barton shut the doors. Sullivan placed a torch on one of the large boxes then pulled some smaller ones around for chairs. Burke noticed that Wilkes and Barton were in non-British fatigues and carried Uzis. Sullivan pulled two black balaclavas out of his trenchcoat pocket. "They won't recognize you with these on," he said as he handed the hoods to them. "Magee's bringing the five lads with him."

Barton pulled the hood over his head, then adjusted the eye holes. "I thought there were eight?"

"We lost three in Libya," Sullivan answered as he walked to the door, his cane clicking on the cement floor.

Burke looked over to where Meagan and Hennessey were hiding and from his vantage point he could just see Hennessey's arm.

Another set of lights flashed in the street and Sullivan pulled the door open. A Zephyr entered, driven by Magee. He pulled in and parked. Five lads got out with him. Though Burke had never seen any of them before, they looked familiar, like so many other young men in the Catholic streets of Belfast. They were wearing coats and it looked like they had weapons under them. But his attention was fixed on Magee.

The nine men gathered around the lamp. Outside in the channel a ship's foghorn sounded and the wind sighed and creaked the warehouse. They were ready to sit down when there was a clatter from the corner where Meagan and Hennessey were hiding. Burke looked over and a rifle had fallen out into plain view. Immediately the men below sprang for cover and three of them advanced on the corner. Burke reached for his rifle and fired a burst at the three. "Drop your weapons," he shouted before he had time to think. They blasted back at him and scrambled in behind some of the crates littering the floor. As he ducked he noticed Barton, his leg limp and bloody, slip in behind one of the cars.

Hedley was smiling at him. "Drop your weapons," he mimicked. "Nice." He slammed a clip into his rifle. "We have to keep them inside."

Burke looked up over the boxes and caught sight of Magee again. Their eyes met and he sprayed the area around Burke and Hedley then shot out the lamp.

Burke felt in the darkness beside him for a roll of rope he had seen earlier and found it. "I'm going down there," he said to Hedley. "Cover me." He moved across the platform to the other end and secured the rope to the railing. He tossed it over and heard it hit the floor. The shooting was intermittent but he noticed, with relief, that there were muzzleflashes from Hennessey's corner. He slid out under the railing and grasped the rope then pushed himself out. The trip was fast but the rope burned his hands. He landed hard on the floor and rolled to the side as bullets ricochetted off the cement. He moved to another box and across the warehouse someone else had noticed the movement and stood to fire. Burke leapt to his feet and fired three shots. The man collapsed.

The firing had stopped and he could hear movement as people jockeyed for position. He formed a mental picture of the inside of the warehouse, then leapt over his cover and raced toward the doors. He was halfway there when someone opened up on him and he rolled to where he knew a stack of crates would cover him. Bullets lifted pieces of wood from the boxes but they came too late. He had found cover but so had someone else. And he was more startled than Burke at finding his refuge invaded. The man was on him. He was larger than Magee and a great deal heavier. Burke wedged his arms around the other's neck. With a quick snap at the right moment it was all over. The man collapsed in a heap, without a sound, still. In the dim light Burke could make out the features. It was Barton. Two down, seven to go.

He moved silently now, like an animal at the hunt. They could wait there all night, but the longer they waited the more chance there was that Magee might be able to plant an explosive and evacuate, then detonate. Or he might have gas. He was a highly skilled killer. Burke knew what that meant. And out there somewhere, in the dark and possibly in danger, were Meagan and Hennessey. Time was not on his side.

He picked up an old can and hurled it off into the darkness against a wall then hopped to a spot which he knew was closer to where Meagan had been before the lights went out. The noise from the can drew fire, though he didn't know from which side. That was something for him to contend with as well. He needed to identify himself, but if Magee had a grenade that might be a fatal move.

His eyes were growing accustomed to the darkness and, peering around an oil drum, he made out the figure of a man moving in the shadows. Suddenly the man darted for the doorway which led into the other section of the warehouse. It was Magee. He rose to follow, but fire from the rafters pinned him down. He fired back but didn't hit anything. Then he saw another figure move through the door. And another. It was Hennessey followed by Meagan. He covered them by emptying his clip into the rafters. As he paused to reload he wondered about Wilkes. Where was that old fool? And Hedley. He could see flashes from the platform. Hedley was trying to contain everyone and kept spraying the doorway. He wondered if he had been able to call in any back-up over the transmitter. Burke was suddenly struck with a fear that Hedley might not come out alive. No one else knew of their deal. He put the thought out of his head. There was no time for that now.

Burke looked up at the rafters again. He had to get that man then go to help Meagan and Hen. There was a slight movement but as he watched he realised it was only a bat; bats don't move unless they are being disturbed. He was patient. There was a dull glint in the rafters, the sort of dull glint given off by a commando-blackened firearm. He strained his eyes and steadied his aim. The chance came. The man above was repositioning himself yet trying to maintain a cover. Burke didn't miss the opportunity. Four well-placed bullets knocked him from his perch, and he tumbled heavily to the floor, a thud followed by the clanking of his rifle. As the rifle landed the jolt jammed the auto-fire and it emptied its magazine, spraying the entire area.

A stray bullet ripped into the gas tank of one of the cars and it exploded. The fire-ball curled up to the rafters then reduced, igniting everything in the dry, deserted warehouse. In the light of the flames, Burke saw that Hedley had moved over and grabbed the rope which he had used to get off the platform. One of the lads stood to fire on Hedley and Burke dropped him. Hedley pulled the rope back behind the crates and then Burke saw a crate crash through the window up there. Hedley had found a way to the outside. It would not be long now. The warehouse was filling with smoke and the flames were spreading. The entire front of the warehouse was cut off. The other car exploded and the heat singed Burke's face.

He dashed over to where Meagan and Hennessey had first taken cover and found Wilkes. He was alive and apparently had been knocked unconscious but he seemed to be coming to. Burke took his Uzi and, after yanking out the clip, tossed it into the fire. Then he bolted for the door which led to the next warehouse area. Someone opened fire on him and he turned as he ran and returned it. He paused just inside the door and looked back. Another body lay on the floor in a pool of blood. He turned and looked into the next warehouse. It, too, was aflame. The stacks of wood stored there were dry as tinder and had ignited as easily. Through the flames he caught a glimpse of Meagan, then of Magee fighting with Hennessey.

Meagan was holding a gun on them but they were moving too much for her to get a clear shot. He leapt through the flames and stared up at them, locked in a dangerous dance, on the top of the lumber. He climbed up toward them but when he was halfway there he heard a shot and saw Hennessey tumble to the floor.

He screamed in rage and Meagan half-turned to see him. Past her, Magee turned on them both and raised his pistol. Burke took aim, close as it was to Meagan and, though he noticed the terror which appeared in her eyes, he had no time to warn her.

His bullet caught Magee full in the chest, he stumbled for a second then fell to the floor, past Burke, still, on the edge of the growing circle of flames. When Meagan saw what had happened she rushed down to Burke who had by now gone to Hennessey's side.

Meagan knelt beside them. "Is he dead?"

"No, but he needs a doctor. We've got to get him out of here." Burke put Hennessey's pistol in his pocket and dropped his rifle. A pile of cedar lumber exploded in flames and almost buried them. They flung themselves back, pulling Hennessey with them, as the flaming boards covered Magee's body.

Carrying Hennessey between them, Meagan and Burke backed to the door where they noticed that the fire which had started from the exploded gas-tank had spread over the whole warehouse. There were flames before them and behind. He noticed a window to his side, just through a growing flame-curtain, and took a chance. There was no time to ask Meagan what she thought. He propelled the three of them towards the wall. The thrust carried them against the window and, mercifully, through the rotting boards around the window. They landed on the outside, bruised, singed, but alive.

Hedley rushed up to them. Burke saw that Wilkes was lying by the side of the road, face down with handcuffs on. Beside him was the last of the five lads, similarly prone. "I grabbed the bastard as he came out," Hedley said smiling and pointing to Wilkes. "How's Hennessey?"

Burke looked down at him and knelt to check the wound. "He needs to get to a hospital but he'll be alright."

"I've got people on the way," Hedley returned. "Any minute. What about the others?"

"I think I got the other four boys. Barton's dead. You haven't seen Sullivan?"

Hedley shook his head. "He hasn't come out, and if he's still in there he won't be coming out."

Burke turned to look for Meagan. She was standing apart from them, quiet, almost in shock. He walked her over to the other side of the street and sat her down on the curb. The roof sang as it erupted into flame and began, slowly, caving in.

Burke saw a figure move in the darkness and he saw first the cane and then Sullivan's face as he turned and hobbled down the alley toward the Victoria Channel. Burke left Meagan to follow him but as he entered the alley shots rang out and he pushed himself against the wall. Up ahead he saw Sullivan but before he could get a shot off a blazing rafter crashed down beside him and he lost his sighting. He leapt over the flames and raced on towards the water. Sullivan was standing by the channel and had his Ruger trained on Burke as he emerged from between the buildings. He fired first but the bullet hit the wall. Martin took a second longer and his aim was true. Sullivan spun from the impact and toppled into the channel. Burke went over to the water's edge. The Ruger lay on the pavement. He put the Smith & Wesson in his pocket and picked up Sullivan's weapon then checked the black water but there was no sign of a body, or a cane. The wailing of sirens and the screech of tires over by the warehouse caught his attention and he headed back.

As he turned the corner to the street the warehouse was on a rifle butt slammed into his stomach and two soldiers jumped him, forcing him face down in the street. He heard Hedley telling them to let him up and they got off, took the Ruger from his hand then frog-marched him to the Supremo. Hedley pulled him free and the soldiers went back to their duties.

They watched as the warehouse tumbled in on itself, the pile of embers alive with heat which seared their faces though they stood far back. Above them a smokey pall hovered over Belfast while the firemen worked to contain the fire which would probably burn through the night. The slight scent of burning flesh caused a ripple in Burke's mind and reminded him of the first time he had met Hedley. He looked at Hedley and knew he was thinking of the same thing. It was up to Hedley now. Burke had finished his job.

Burke and Meagan climbed the stairs to Hennessey's flat in silence and opened the door. It was quiet inside, peaceful. They had had no rest for so long and now they seemed to be past rest. They clung to each other for physical and spiritual support. As they stood by the bed in each other's arms Burke's mind closed in. He wasn't thinking of Hennessey or Finnerty or British Columbia, just of Meagan. He had fought against ever needing anyone but he needed her now.

THE VALLEY OF DEATH

12 Meitheamh

Burke woke and felt Meagan by his side. He had been afraid for a moment to reach for her, in case she was not really there and the last two weeks had been a cruel nightmare brought about by the sandwiches at McDaid's. But there she was, her lips slightly puckered, hair tousled, a hint of a frown as though she was again a young girl, wrestling with some deep problem. Then her face relaxed and she opened her eyes. "Hi."

"Hi," Burke said and then leaned over and kissed her. "Want some breakfast?"

"After a shower." She tossed the blankets back, tensed her body in a morning stretch, then stood and wrapped her arms around her goose-bumped breasts and shivered her way into the bathroom. Before closing the door she looked back at Burke, laying on his back with his hands cupped under his head. "And don't you be laying there when I'm finished either."

Burke lay there with the white noise of the shower soothing him, but not soothing him enough. He thought of Hennessey in the hospital and decided he would see him later in the day. He wasn't sure that Hennessey would want to leave Ireland. Meagan had assured him last night that she would but it was all too much of a change for him to believe it until it happened. Now in the mid-morning sun he wondered if it was the best thing for him. Somehow, the action last night had cleansed him and he felt a sense of normalcy returning. But he knew it was false. There had never been normalcy in his life, never would be. He had gone beyond what the IRA considered acceptable. They had made it a policy not to punish those volunteers who had been broken in the Maze, so long as they had not caused a loss of personnel. It was just policy that they would be excluded from all future operations, shunned. But he had not been broken. He had gone to Hedley. Admittedly it had been to free his friends, but Catholic volunteers had died because of it. He would have to leave.

He got up and wrapped a towel around his waist then went out to the kitchen. The cocoon he had retreated into three years ago had been ripped from him and, in the space of two weeks, his world had spun madly. But the mad spin had brought Meagan.

What would they do in Canada, he thought as he cracked the eggs and they sizzled in the hot pan. There would be money — Hedley was arranging for that along with their passports — and it would cushion them for a long time. Perhaps he'd return to school, maybe law school, or find a job of some kind. But what kind of job would a gunman take. He thought again of last night. It had felt good. There was no use denying it.

He turned the ham with a fork and wiped the splatter from his fingers. There'd be plenty of time to figure that out later. They could spend the next year talking and planning, dreaming, but mainly just being together. For the first time in a long while he felt he had a future ahead of him with potential. There would be time to get to know Meagan and that was one challenge he welcomed.

The shower finished and Meagan hopped into the bedroom only to emerge two minutes later in jeans and a sweater with her hair wrapped in a towel-turban. She flipped her long leg over the back of the chair and sat down at the table Burke had set. "Breakfast. I'm famished."

Hedley had been up all night and he was trying to eat a small breakfast at his desk in MIHQ. Everything seemed to be in order, but he wanted to make sure. The SAS had been pulled off all details and confined to barracks. Security had been tripled at the function Charles was attending. Early this morning another train had set out along the route, dropping troops and RUC constables at every station, as well as one man each mile from Belfast to Londonderry. The Engineers had checked and re-checked every mile of track; a Sea King helicopter would ride point along with the Royal Train, which itself would carry a complement of Guards; and besides all this Magee was dead. He had briefed Their Royal Highnesses, but they had been adamant about proceeding with the trip exactly as planned: Charles and William would take the train while Diana and Harry would be flown to Londonderry.

It was only ten o'clock. He had two hours before they would leave. He could think of nothing which he might have overlooked. But something was disturbing him. He was letting Martin Burke go. More than that he was giving him money and arranging to relocate him with a new identity. It was something he had done before, but this was a man he had wanted so badly to trap. True, things had worked out. It had been touch and go down to the wire, but he had to admit to himself that Burke was some fellow. And his service to MI in these last few days had been such that, had it been anyone else, there would have been a knighthood.

As he sat with his breakfast, word was coming in to him of arrests made in relation to Broken English and the dossiers kept piling up on his desk. Wilkes had spent much of the night in interrogation but had said nothing. The SAS were well-trained, perhaps too well-trained. And the Catholic lad hadn't known much though he might be useful later. He would work on him. But the Protestants they had picked up were more than ready to sell their comrades short and the agents had been busy picking up a number of highly-placed individuals both in Ireland and in England. Many of the details of this operation would have to be kept from the papers, but Hedley knew that his part in it all would secure him a title at year-end.

And what of Burke? That fellow would take care of himself. And just to be sure, MI would keep tabs on him. It always paid to be cautious and to watch over foes turned allies. He had informed and worked with MI. That made him a traitor to the cause. The IRA would have him on their death list if they knew, even though he had saved their skins. To everything there is a season.

But there was a bad smell about this thing. He had felt it as he stood with Burke outside of the burning warehouse. It reminded him of the unsavory interlude during the campaign he had witnessed in Mozambique, when he had first met Burke. Hedley had a sense that he could trust the man, but the stakes were too high. Just to be sure he decided to head over to the apartment where Burke was staying. He got his Browning out of his drawer and slipped it in his shoulder holster. As he walked down the hall, a sense of urgency overwhelmed him and he raced to the garage and got in his car. There was no time for an escort. He would go alone. He could radio later for help, if it was necessary. He hoped it would not be.

Burke put his shirt on and fastened his pants. "I'm going over to see how Hen is doing," he called out to Meagan in the kitchen. "Want to come?"

Meagan stuck her head through the doorway. "No need to yell," she said smiling. "You go ahead. I've got some things to do if we're going to leave tonight. I can see him later. Will he be coming?"

Burke put his arms around her waist. "Don't know. Maybe." He tried to kiss her but she shoved him away playfully. "Get going then. I'll be back by 4 o'clock. You'll be here?"

"Sure." Martin grabbed his jacket and left.

As he walked along the Falls Road he felt Hennessey's Smith & Wesson in his jacket pocket. In Belfast he would feel naked without one but where he was going he wouldn't need it. One more thing to get used to. He wondered how Sean was doing. The little bugger had certainly come in handy. Burke thought of what Sean had said about the failsafe location north on the train route. Sullivan's body had not come up. There was a remote possibility that he had survived. And if he was alive there was a chance he might have the guts to try and pull it off himself. For a moment Burke thought of contacting Hedley but he decided against it. It was probably nothing but, if there was any trouble he could take care of it himself. He had to get a car and, as he rounded a corner he saw a parked Austin Marina. There was no one around. It would do. He could see Hennessey later.

Beggars weren't supposed to be choosers but as Burke drove he found himself wishing that the owner of the car had had a more modern taste in music. Not that he minded Bach's Concerto for Oboe d'Amore in A Minor; it was just that he was in the mood for something more current. But the rich sound was a comfort and so he rolled down the window and drove on. It was a peaceful Friday and a pleasant day with one of the rare blue skies of Ulster summer.

Burke took the M2 north from Belfast then up the A26 and west on the B64 and north on the B16. The drive was beautiful, green and bright, refreshing. Past Dunloy he followed Sean's instructions and took a right then a left. He pulled the car off and in behind some trees then headed for the hill in front of him. He crossed over it and saw below him the rail-line along which, here and there, solitary soldiers stood guard. There was a rocky outcrop covered over with trees and brush which afforded a view of the tracks and the river and his intuition told him to head for it. He reached the top and leaned against a rock, warming himself in the sun. A slight breeze was blowing and here and there hawks soared in updrafts, floating over the fields, looking for mice. About the rocks and potholes, squirrels scurried and chattered. 'God's in his heaven, all's right with the world' he thought. As he surveyed the area something below him and to his right attracted his attention. It was a dim flash of light, like sunlight on metal. He went closer to the source and leaned out past a rock. In a space below him he noticed, in what appeared to be the mouth of a cave, a breastwork of bushes. Just behind the bushes, under some branches, he made out the shape of three boxes, painted in a woodland cammo pattern. He had found the failsafe location. It was as Sean had said.

He took his pistol out of his pocket and moved more cautiously now, back again in the jungle, cracking no twig, bending no branch, flowing through the brush silently. He edged around the corner, holding the Smith & Wesson above his head and inched to the cave-mouth. Using his right leg as a pivot, he swung around through a 180-degree arc into the mouth of the cave. There was no one there. He slid the pistol back into his pocket and removed the branches from on top of the boxes. They were military cases stamped USMC. Inside the first was a small TOW missile mechanism. He checked the next box — missiles. He ran his hand along the smooth metal. The high explosive warhead was designed to easily pierce heavy armour and deal a lethal blast with its remaining firepower. Against a train it would be devastating. The crash of the train would make certain. The last box held two rockets, M-136s, sufficient to take care of any helicopters. He glanced out across the valley to the train tracks. Sullivan had chosen his failsafe location well.

Burke closed the lids and sat. He was not in the mood for lugging them all the way back to the car. He decided he would wait until after the train passed. The thought crossed his mind that fate had dealt him a strange hand. He had helped the Brits foil a plan to assassinate Prince Charles, a plan which had included him being framed as the assassin. And now he was here, with all the necessary firepower to pull it off. And if he did? The plot had been revealed; wouldn't the Brits themselves be blamed? His train of thought was broken by what sounded like a foot slipping on a rock. He listened intently and heard more, someone moving through the brush towards him. Replacing the branches quickly, he vaulted over a rock and scrambled in behind some underbrush. A shape moved past the trees. It was a second before he recognized who it was. Something inside of him turned very cold. Meagan stepped down into the clearing and crouched over the box.

He watched as she took off her coat. There was a Ruger .352 stuffed into her waistband. She undid the fasteners and took out the TOW, arming it and moving to the edge of the clearing where she had a clear view of the tracks. She placed the TOW on the ground and went back to the boxes. Martin stood, his hands in his jacket pockets, and saw her unpacking and arming the M-136 with a practiced hand. A great many questions were answered for him. He knew now how Magee had been able to find him, why Finn was dead and who had promised to deliver his body to complete the operation. Like the bolt of a rifle sliding into place, the inescapable conclusion presented itself. Meagan placed the M-136 next to the TOW and stood. A train whistle blew in the distance and she looked in the direction of the sound. Their eyes met.

The wind caught a wisp of her red hair and she raised her hand to pull it back. Martin gazed directly into her eyes but there was no emotion there. They were ice. She swept the hair from her face and her lips relaxed into a smile. She was about to speak. He shot her.

Jimmy Matthews stood with his back against a fence post watching the approaching Sea King as it wove back and forth over the Royal Train speeding toward him. To him it had been a waste of time being out here all day but it wasn't too bad. He had heard that they would get a good meal tonight and a week's leave in London after the Royal Family left the Isles. His imagination started up again: The Train speeding down the track suddenly begins careening in slow motion off to the side in a stiff horrible sideways spiral. The engine hits the ground and the whole thing piles up on itself and explodes. During the six hours he had been stationed here he'd seen that image a hundred times and even though the tracks had been checked and re-checked for explosives, he saw it now. He had chosen a vantage point judiciously distant from the tracks just in case.

He wanted to shut his eyes but he couldn't. Suddenly, the engine shot past, deafening him. He caught a glimpse of Prince Charles leaning over, looking out the window with William beside him and then the train was disappearing down the tracks, the helicopter still swinging back and forth. He breathed a sigh of relief and stepped up onto the track to wait for the pickup.

GLOSSARY

Andersontown militantly Catholic area of Belfast

ASU Active Service Unit; the IRA term for a cell involved in military operations

Belfast Capital of Ulster, situated at the mouth of the Laggan, means 'mouth of the ford of the sand banks', claimed after the Flight of the Earls and developed as an industrial centre, attracted the poor of the Protestant Plantation and the Catholic South, all of whom were settled in ghettos. (pop. 362,000)

Bobby Sands Celebrated IRA hunger striker, born in Belfast in 1954, first arrested and imprisoned in the Long Kesh Cages as a Special Category Status prisoner in 1973, released in April and rearrested in October of 1976, was sentenced to 14 years imprisonment in September 1977 in the H-Blocks, without status. During his hunger strike he was elected as Westminster MP for Fermanagh and South Tyrone. He began his last protest on 1 March 1981 and died on 5 May. It is estimated that 100,000 people attended his funeral

Brady Petty criminals posing as IRA in order to commit crimes or cause trouble

Brits Generally refers to British people, but more specifically to the British Army regulars stationed in Northern Ireland in large numbers to keep the peace and constantly patrol both urban and rural areas in small squads. From a high of 21,000 in 1972 down to about 10,000 in 1986, the British government has stated an intention to gradually reduce the combat strength to a target of 7000

cell Small unit of 4 or 5 members in a revolutionary organisation, which has little or no contact with other cells and is given special tasks to perform

COBRA Cabinet Office Briefing Room; anti-terrorist government committee chaired by the Home Secretary with representatives from the Ministries of Defence and Foreign Affairs, the police, MI-5, MI-6, the SAS; convened during a crisis situation

CO/OC Commanding Officer(Amer)/Officer Commanding

CRW Squad Counter Revolutionary Warfare Squads of SAS trained in special operational procedures to combat terrorism

criminalisation The British government's position that all revolutionary or terrorists acts associated with the Irish problem should be viewed as criminal rather than military activities

croppie a poor Catholic

Dail The Irish parliament in Dublin

dicking Children assisting operations by acting as look-outs or diversion

Diplock Courts Lord Diplock suggested the relaxation of rules of evidence and procedure to allow for conviction of suspected terrorists based on uncorroborated testimony of paid informers or written confessions which were often the result of police interrogation carried out at 'interrogation centres'. The Diplock Courts have no jury

Derry 'An oak grove'. Following the Flight of the Earls, Derry was seized by the English and given to the London merchants to exploit under a corporation named the Honourable Irish Society, hence the name change to Londonderry. (pop. 32,000)

Dublin 'Black Pool', known in Irish as Baile Atha Cliath (the town of the ford of the hurdles) situated on the Liffey, capital of Eire. (pop. 600,000)

Eire The Republic of Ireland; the South; the Twenty-six Counties (pop. 4 million)

Falls Road A main street in Belfast, a militantly Catholic area

Fenian Generally, a Republican; a secret society which originated in the mid-1860s dedicated to driving the British out of Ireland, had strong American connections and launched raids against the British in Canada. Originally, the warriors who accompanied the ancient Irish hero Finn McCool

Flight of the Earls The O'Neills left Ulster in 1607 for the continent and their lands were then seized by the English and planted with English and Lowland Scottish Protestants

Flight of the Wild Geese   Following the defeat of the Irish forces by the English forces under Prince William of Orange in 1691 the Irish Army began fleeing to the continent as mercenaries and were gone by 1695

Garda   The police force of the Irish Republic; garda (pl. gardai) — a police officer or guard

geas   An obligation which is placed on an individual to perform (or refrain from performing) a certain act at a specific time or place no matter what the consequences. Often the consequences are bad but to fail to perform the *geas* might occasion worse disaster

git   A stupid person

gos   colloquial shortening of *gasur*, Irish for young boy

heading   A beating

hunger strike   A traditional Irish protest. When wronged, the person offended would camp at the offender's portal and refuse to eat until the wrong was corrected. To fast for no good reason or to leave the wrong uncorrected and allow a legitimate hunger striker to die was uncivilized

INLA   Irish National Liberation Army, a small but violent splinter group of the IRA that split off in the late 1970s as they grew dissatisfied with the more moderate stance of the PIRA. Described by the British as being Marxist-Leninist and having a combat strength of 20

IRA   Irish Republican Army *(Oglaigh na hEireann)*, generally estimated by the British to have a combat strength of between 200 and 300 active members in Ireland, and operates with the assistance of 'volunteers'. IRA is taken now to mean the Provisionals. The Provos (PIRA) split from the Officials (OIRA) in 1969 as they preferred the bullet to the ballot. The OIRA called for a political solution and seemed unable to protect the Catholics of Derry and Belfast against attack by the British forces and Protestant terrorist groups. However, the PIRA has now moved much closer to the policy they initially rebelled against, and are now committed to 'bullets and ballots'

Maeve   Bellicose and libidinous queen of Connaught who, in the pre-Christian Irish epic *Tain Bo Cuilagne* (The Cattle Raid of Cooley) leads her army in an attack on Ulster but is defeated by the Irish hero Cuchulain

Maze   (a.k.a. Silver City, Long Kesh, H-Blocks) — a prison complex outside of Belfast which houses those accused and convicted of revolutionary or terrorist activities (both Protestants and Catholics). Originally know as Long Kesh, the addition of the H-shaped prison units led to the name H-Blocks or The Maze. The tin-roofed huts gave rise to the term Silver City

Meitheamh   Irish for the month of June

MI-5   British domestic intelligence (comparable to FBI)

MI-6   British foreign intelligence (comparable to CIA)

nicked   Arrested

Noraid   Irish Northern Aid, an American fund-raising organisation which supports a pro-Republican lobby in the United States, offers financial assistance to Republican families in Ireland, and allegedly provides a small portion of the annual Provo budget. The Provisionals, and other groups, raise funds in Northern Ireland from the operation of taxi cab companies, clubs, security services and through various illegal activities

on the blanket   A form of protest that came about when IRA prisoners, denied Special Category Status as political prisoners in 1976, refused to wear prison clothes and remained naked except for blankets that they wrapped around themselves. When they were not allowed to leave their cells to go to the lavatories they remained in their cells, unwashed. Their chamberpots overturned by guards, the prisoners took to smearing the excrement on the blinding white walls rather than have it remain on the floor and soil their mattresses

Orangeman   Member of the Loyal Orange Institution of Ireland, a Protestant organization, formed around 1795, which grew out of night-riding anti-Catholic vigilantes who attempted to terrorize the Catholics into submission. Named in honour of William of Orange

ODC   Ordinary Decent Criminal — used by the authorities to differentiate other inmates from men and women incarcerated for revolutionary or terrorist activities

paddy   An Irish person

papist   A Catholic

peelers   The police

prod   A Protestant

QRF   Quick Reaction Force — SAS squad standing by with helicopter and called in after 'contact' with suspected terrorists

Ra   The IRA

Republican   One who believes that the North should be reunited with the South and not affiliated with England, loosely a member or supporter of the IRA

RUC   Royal Ulster Constabulary — the police force of Ulster

SAS   Special Air Services — elite corps of the British Army

shebeen   An illegal drinking establishment, a "speak" or "booze can"

Shankill   One of the main streets of Belfast, a militantly Protestant area

sin-eating   An ancient ritual whereby food is laid out on or beside the body of one recently deceased and eaten by a sin-eater. It is believed that the sins go into the food and the spirit of the deceased is then free to pass over. Traditionally, sin-eating would be passed on from father to son

Sinn Fein   Considered to be the political wing of the Provisional IRA, the name means 'Ourselves Alone' in Irish

sitrep   situation report, a military term

sixer   General term applied to six-wheeled armoured cars operated by the military or the police

SOP   Standing Operational Procedures

supergrass   A term used by the British to describe their sources of information; it has a criminal sense which is objected to by the IRA, who prefer to call these people informers

Supremo   Specially appointed civilian head of intelligence and operations in Northern Ireland

TOW   Tube-launched, Optically tracked, Wire-guided missile. The BILL is a Swedish-made TOW with a maximum range of 2000 m and a combat weight of 36 kg

torch   Flashlight

Ulster   Traditionally, a province in the North made up of the nine counties of Donegal, Cavan, Monaghan, Fermanagh, Tyrone, Armagh, Down, Antrim and Derry; politically, Northern Ireland, the latter six counties partitioned from the rest of Ireland in 1922 when the Irish Free State was proclaimed. Northern Ireland has remained part of Britain with a Protestant to Catholic ratio of 2 to 1. (pop. 1.5 million)

UDA   Ulster Defence Association — the largest of the Protestant paramilitary organisations estimated to have over 50,000 actives and which claims control over the UDR

UDR Ulster Defense Regiment — a paramilitary Protestant organisation which replaced the B-Specials as Protestant 'auxiliaries' to the RUC, numbering over 8,000 members

UFF Ulster Freedom Fighters — a small group of violent extremists who splintered from the UDA in 1973 and are reputed to carry out executions which would be politically unacceptable to UDA

UVF Ulster Volunteer Force — first formed in 1913 to force British to remain in Ulster, resurrected in 1966 as a Protestant terrorist group opposed to any form of union with the South. The UVF rejected terrorism, but not criminal activities, in 1976

Unionist Loyalist; one who believes that Northern Ireland should remain part of Britain; a member of the Unionist Party